The
Shakespeare
Thief

The Shakespeare Thief

An Elliot Todd Mystery
Book 1

Lionel Ward

Onyx Publishing

ISBN 13: 978-0-9532876-5-9

Revised second edition

"I have unclasp'd to thee the book
even of my secret soul."
— Twelfth Night

In death, Harry Nielsen looked nothing like he did in life. His handsome, confident countenance had been replaced by a startled and uncomprehending look; a comic-tragic face more to be pitied than admired. That image has stayed with me and intruded on my thoughts countless times over the years and its vividness has not faded with time.

An acquaintance rather than a friend, his death at that time did not affect me deeply on a personal level but it was never-the-less shocking and disquieting, taking place as it did on my own bookshop premises.

Nielsen's reputation had been gained as a Shakespeare 'expert'. It was commonly said that he was more knowledgeable than anyone else on the subject and it was for this reason that I had sought him out to talk in my bookshop, *Ex Libris*, when I discovered that he had written an eagerly awaited new volume, timed to appear on Shakespeare's birthday, the 23rd April, or Saint George's Day as some will have it.

A good deal of thought and preparation is required to host a talk, so I was relieved as well as satisfied when it proved to be a success. Places had sold out long before the start of the event and, following resounding applause for Harry from our audience, I felt able to relax for a while in our upstairs cafe, accompanied by the gratifying sound of lively conversation and clinking glasses, while the capable Esther supervised the book signing downstairs.

I sipped a glass of Prosecco and chatted to customer and friend, Simon Bonneville. He was trying to recruit me for a gala cricket match that heralded the beginning of the cricket season. However, my equanimity was shortly disturbed by the approach of Mrs De'Ath clutching a copy of Nielsen's *The Real Shakespeare*.

'Do you think Mr Nielsen will sign my book?' she asked fretfully.

'I'm sure he'd love to,' I said, trying to reassure her. An agitated manner was not new on her part so I was not overly concerned. I turned back to Simon believing our little exchange was over. However, Mrs De'Ath was not satisfied.

'He's not left has he? I do so want him to sign it. My father taught him at school.'

She obviously had not heard my announcement after the talk that the signing would take place downstairs. I decided I would accompany her to the author myself. I offered my arm and guided her towards the stairs. However, as we reached the top step I saw two more customers mounting the stairs holding Nielsen's book. The striking dark figure of Esther was not far behind.

'You haven't seen Mr Nielsen have you?' she called up the stairwell to me.

'I thought he was with you.'

She gave a wry smile.

The bookshop was rambling and had several nooks and crannies. It was easy to lose someone, especially when there were a number of people milling around as there were that evening.

'Perhaps he needed to "go somewhere"?' I ventured, though a glance towards the partly open door to the toilet revealed that it was unoccupied. I regained the top of the stairs and walked through to the back room where the talk had taken place. I wondered if Nielsen had left something behind and returned there from the signing downstairs. There was still a small crowd but no Harry Nielsen. One or two smiled back at me from the other side of the room.

'I'm looking for the author,' I attempted to enunciate across to them, but I do not think I was heard above the noise of chattering voices. There were more smiles and a few quizzical looks. Esther had disappeared from view. No doubt she was continuing the search in the shop below and placating Mrs De'Ath and other customers. I inwardly admonished myself for not staying by Nielsen's side. I went downstairs. There were a few customers queuing to pay for their books at the till. Susie, the work experience girl, was serving.

'Seen the author, Susie?'

'He was here earlier.'

I resisted the urge to say something caustic.

Another customer approached the counter.

'Do we pay for the books now or when the author has signed them?'

'It doesn't matter, whichever way is fine.'

I tried to sound nonchalant, trusting that Nielsen would appear shortly. I went into the courtyard at the front of the shop. We were experiencing an unusually warm spell of April weather. I found Aggie, who had been with me since I had taken on the bookshop and was now part-time, and a couple of the other customers, sneaking a cigarette and laughing loudly.

'Have you seen the author, Aggie?'

'Is he not in there?'

'Of course… no.'

'I suppose he could've gone to his car,' she offered, 'though I didn't see him go.'

'Yeah, he might have gone for his favourite pen or something.'

'I don't know, I'm sorry.' She stubbed out her cigarette. 'Do you want me to have a look?'

'It's OK, I'll go.'

'I'll see if I can help inside,' I heard her say as I half-walked and half-ran down the connecting alley.

When I reached the car park I realised that I had embarked on a hopeless task. I had no idea what his car looked like. I peered around in the vague hope that I would spot him. By the time I had reached the other side of the car park my eyes were hurting with the effort of looking.

I walked back to the entrance to the ancient alleyway which was believed to be, at one time, the main thoroughfare and route to London. It had once had a notoriety which belied its current status as a respectable shopping area. There had been an open drain running down the middle carrying effluent from the courts and houses nearby and it had been populated by sedan chair carriers and prostitutes before being rebuilt in the eighteenth century. I walked along the now quaint cobbled walkway past the pleasant facade of terrace buildings that dated from that time and some of its current incumbents: a mixture of independent retailers, a butcher, a baker, a fish shop, a jewellers, a hairdresser and a clothing shop. Finally, reaching the end of the alley I came back to the courtyard and the bookshop, originally an art institute long ago incorporated into the local university. I felt a pleasant warm feeling as I often did as I approached its attractive frontage. The clock tower in the High Street nearby, chimed the hour. I usually found this a comforting sound and half expected to see Nielsen's smiling face on my return. In my experience, problems such as these had a habit of resolving themselves.

However, when I entered the shop, I could see Esther surrounded by a group of customers clutching their copies of the book and I detected irritation in one or two of the faces. Esther appeared stressed and turned to me as soon as I entered the shop.

'Not in the car park?'

'No. Definitely not upstairs?'

'I don't think so.'

I ran up the stairs for one more check. I remembered that I had not looked in my office. Could he have been locked in there by accident or perhaps he was making a private phone call?

Simon Bonneville greeted me, picking up the conversation where we'd left off.

'Very good talk, Elliot. I must say you put on a damned good show.'

'Thank you.'

'You think there's any chance he'll sign my book?'

'I hope so. Unfortunately, I seem to have lost him at the moment.'

I opened the door to the office and stuck my head around. No one there.

'That is unfortunate,' muttered Bonneville, who was hovering behind me. 'Very unfortunate.'

I left him puzzling and started descending the stairs again. I met Esther on her way up.

'This is getting serious,' she said. 'You'll have to do something.'

'I must say it's rather rude,' I heard someone say from the bottom of the stairwell. This was the signal for a lot of excited babble from the group that had now formed around the main serving counter. Susie, behind the till, looked terrified.

Esther was immediately behind me as I made the bottom of the stairs. I clapped my hands.

'Quiet please... quiet!'

Esther gave the top of the serving counter a thump.

'Look, I'm really sorry,' I smiled, putting on a brave face, 'we seem to have lost the author.' I gave a nervous little laugh and felt like Basil Fawlty.

Mrs Peters gave an audible sigh.

'I was so hoping to have my book signed. My grandfather knew his grandfather in India.'

'Could I ask who has had their book already signed?' I asked.

A few hands went up. Not as many as I had hoped.

'Someone must have seen him go!' Esther implored.

'He seemed quite happy signing my book,' said Mrs Adams.

'Perhaps he had an urgent call and had to leave,' I speculated. 'I don't suppose he left some already signed?'

Esther dug into the pile of books and looked inside at the title pages and then shook her head.

There was a tug at my shirt. I turned around, irked by the intrusion. It was Bonneville's precocious grandson who had accompanied him for the talk while his mother was 'on some damned shopping expedition.'

'He went off with a man with a beard just here,' said the young boy in his screechy high pitched voice, while pointing to his top lip.

'A moustache?'

'That's it, a stosh.'

'Which man?'

Mrs Kay, who was at the back of the group of customers, raised her hand.

'I was waiting my turn and he sort of pushed in from behind. I didn't mind too much as I was talking to Clive about - I can't remember now. Isn't it annoying when you can't remember?'

'It doesn't matter,' I said, anxious to keep her to the point. I had in the past had a number of meandering conversations that did not lead anywhere with Mrs Kay.

'Did he say anything?'

'He was polite, you know - smiled - but he did rather mumble - everything was *sotto voce* - but you knew he meant to have his own way.'

I could see Esther suppress a snigger. She recovered herself.

'Did you recognise him as one of our customers?' asked Esther.

'No, I'm afraid not. The boy is right though, he did have a moustache, and also one of those tiny beards.'

'A *goatee*?'

'Yes, a *goatee*.'

'Did anyone else recognise him?' I asked.

There were mumbled 'noes' and another tug at my shirt.

'He went that way with the man.'

Bonneville's grandson pointed to the far end of the shop, which narrowed into the children's section.

'He was quite animated, I remember,' said Mrs Kay, picking up on the thread of her earlier remarks, 'in a quiet sort of way. Mr Nielsen said he would be back in a moment. I thought it was all part of the fun.'

The boy trotted off to the end of the shop. Esther, myself and several other customers followed in a troop.

At the end of the children's section was an L-shaped storage area for overstocks and display material. There was no door but a staggered entrance made up of a couple of freestanding screens.

Bonneville's grandson ran straight between them into the alcove and then, rather comically, ran straight out again.

'I told you he was there,' he squeaked triumphantly.

'Oh, he's hiding from us,' said Mrs Kay, mollifying the child.

'Why's he standing all funny like that?' he continued.

I stepped inside the alcove. He was, as the boy described, standing awkwardly, propped against the wall. His head was hanging down at an acute angle, his mouth was open, his tongue was prominent and he was staring fixedly into space.

2

My office was like a large broom cupboard and, I suspect, less well organised than most. I only inhabited it occasionally. Mostly it was a dumping ground for books and paperwork. There were very few occasions, excepting when the bank manager visited, when it received a really good tidy up. I did not have enough notice to do the same for Inspector Clinton before he arrived to interview me the morning after the demise of Harry Nielsen. I showed him into the office and moved books and bags so that we had enough room to face each other across the small desk.

The phone rang. It was Aggie on the internal line.

'Sorry to disturb you, there's a man with lots of books to sell. I wouldn't have bothered you except they sound like a really interesting selection.'

'Can you take a phone number, and if he's local I can always pop over after the shop closes? Better say I am not available if anyone else wants me. '

I turned back to Clinton, who gave a sigh. In fact that was the third time he had sighed in my presence. I was not sure if this was irritation on his part, with me, or whether he was a serial sigher.

'Sorry, Inspector,' I said. 'Now you have my full attention.'

It had turned out that the instrument of Nielsen's death was the pointed spike of a military helmet, a *Pickelhaube*, that had been mounted on a board as part of a window display for a recent author talk on the rise of militarism in Europe. It had been stored awaiting collection by the author as, I had thought, 'out of harm's way'. The spike of the helmet had impaled Nielsen. As well as causing his death it had supported his body in the awkward standing position that we had found him. My sorrow at Nielsen's death was tempered with a degree of anxiety that I should be considered negligent and the subject of a Health and Safety Inspection and a huge insurance claim.

'Do you hold many of these author events?' Clinton asked me once we were settled.

'Quite a few. They can be quite rewarding. With all the competition out there it is a way of fighting back.'

'Fighting back?'

'You can't hold author events on-line - at least not yet.'

'I see,' he said, though he obviously did not as the next thing he said was, 'I order from that internet crowd myself - one click and straight to the door. Amazing!'

Or perhaps I was wrong, I reasoned. Perhaps he was playing a cunning psychological game and trying to upset me and put me off my guard in case I was the murderer of Harry Nielsen. He continued.

'Did you know the deceased?'

'We met a few weeks before the talk to discuss the arrangments. I also knew him by reputation from his work. He was very highly regarded in his field.'

'And you can think of no reason why anyone would want to kill him?'

I shook my head.

'It seems bizarre. Why would anyone want to hurt a university professor - and a highly respected one at that? Do you think it could be an accident and that he somehow just fell against the spike?'

I was not sure that I was doing the correct thing, highlighting my possible negligence.

'We need the pathologist to get back to us but from my experience, for what it is worth, I think it's unlikely. For the spike to penetrate Dr Nielsen's skin, considerable force would be required and, therefore, the actions of another party.'

'Murder in our little shop!'

'Or manslaughter. But I have to emphasise this is just speculation at this stage. I grant you it's an uncommon case – but then, I have seen some unusual ones over the years.'

I imagined children kept in underground cells and the limbs of murdered 'loved ones' stored in freezers.

Clinton continued.

'We already have a summary of the incident but what I would like you to do, if you don't mind, is describe in detail everything that happened before and after the talk exactly as you remember it. Sometimes what appears to be the most trivial piece of information is vitally important. Take your time.'

He sat back in his chair and linked his fingers together.

'Well, immediately before the talk, I was greeting customers.'

'This was at about seven-thirty I believe?'

'The talk began at seven-thirty but the first customers start arriving around seven.'

'What time did Nielsen arrive?'

'I think it was about seven-fifteen, but I can't remember precisely.'

'Do you remember his arrival?'

'Yes, I was talking to Simon Bonneville, one of our customers.'

'What was that about?'

'Now that I can remember almost exactly. He, Simon that is, said something along the lines of, I wonder if Tolstoy did this?'

'Did what?'

'That's what I said. He said, "Go to his local bookshop and talk about *War and Peace*." We joked that it would've been a long talk and I pointed out to him that in any case it was called 1805 to begin with and was written half in French and had a completely different ending. It was interesting that Simon chose Tolstoy as his example.'

'Why was that?'

'Well, Simon probably did not realise it, but Tolstoy did not particularly like Shakespeare. In fact he said something along the lines that the high regard we have for him is a great evil.'

'Did you tell him that?'

'No, I didn't want to bring a discordant note just when the author was arriving.'

'What did you talk about after that?'

'We discussed the talk on militarism the previous week. That was the reason we had that spiky helmet in the first place.'

'This Simon Bonneville, he a regular customer?'

'One of my best, though, I have to admit, a little eccentric. More than a customer, really. I count him as a friend.'

'He would have known Mr Nielsen?'

'No, I know for a fact he didn't because when Nielsen arrived a few moments later, he remarked on how well he was dressed, unlike a lot of the current lecturers. He claimed you couldn't tell them from the students.'

'What did you do after Nielsen arrived?'

'I introduced myself to him, though I had to fight to get past some women customers who were fawning over him.'

'Fawning?'

'He was considered attractive and charismatic, especially to women of a certain age. He was the sort of academic you might expect to end up with his own television programme one day.'

'How did you find his manner? Was he in a relaxed mood?'

'Yes, I suppose, very much as I would have expected. We shook hands, he said how nice it was to be in a proper bookshop…' I could see another question coming so I expanded. 'A dedicated independent that sells nothing but books. And then he asked me how many copies of his book I had sold. Nielsen was very commercially minded, unlike many academics. The publicist made this clear when we were pitching for the talk.'

'What was the answer – about the number of books sold?'

'We had only had his book in stock for two days, though six customers had asked for copies to be put aside for them and signed as they could not attend the talk. He signed them right away while I poured him a glass of Prosecco.'

'Did he just have one glass?'

'As far as I know. He may have had one afterwards though I am not so sure.'

He made a note in his notebook.

'You didn't notice any unusual behaviour when he made his talk - slurring of his speech or anything of that nature?'

'No, in fact, quite the opposite. He was very sharp and I would say, on top of his game.'

'So what was this talk about?'

'The *First Folio* of Shakespeare.'

'You will have to fill me in on some of the detail.'

'Well it – the *First Folio* - was the first proper collection of Shakespeare's plays, put together by two former actor friends of his, John Heminges and Henry Condell. They have an original copy at the university where Nielsen lectures. Nielsen was the resident expert and had just published a book about it. Apart from its historical value the commercial value of the *Folio* is three million pounds – perhaps more.'

The inspector looked at me for a moment with something between a surprised and quizzical look. I felt he was giving me the opportunity to correct the attribution of such a high value to a mere book. I assented with a nod and he made a note before he continued.

'So what did Mr Nielsen have to say?'

'Well, he explained how they put it together, which was not like modern books. He did it in a dramatic way. He held up three sheets of paper in front of the audience – a bit like a mime artist or a magician. Then he explained that he had the sheets of paper to help describe how the *Folio* was put together.'

I picked up a sheet of A4 paper that was lying in the tray of the printer on my desk to help me remember.

'The three sheets of paper were folded to make six leaves and then were folded again to make a booklet of twelve. But when they were printed they didn't start with number one as you might suppose but from the middle outwards.'

'I think you might be losing me but presumably there was some point to this?'

'The point was that the compositors had to guess how much text was going to fit on each part of the *Folio* which means there were inevitably some errors. So sometimes there was a piece of text missing, sometimes it was squashed in or duplicated or there were big spaces. And because of the way the *Folios* were put together with the intervention of the compositors, there were variations between the *Folios*.'

'And that was what the whole talk was about?'

I thought I detected a raised eyebrow. I could see that I had seriously under-whelmed the inspector.

'I'm sorry, I don't have Nielsen's skill. He made it sound much more interesting. He said that without the *First Folio* many of Shakespeare's plays would not exist. He apparently had done some acting in his youth and began pacing up and down quoting from some of the plays we might have lost, Friends, Romans, Countrymen, To be or not to be - that sort of thing.'

'And the audience enjoyed his performance?'

'Very much so. He went on to explain that, though there were some problems with the *Folios*, they were often the best source for acting Shakespeare's plays.'

'Why would that be?'

'Well, he explained that the changes that had been made to many of the modern editions had influenced the way the plays had been interpreted – in his opinion, for the worse.'

'What sort of things?'

'Well, it could be as little as an exclamation mark in the wrong place or the layout of the lines which could alter the whole meaning of a part of the play.'

I was not sure I was holding the interest of the inspector. I desperately searched my mind for an interesting example.

'There was even a case in Victorian times when they completely altered the ending of *King Lear* so that there is a happy ending and they don't all die, and Cordelia marries, even though she had already married the King of France earlier in the play.'

I did not receive the appreciative response from the inspector that Nielsen received from the audience just two nights before, but I carried on.

'He also described how, because of the way we speak the language, sometimes the lines of the play, lose their meaning. In fact he used me as an example.'

He looked at me over his glasses. At last I had aroused his interest.

'I had to read out a speech by Jacques from *As You Like It*.'

'That didn't bother you?'

'I didn't see how I had any choice without losing face. He had originally asked for a volunteer from the audience, but they seemed too preoccupied with a hand-out of the *Folio* he had just passed around. And I did enjoy it once I got into it. I actually received a round of applause when I sat down.'

There was the faintest hint of a smile on his face

'The trouble was, he then went on to pull my reading apart. It was supposed to be a funny piece.'

The passage was etched on my mind. I recited part of it for the inspector.

Tis but an hour ago since it was nine
And after one more hour 'twill be eleven
And so, from hour to hour, we ripe and ripe
And then, from hour to hour, we rot and rot;
And thereby hangs a tale.

The inspector did not appear unduly perturbed by my sudden out-burst but I could tell he was unsure of its relevance. I attempted to elucidate.

'The reason it doesn't sound funny is that in Shakespeare's time "hour" and "whore" were pronounced in the same way. When you realize that, it suddenly becomes funny.'

There was an uncomfortable silence.

'I'll take your word for that, sir. While all this was going on, did you notice anything unusual?'

'No, I can't say I did.'

'You say you were sitting across from Nielsen.'

'Yes.'

'So you would have had a good view of the audience?'

'Quite a good one, but I was behind a desk so my view was limited.'

'Did you notice the man with the *goatee* beard?'

'No, I've been racking my brains. I'm afraid I don't remember seeing anyone with a *goatee* all evening. But then, I was not consciously looking for someone who had one. He could easily have been there and I just didn't notice.'

'What was the audience like?'

'Our usual sort of audience, I suppose, quite knowledgeable and they asked some good questions.'

'No hostility?'

'No, they were an appreciative audience – except... there was one hostile question near the end. I suppose it was less of a question more of a series of observations and opinions.'

'What was that about?'

'He was challenging, I suppose, the position of Shakespeare as our most important playwright – rather like Tolstoy did - though he went further and claimed he didn't write half of his plays, if any at all, and that Christopher Marlowe would have been a far greater playwright had he lived. You often find the odd maverick at these events wanting to air their knowledge or thinking they have a greater insight than the speaker. It's not such a bad thing. It can often make the evening more stimulating.'

'How did Nielsen react?'

'It took him aback a little I suppose. There we all were in awe of Shakespeare and of Nielsen and then suddenly someone was challenging it all. However, he is (was) an experienced speaker and was able to handle it without too much difficulty, though the man did come back at him strongly.'

'Do you know who this man is?'

'I don't know his name and I don't know that I have noticed him before. But then, we see so many people over the year.'

'Now we come to the critical part. The talk finished, about what time?'

'Again, I'm not absolutely sure but I believe, after questions, about eight-thirty.'

'What happened then?'

'I thanked him for coming and for his interesting talk and said there would be a signing downstairs. I also requested that everyone remain seated while Nielsen went downstairs to prepare for the signing.'

'Ah, why was that?'

'Simply to allow him to avoid the crush. There would be no point in customers rushing down the stairs to get the author to sign their books if the author was stranded upstairs.'

'Did you accompany him?'

'No, looking back I wish I had. I stayed upstairs talking with some of the customers. Esther, my main employee, accompanied him and looked after the signing.'

I explained Mrs De'Ath's interruption of my conversation with Simon Bonneville and the events that followed. When I had finished he asked me about any details we had for the customers who came to our talks.

'We take details of any customers who book in advance. We ask anyone who has not booked in advance to write their names on our guest list.'

'So, he could lie about his name?'

'Yes, or just not bother at all, especially if he was late. We don't ask for proof of identity or anything like that.'

'Still, it would be worth having the guest list and the list of advance bookings. I would like to talk to as many people as possible who were here on the night. Any details - names, addresses and phone numbers - would be useful. Oh, and do you have any photos of the evening?'

'Yes, I think so. We usually take one or two. I will ask Esther.'

'You never know, you might have one of the man with the moustache.'

There were police interviews in the bookshop throughout the day. I placed a sign on the door apologising for the fact that we were closed. In a typical day we received a number of phone calls and that day was no exception. I took the first two and explained that we were closed due to unforeseen circumstances. I was not clear about my responsibilities regarding what information I should reveal about the current investigation and quickly became aware that I was unable to give a definite time for when we would re-open. The second caller was rather put out and questioned my vagueness. As well as being unsure about whether I should admit that there were police interviews being carried out at that time, the incident with Nielsen was so fresh in my mind that I felt unable to say the words that someone had died in my bookshop the previous evening. After that call I decided to leave the phone ringing and let customers speak to the answer-phone.

After they had both been seen by the police, I suggested that Esther and Aggie go home. I catalogued some second-hand books while I waited for the interviews to end. Feeling disconsolate, I went home in the late afternoon as soon as the police were finished for the day.

3

I had not reckoned on having a suspicious death on my hands when I first considered opening a bookshop.

For a number of years I had been employed by a major retailer in an uninspiring marketing job where I was never quite settled or happy. When I received a legacy of £50,000 following the death of my father and came out on the right side of a property boom which gave me a substantial amount of equity in my London home, I found myself with a degree of financial independence that gave me the possibility of setting up my own business.

I was in a very loose off-on relationship at the time and lived on my own. I remember sitting down one night with a glass of Jameson's re-reading *The Glory of My Father* by Pagnol, part in tribute to my father, part grieving for him. Though the story is enchanting it brought out in me a sadness for the loss of my own father and the loss of my childhood, which, though not unreservedly happy, had many moments of sunny uplands in which my father and mother and brother were at the centre. The relationship of my mother (who was still alive) and my father was often stormy but it had endured and mellowed in later years into something approaching mutual understanding and tolerance.

By contrast I was approaching my thirtieth year and yet to find my soulmate. I thought, not for the first time, how important children's and adolescent literature and the experience of childhood was, not just for children, but for adults. It can sometimes encapsulate our dreams and aspirations and can crystallise thought, uncluttered as it is with all the baggage and complexity that so often accompanies adult literature.

The legacy from my father gave me an opportunity to pay off my house in full but, I thought, what good is a house to me when I could put the money to some better use?

Then I had a kind of revelation. The answer was staring me in the face: rows and rows of volumes, in bookcases, piled on the floor in every conceivable corner, some read, some not (though the intention was always that I would get round to them some time). I loved books and was an inveterate collector. What better than to become a bookseller so that I could be involved with them all of my working day?

My childhood had been blighted by a fall and a resulting bad bruise to my spine (just like the young Katy Carr in *What Katy Did*) when I was the tender age of 11. Like Katy and the young Robert Louis Stevenson, I spent long periods away from school. Propped carefully among a mountain of pillows in order to minimise the pain, my greatest relief came from reading. This exposure to books soon became my obsession. My books meant more to me than anything, so much so that I was aware that later on, even after my back had healed, it was a constraining factor on any attempt at a long term partnership.

My first attempt at a settled relationship ended rather abruptly when my girlfriend, on staying over at my flat, had the temerity to think she was improving my life by tidying up my books and selecting several old volumes for the rubbish bin. I was close to tears as I sorted through the bins in an attempt to retrieve my precious volumes. Some of them were too imbued with the detritus from the remains of the previous meal to be saved. I tried to rationalise the situation and tell myself that a few books did not really matter, but within weeks the relationship was over.

That evening when I realised that I wanted to open a bookshop, I was so taken with the idea that my imagination went into overdrive, though fuelled, I had to admit, by an excessive consumption of alcohol. I finished the whole bottle of whisky, conceiving in my mind the purchase of an elegant old building in the centre of a bustling town, stuffed full of an exciting range of books and surrounded by a constant stream of eager customers. I went to bed in the early hours of the morning in a happy alcoholic haze.

Awaking the next day with an evil hangover, I vowed never to drink whisky again. It did not, though, erase the idea of opening a bookshop from my mind. I took out a subscription to *The Bookseller*, which carried advertisements for bookshops for sale, and registered with several business agents in the parts of the country where I had decided I would like to live. Within six months I had sold my house in exchange for a piece of commercial property in a small but expanding market town and set up my bookshop. I went into it with my eyes open, knowing that it would not make me rich but if I could make a living doing something I loved then that would be fulfillment enough for me. I felt a tremendous excitement and a kind of relief that I had stopped letting my life drift.

I can still remember the exhilaration I felt on finding what I believed was the perfect building to house my bookshop, in a quaint street off the main area of the town of Ashby Morton. Following its time as an art institute, the building had become a bicycle shop which had been allowed to run down over the years and had closed a year before, so I was able to buy it for a good price, though it required a good deal of work to get it up to scratch. I had appointed a local builder who was willing to go along with my preference for keeping as many of the original features as possible. There was much to be done. An internal wall had to be knocked down and an RSJ installed in order to give the required amount of space, for I was determined to keep a good wide range of stock. I knew one of my biggest challenges would be reigning myself in and not buying too many books, as my instinct had always been to acquire books I liked whenever I saw them, with no regard to my financial situation.

Once the extra space had been created the walls needed to be made good. As far as possible I left the roof beams and tiles exposed on the first floor. The floorboards were mainly pitch pine in remarkably good condition, which I decided made the perfect floor surface. With some patching and hours of scrubbing to remove some unattractive dark staining I produced a floor that I was proud of. There were several broken roof tiles to replace, much of the brickwork needed re-pointing and the timber window and frontage needed attention. Then I began the job of fitting out the shop with bookcases from a DIY Store. I adapted them to fit the various nooks and crannies of the old building and extended them up as high as I dare. I knew this might alienate some customers but was all part of my quest to present a wide range of interesting books. In order to make the top shelves accessible, I hunted out from a local antique shop a pair of sturdy wooden library steps that I believed added to the overall effect.

I worked tirelessly for weeks, painting and decorating the inside walls. I brought a sleeping bag along with me and on several occasions slept in a corner. By this means I saved some precious time travelling to and from my home and avoided any distractions that might weaken my focus on the job in hand. The ceilings had been a particular challenge as I had never been over-confident with heights, especially when hanging off the top of a ladder. I felt tired and a little nervous about my new enterprise but at the same time a great feeling of adventure.

It was while I was hammering away fitting my first run of shelving units that I noticed, through the fanlight at the front of the shop, a bicycle parked up against the railings outside. I walked up towards the door, curious to see who it was and what business they had. Peering through the temporary door of plywood which had a letterbox size slit for post, I could see two large cow-like eyes. Eyelashes flickered and the eyes became a little animated.

'Excuse me, I don't suppose you know what happened to the bicycle shop?'

'Closed down I'm afraid.'

'I need my bike repairing you see. When did it close down?'

'I think about a year ago now.'

'I haven't been into town for ages. Usually my son does it for me but he's too busy at the moment. I didn't realise.' She sighed. 'It's a shame, all the best places are closing down.'

'Well, I'm here now,' I said, feeling a little on the defensive.

'Who are you?'

I dragged the plywood door open a little. The sun flooded in to reveal the owner of the beautiful cow eyes as an elegant lady in her fifties with short greying hair. She laughed and smiled.

'I meant what are you?'

'I'm Elliot Todd and I'm a bookshop.'

'A bookshop!' she said with sudden enthusiasm. 'This town needs a decent bookshop.'

'Well, I hope I'll be that.'

'I spend most of my time in second-hand bookshops or charity shops.'

'Well, I'm going to be both new and second-hand.'

'Really, that's marvellous. When are you going to open?'

'Well, obviously I need to get this door fixed first.'

'You're right,' she laughed, 'it is a bit off-putting.'

'And a few more shelves.'

'That's always a good idea.'

'And then it's up to me, really. It could be any day. Next week, a fortnight.'

She looked over my shoulder.

'Do you mind if I have a quick peek?'

'Be my guest.'

I stepped back from the door to allow her in while she parked her bike against a wall.

'It's lovely! I like the way you haven't messed about with it too much.'

'Thank you.'

'Some books might be a good idea.'

I laughed. I was beginning to like her.

'How on earth are you going to choose what to stock?'

'Well, I have lots of my own to put in - for the second hand ones - and then I was going to order a few new ones.'

'Make sure you have a large crime section,' she laughed. 'I like a good murder. But nothing too bloody.'

I nodded my head to indicate that I would do as she requested.

'Sounds like you're going to be my first customer.'

'I would love that. What are you going to call it?'

'Perhaps I could ask your advice. I was thinking of calling it *Ex Libris* but I didn't know if it sounded too fancy.'

'Of the books.'

'You don't think it's too fancy?'

'Well, this is not the most literary town in the world but who cares if they understand it, it sounds good.'

'I suppose that's all part of marketing.'

She was thoughtful a moment.

'I suppose you have plenty of staff.'

'No, actually, I haven't got any yet. I thought I would start by myself and see how I got on. I'm a little bit nervous about that. I've never had to employ anyone before.'

'I imagine it's pretty easy.'

'Really?'

'Well, you know, give a person a trial and if it doesn't work out, no hard feelings.'

'You make it sound simple.'

'Life is only difficult if you make it so.'

'You obviously like philosophy as well as crime.'

'No, I wouldn't know where to start. It's just something my dad used to say. Mind you he made life for himself pretty difficult, he drank himself to death.'

'Poor man.'

'Well, if you need anyone.'

'You'd be interested?'

'Well, I am severely underemployed at the moment. At present I am a supply teacher – but only in name. I can't seem to get anything without travelling to the ends of the earth. And I would so love to work in a bookshop.'

'Perhaps you could come and be my first customer and we could see how we get on.'

'All right, you're on Mr Todd.'

She began to walk away towards her bike.

'Hang on. What's your name?'

'Agnes, though everybody calls me Aggie. Agnes Stevenson. You had better tell me when you are opening. I can't keep turning up here every day on spec.'

She reached into her pocket.

'Here's a card I use for supply teaching – when there's anything going - so they don't keep getting my name wrong. They do like to make the "v" into a "ph".'

'What about your bike?' I called after her, remembering the original reason for her visit, as she pulled off, wobbling slightly.

'It's OK, it's only the brakes and they still work in a vague sort of way. I'll just have to go a bit slowly.'

So it was, Aggie joined the bookshop from the very first day. She was, as predicted, the first customer. She bought Margery Allingham's *Sweet Danger*. I tried to give it to her as a present but she insisted on paying for it as she said she would not count as the first customer if it had not been paid for. After our little ceremony of the first transaction we both stood around for a moment unsure of how to proceed. Then Aggie took her coat off and laid it on the floor behind the makeshift counter (a chest of drawers), proceeded to roll her sleeves up and started arranging books on the shelves. At that time we only had six rows of bookshelves and most of the rear of the shop and all of the upstairs was cordoned off. We had three other customers that morning and by the end of the day had taken the grand sum of just over £20. I spent half of my day putting up shelves in the far end of the shop while Aggie spent most of the day cleaning and hoovering and filling me in about her spinster-like existence. She had 'done husbands and children'. The children kept in touch, the husband didn't. A number of cats and dogs appeared to have taken his place. She seemed comfortable with her own company. I liked her a lot.

Whenever a customer came in we kept a discreet eye while they perused our limited shelves, anxious to help but unwilling to pounce on them and interrupt their browsing experience, sparse though it was at that time.

Then one of our customers asked: 'Do you order books?'

'Do we?' Aggie asked me.

'Of course we do, 'I replied.

I rang up the only supplier I had an account with. They had the book in stock and could supply it the next day - except the minimum order was £100.

'But as this is your very first order,' the Customer Services lady said helpfully, 'I will supply it carriage free so that you can see how good we are.'

We wrote down the customers details onto the back of an envelope and sellotaped it to the side of the chest-of-drawers. We felt great excitement when the order arrived promptly the next day. Aggie said it was only right that I should open the first order as she had bought the first book. In that case I pointed out, she could phone the customer to let them know the book was in. The delighted customer said that she would tell her friends. The following day our first stock order of new books arrived and we doubled our shelving space. Aggie worked hard on lobbying her friends and an article was printed in the local newspaper. By the end of the week we had achieved our first day when we had taken over £100. Within a month we had filled all of the shelving downstairs and began to eye the upstairs part of the shop.

We saw our initial modest enterprise grow into a well-stocked and busy bookshop. And our friendship grew over the years. She always had something interesting to say and was never judgmental. She was the sort of friend who always sounded pleased to hear from you and never failed to turn out.

Of course, the dream did not work out quite as expected in every way. With the outlawing of the Net Book Agreement and the rise of supermarkets and on-line selling, it became more and more difficult for small independent booksellers to survive. However, I worked hard at stocking an interesting range of new and old books that would not readily be found elsewhere and held a number of events with authors. Some were high profile, some local, some just had something interesting to say - and the events were well attended on the whole. After ten years I felt I had established myself at the heart of the community and for the most part was content with my lot. There was always something new on the horizon: an inspiring book from a new author, an eagerly awaited one from an established writer, or a hidden treasure found among my latest batch of old books. There were, I knew, far less happy places I could be.

There was, though, something missing: someone to share my enthusiasm and life with. I had my great friend and colleague, Aggie, but she was twenty years older than me and more like my favourite aunt and confidante. I began to realize that the longer I remained in my single state, the more independent and inflexible I was becoming. I feared a life of bachelorhood and a probable retreat into pipe-smoking. The bookshop did not, as I had originally envisaged, give me much free time. Very often I worked late into the evening making countless visits to look at second-hand books. If I was not making visits I was sorting books or holding author events. On a number of occasions I found myself sitting alone at the end of a long day feeling a little sad, and sometimes drinking a little too much. There was, though, always a book to find consolation in.

4

Then one day Esther walked into my life, though far from solving my dilemma, everything just became more complicated.

The very moment she walked into the shop, I was attracted to her. She was so enthusiastic about books and before I knew it we had effortlessly fallen into a conversation about Graham Greene (my favourite was the *The Power and the Glory*, hers was *The Heart of the Matter*), Evelyn Waugh (mine was *Scoop*, hers was *Decline and Fall*), Robert Frost (mine *Mending Wall*, hers *After Apple Picking*) and Edward Thomas (mine *Nothing Like the Sun*, hers *Addlestrop*). She left with a pile of books and took away some information about forthcoming author events. Two weeks later she phoned and asked if there was any possibility of a job at the bookshop. Though there was no vacancy at the time, Aggie, who was already beyond retirement age, had already given me notice of her intention to leave in three months (though she was happy to 'help-out' for odd days). I said to Esther that if she was still interested I would contact her in two months and, if Agnes was still feeling the same way about retiring, I would call her in for an interview. I owed so much to Aggie and did not want her to feel that I was in any way putting pressure on her to retire and, the truth was, I would miss her greatly – as I knew many of the customers would.

I tried to forget about Esther though I had to admit the memory of her visit came into my mind on more than one occasion. It was, therefore, with a degree of eager anticipation just over two months later, now that Aggie had confirmed her decision, that I phoned Esther about the vacancy.

Of course, lots of things can change in two months and I was half expecting that Esther had found another job or interest. So it was that I was disappointed (though not entirely surprised) when I had not received a reply to the answer phone message that I had left for her. Two further messages over the following week also elicited no response. I had not considered anybody else for the job, already in my mind considering that she would be the perfect candidate. Resigned to finding someone else I put an advert in the local paper and turned to one or two recent CVs which I had on file.

After I had placed my advert, I received over sixty applications for the bookseller post. I whittled them down to a dozen possible candidates. Two weeks later I interviewed those who I believed were the four strongest. I had difficulty choosing between a young academic who wanted a job for two years while she studied for her law exams and a former librarian in her fifties. I decided in the end on the young academic, feeling that the book business was changing so rapidly it might be good if I was forced to review things in two years' time. I had just written the letter offering the job to the successful candidate when Aggie came knocking on the door of my office to ask me if there was anything for the last post that evening. The letter offering the job was on the side of the desk ready to go. I reached towards it and then something made me hesitate. I withdrew my hand. 'No, it's OK, Aggie, it will do tomorrow.'

I decided not to work late in the bookshop that evening and a little after six I switched off the lights and made my way over to set the alarm system. The phone rang. Usually I could not resist a phone call, but as all the computers and the lights were switched off, I decided to leave it unanswered. If it was a customer they could leave a message which I would pick up in the morning. If it was someone who knew me they could get me at home or on my mobile. I was one of those people that did not like mobile phones but I had reluctantly learnt to keep mine switched on as it had become a useful means of contact when I was sourcing second-hand books - even though I often had trouble finding the thing when it did ring.

I set the alarm and closed the door only to find that I had left my car and house keys behind so, annoyed at my forgetfulness, I went through all the palaver of finding the keys and resetting the alarm. I rushed out determined to be on my way - straight into…

'Esther!' I cried as I flew into her, dropped my book and knocked a piece of paper and pen out of her hand. She immediately scooped the book off the floor for me and picked up the pen and paper.

'I'm sorry, I tried ringing. Then I thought I could leave a note.'

She smiled with her eyes as well as her face, exuding an enchanting warmth.

'That's all right. I heard the phone but left it as I was already on my way out. It's nice to see you again.'

'And you. Is it too late?'

'Too late?'

'To apply for the job. I quite understand if it is.'

'Oh… no. You're just in time … I mean you could be included if you want to.'

I was conscious even at that stage that I was sounding a little too eager and part of my conscience was nagging at me and telling me that what I should do was give the job to the law student for whom I had already written the offer letter. Another part was telling me that my undoubted attraction to Esther was not the best basis for a working relationship.

'If you are sure?' she continued.

'Absolutely,' I replied, realising that my conscience was going to play no part in my decision.

'Well, yes I would like that.'

So she came back the next day.

'I am so sorry that I took so long to respond to your call, 'she explained. 'You see I was away - had to be away - and then I picked up your messages.'

'It's fine, honestly.'

We entered my office.

'Please sit down - and tell me what you have been reading.'

I beckoned to a chair.

'I read *Scoop* again, you know after our conversation. It is wickedly funny, I have to agree. But I still stand by *Decline and Fall*'.

'Yes, I read *After Apple Picking* again. It is a great poem.'

An interview that should have taken fifteen or twenty minutes took an hour as we became side-tracked on the relative merits of Hardy, Dickens and Trollope.

'Though we have had a couple of very good candidates,' I said, winding up the interview (which had really not been like an interview), and trying to sound like I had made a considered decision (and there was more than an element of truth in the next thing I said), 'no one else comes near your knowledge of literature: so I would like to offer you the job.'

I had already established that she was happy with the paltry pay.

'Thank you,' she said. 'I am really very pleased'.

I stood up and she followed suit. I held out my hand.

'Welcome to the bookshop. I look forward to working with you.'

Esther turned out not only to be very knowledgeable about literature but also extremely capable. She became quickly adept with the ordering, stock receipt, customer enquiries, cataloguing and all the other ins and outs of bookselling. While Aggie was perfectly competent she had not quite mastered computer skills. A new dimension was added to the marketing of the bookshop as Esther churned out promotional material and sent out newsletters to our customers. However, I was worried that we would lose some of our long established and, particularly, older customers once Aggie only became part-time. Esther, though, turned out to have a compelling and charming way about her and, though some mourned the absence of Aggie, very few were prepared to abandon our shop now that they had seen how good her replacement was.

On the Friday following Esther's first week at the bookshop I closed the doors promptly at five-thirty and turned to her. She was still busy cataloguing books.

'Well, Esther, you have now completed a whole week. How do you think it has gone?'

She put the large Michelangelo art book, which she had finished cataloguing to one side.

'As you warned me, there has been a lot to learn but ... I have loved it.'

'Well I think you have been brilliant - you fit in perfectly. Do you fancy a celebratory drink at The Crown?'

'That would be great. My chickens can wait half-an-hour.'

'Chickens?'

'Yes, Flossie and Dewdrop.'

'They have names?'

'Of course!'

She rummaged in her handbag and pulled out her purse.

I put up my hand.

'No Esther,' I protested, 'I think you have got it wrong, I pay you to work not the other way around.'

With a smile she extracted some photographs and passed them across to me.

'I know that most women would have photographs of their boyfriend or husband but these are my pin-ups.'

I looked at the photographs of two fine and proud looking chickens.

'That's Flossie on the right.'

'I think I am rapidly finding out that you are not like any other woman.'

There was a cheeky defiant smile that I was to come to know so well.

In fact we decided to eat as well as drink at the pub. Esther had spaghetti carbonara while I favoured chilli con carne. I was enjoying the novelty of her first week at the bookshop.

'Do you realise I never asked you for a CV?'

'Yes.'

She scooped up a forkful of spaghetti.

'Do you want one now?'

'Nothing too formal. I am particularly interested in where your love of books comes from.'

'My mother, I would say, mainly. She was an actor and dancer. She had lots of spare time between rehearsals and always had a book with her. And she used to read to me and my brother at night time - she really made the stories come alive. She had a lovely expressive voice.'

'Do you get your sense of humour from your mother too?'

'I would say mostly from my father. This food is not at all bad.'

I drank a sip of beer.

'Did you do any acting yourself?'

'At school, though I did seem to mix with a lot of "resting" actors when I worked in a bar.'

'And after the bar work.'

'A number of things. Publishing, publicity, a museum - I never quite settled. Then I met my husband, David.'

My stomach lurched. I knew all along that there was likely to be someone. I tried to carry on without betraying disappointment.

'Where did you meet?'

'I had a small part in an opera.'

'I thought you didn't act.'

'It was hardly acting. I had done some singing. I played one of the three ladies in *The Magic Flute*, David played Tamino, the handsome prince lost in a distant land. We got chatting in rehearsals.'

'The prince found his princess.'

She smiled.

'Yes, I suppose you could put it like that.'

I was afraid of asking the next question but I felt I had to.

'And David...?'

'Is dead.'

It was not the answer I was expecting.

'I'm sorry.'

She seemed perfectly calm for a moment, then her eyes momentarily welled with tears.

'I am sorry. I didn't mean to be dramatic.' She covered her eyes with her hand for a moment. 'I should have said that in a more measured way.'

I observed, not for the first time, that there could be a kind of beauty in tragedy, as there was in her tears at that moment.

'I don't think there is any easy way to say these things.'

'It's only been a year.'

'Which is no time at all.'

She hesitated.

'I know this might seem strange but I still feel wedded to him. Can you understand?' she searched my eyes. 'I know everybody says you will get over it in time but in a way I don't want to. I want to feel that way. It's not a morbid feeling. It's just the way I do feel.'

'I lost my father ten years ago and I still think about him every day, still talk to him and think what he would have said in a particular situation. I don't think there are any rules. It's what you feel is right for you that is important.

'I'm sorry,' I continued, 'I shouldn't have quizzed you like that.'

'It's OK really, you would have found out at some stage.'

I squeezed her arm.

'Well, I promise not to ask you anything about it again - unless you ever want to talk about it. Let's just talk about books.'

She screwed her eyes up.

'That could be a bit limiting.'

'With your knowledge I wouldn't think so. But all right, we could talk about chickens as well then, though I warn you all I have heard of is a Rhode Island Red.'

She laughed.

'You are not so far off the mark. I keep Black Rock hens, a cross between a Plymouth Rock and Rhode Island Red. They are great for free range and resistant to disease. I'll bring you some eggs.' She reached behind for her handbag. 'Which reminds me, I must get back to them. But, thank you Elliot. And, you know, the bookshop feels so right for me. Thank you for giving me the opportunity.'

After she left I stayed for another drink. Her moving declaration about her late husband had done nothing to decrease my attraction to her - on the contrary it had done quite the opposite, making me feel more protective towards her.

We began to establish a close but platonic relationship. There was, I felt, a kind of unspoken agreement between us which gave us a lot of freedom to be close as friends and work colleagues while knowing exactly where the boundaries lay. We would go round to each other's house, keep a regular dinner engagement, go to the cinema or visit a garden or a museum. We were the couple who were not a couple. So many people thought that we were partners, that sometimes I did not bother explaining. In some ways we were a bit like the idyll of an old-fashioned courting couple and without the pressure of a physical relationship there was a freedom just to be. I learnt not to push things or make assumptions. If she was going out on her own, unless she told me, I did not ask where she was going or who with. I think I was afraid of knowing because if I knew she was going out with another man, even though I tried to deny it to myself, I would be jealous. So, for the moment I accepted my celibacy. I knew this situation could not last forever but I had to admit I had achieved a degree of contentment. It was like the joy of childhood friendship before the onset of puberty and the complications of sexual feelings, and I tried to think of it as such and enjoy it for its own sake.

5

After I arrived home following the police interviews at the
bookshop I picked up an answer phone message from Esther
inviting me to talk to her if I wanted to, and if not, that she
would see me the following day. I rang her and she answered
immediately. I asked her how her interview with the inspector
went.

'I think he was surprised that I was not at the author's side all
the time. I explained how I showed Nielsen to the table, made
sure he had a comfortable chair and so on and showed people
where to queue. Then - you know how it is - I got called to the
till to help Susie.'

'I should have come down to help you.'

'No, you shouldn't have. Customers needed looking after
upstairs as well. The queues normally look after themselves. It
didn't seem any time at all between helping Susie and customers
asking where the author was. It's really bizarre.'

'Yes, it's so strange to think that right under our very noses
Harry Nielsen was breathing his last. I still can't quite believe it.'

'No, nor can I.'

Thankfully, they allowed me to open the bookshop the following
day as forensics had completed their work, though the stock
room remained cordoned off.

I wanted to make sure everything was in order before we
opened, following the disruption caused by the police and the
forensic investigation. After re-arranging a display table and a
couple of bookshelves, I soon found myself drawn towards the
centre of the shop where the signing had taken place after the
talk. The table we had used for the signing was still in position.
I stood beside it imagining the scene and the moment when
Nielsen had been spirited away by the mysterious man. During
a signing we placed the table so that it was bounded by a row
of freestanding bookshelf units on either side. This arrangement

was intentional as it encouraged customers to queue closer to the till, making it easier for them to pay for their book before or after the signing. It also meant that the author was in the view of the person serving there. Of course, I had not been present at the moment of the signing in this case, though I had been a witness to many of them over the years.

As I contemplated all this, I heard the turn of a key in the lock of the shop door. It was Esther. As she approached I voiced my thoughts to her.

'I was just trying to imagine how on earth it could have happened.'

'And?'

'I don't think I'm any the wiser.'

I felt rooted to the spot as though occupying the place where the incident had happened would somehow give me an insight into what had occurred there. Esther stood looking at the scene for a second before walking past me to the end of the shop and back towards the entrance with her arms folded in a thoughtful way. Then, I realised that she had disappeared from view.

'Esther!' I called.

'Boo!'

I jumped. She was right behind me, a little out of breath.

'I ducked down behind the run of units and came round. I bet that's how he got to Nielsen without anyone noticing.'

'And probably left the same way.'

'That could be it. There would only be a small area at the front of the shop to negotiate where he could be seen.'

'And with everything that was going on, he probably would not be noticed. But he didn't just come and go. He took Nielsen to the back of the shop and … Nielsen's death resulted.'

'Delicately put.'

She sat on the edge of the table with her legs dangling down.

'If you think about it,' Esther continued, 'most customers keep a respectful distance while the author talks and signs the book of the customer in front of them. Look if you stand there,' she slipped her small but perfectly-formed frame off the table and propelled me backwards to a kind of entrance formed by the freestanding shelf units either side, 'when I am behind you …' she walked towards the counter, ' I can't really see what is going on, especially as the author is usually sitting down.'

'Except we know that Mrs Kay was interrupted by this *goatee* beard man.'

'Well, that's a key point. For all we love Mrs Kay she is a bit dotty. When she was interrupted she said she thought it was all part of the fun, and - no doubt - probably forgot what she was doing for a moment and chatted to all sorts of people before anyone had the temerity to insist that something was amiss.'

'That was when you were accosted, no doubt.'

Esther nodded.

'It might explain how he was whisked away but what was the motive?' said Esther.

'Professional jealousy, a madman off the street.'

'Or an angry husband.'

'He did have a reputation with the ladies, according to Mrs Pargeter, though I'm not sure where she got her information from.'

'She's not the sort who usually resorts to tittle tattle.'

'No.'

'Though it does make you wonder where she would hear such things.'

Then I suddenly remembered.

'Oh, Clinton wants us give him names and numbers from the guest list and we need to go through the photos. Do you think we could split it between us?'

We worked through the list throughout the day in-between running the bookshop. I felt subdued at first but it was difficult to stay that way for long in Esther's company. Not too many of our customers were aware that anything untoward had happened and those that were had the good sense not to make too many demanding enquiries.

There was also a long-standing engagement to consider. That evening Esther and I had been invited to visit Aggie in her quaint old cottage. We decided that, despite the drama of recent events at the bookshop, it was an appointment we should keep. I also thought that, as Aggie was such good company, it might lift our spirits a bit.

6

Aggie lived close by a river just a few miles out of town, her house hidden away and accessed by a tiny narrow lane with high hedges on either side. She was not entirely alone. A few yards further down the river bank was a smart pub-cum restaurant and beyond that a private dwelling which had formerly housed a family who ferried people across the river, from which the restaurant next door, The Ferry Boat Inn, took its name. It always made me think of the inn in *The History of Mr. Polly*.

There was an area at the back of Aggies's house that faced the river. Over the years it had become a dumping ground for rubbish. To deal with the eyesore Aggie had installed a blind in the window facing towards it, seeking to ignore what was there. She had a fit of inertia whenever she contemplated doing something about it. Help, however, had been at hand. By way of a birthday present, her son had cleared the area and made it into an attractive courtyard for sitting and relaxing in. He had worked on his project over several weeks clearing away the mess, checking with Aggie what was essential and what was not (desperately trying to persuade her that most of it was only fit for the dump). Then he laid down the area with some superior looking stone chippings and populated it with an ancient cast iron table and chairs (rescued from a dump) and a selection of potted plants. We were there to help her christen it with 'a little something', which in Aggies's case meant a little something of alcohol.

We had continued to be blessed with unseasonably warm spring weather and that day was one of those special warm days that turned into a caressing warm evening, where one could think of nothing better than sitting outside and passing it in good company.

We admired the courtyard and the way her son had carefully arranged Aggies's vast array of pots and plants. Aggie had a knack with gardening that did not seem to be based on any scientific principles. She claimed that her plants survived through 'benign neglect and occasional haphazard watering.'

Though we did not expressly mention the death in the bookshop it did not preclude us from talking about 'The Bard'. I had read Nielsen's book about him and some of the details were at the forefront of my mind.

'What do you know about Shakespeare Aggie?' I asked her.

'I know that Shakespeare *had small Latine, and less Greeke*.'

'So he wasn't a very good writer?'

'No, I didn't say that. He was just not as well educated as some of the others like Christopher Marlowe.'

'And that he didn't leave his wife the best bed,' put in Esther.

'But it was his second best bed,' I said.

'It was still not the best.'

'But wasn't there a reason for that?'

'What, for not caring enough to leave the best bed to your wife, the one they slept in. I think it's just called callousness. '

'When he was around,' added Aggie, 'he spent half of his life gallivanting about in London. Beside, in respectable households ,husband and wife often had their own bedroom and bed.'

'We don't know the half of what he did because there's a big gap in what we know about him after the birth of his twins - for about seven years I think,' said Esther.

'I bet you don't know this. One of the twins was called Hamnet.'

I challenged her 'you mean Hamlet - as in the play - he must have got the name from there.'

'No, it was Hamnet; that was his name and he died when he was just eleven.'

'You're just slurring your speech. It's the drink. It must be Hamlet.'

'It is Hamnet, I swear.' Esther thrust her hand into mine. 'I'll bet you £100.'

'If you make it a twenty you're on.'

'I am a witness to that. You can't wriggle out of it Elliot,' said Aggie.

'How do you know she's right?' I said.

'When she is sure you can bet she is right.'

'But going back to what we were talking about earlier: wasn't there something about leaving the best bed to one's son?'

'I don't know.'

'Anyway, are you going to leave me anything Aggie?' I said to Aggie

'Yes my dogs.'

'But, you know I can't abide ...'

'What are you going to leave me?'

'There's no point, you'll be dead before me.'

'You don't know that,' broke in Esther. 'Aggie is extremely fit.'

'For someone who smokes and takes ten sugars in her coffee.'

'I'll give you a list. And what are you going to leave Esther?' said Aggie.

'I hadn't really thought. I haven't known ...'

'I'm sure he will be interested in your crime novels when you have finished with them.' Esther chimed in as she simultaneously kicked me under the table.

'Yes, even if I haven't popped my clogs you can borrow them.'

'How did we get onto this?'

'Shakespeare and his blessed bed.'

Aggie's son Henry joined us and we continued to talk late into the night. His main trade was thatching and by the end of the evening I felt quite expert in the different types of materials used for thatch and thatching techniques. I was also surprised to learn that thatching had increased in popularity in the last 30 years and that there were now almost as many Master Thatchers as there were independent bookshops. I wasn't sure whether to be cheered or depressed by this news.

There followed a brief foray into the rights and wrongs of intervention in foreign climes.

'Elliot, you're driving,' Esther reminded me, as I downed another glass of wine.'

'Sorry, I wasn't thinking. I got carried away.'

'It's OK, we can walk. It's only about three miles to the house if we go along by the canal. We can do something about your car tomorrow.'

'To yours. It must be about six to mine.'

'You'll just have to sleep on the floor - on the sofa bed anyway - the spare bedroom is being decorated.'

'There's always the hen coop,' Aggie laughed. 'Don't forget to lay an egg or two while you're in there.'

'I was going to take you in to the police tomorrow anyway.'

'Aggie can you ...?'

'Look after the shop. It's like I've never left.'

'Well you haven't really, and I suppose you never will.'

'I do hope not,' said Esther enthusiastically.

'You know, it's one of those nights that you just want to go on forever. Shall we open another bottle of fizzy Aggie?'

'This from the man who was supposed to be driving.'

'It doesn't matter now I know I'm not.'

'There's one in the fridge.'

I walked at a not too straight angle towards Aggie's kitchen.

As I wandered back with the bottle Aggie and Esther were in close conversation while Henry was having a wander around the garden looking at his handiwork. I felt the soft breeze through the willows that bordered the river and felt a flood of warm hearted emotion which I did not believe was entirely fuelled by alcohol. I gave a sigh of contentment.

'This is the life,' I said to them as I approached and sat down with a sigh. 'My two favourite girls, wine, a warm breeze.'

'You are a silly romantic when you get drunk,' commented Aggie.

'I suppose you're right,' I said. 'But I'm having fun.'

For some reason we all started howling with laughter as though this was the funniest exchange of words that had ever been made. Such was the noise we made that Henry came across.

'Is everything all right? It's not my garden you are laughing at is it?'

'No your garden is absolutely beautiful,' said Esther.

A few coffees later and well after midnight, Esther and I began the walk along the river. For a while Esther put her arm through mine.

'That's too annoying,' she said at last. 'I need to have my arms free.'

'I know. You are a free spirit.'

'Yes, and you would do well to heed that Elliot Todd.'

'I feel like I am being reprimanded for something I haven't

done.'

I tapped myself on my head.

'Of course, it's for something I might do.'

'Yes and if you try anything,' She put her fist up at me but she was laughing, 'you will be dead in the water.'

'If my mother could hear you.'

When we arrived at Esther's house we hardly stopped to turn the lights on. Esther flung me a sleeping bag and said she was just going to check her beloved chickens. I began clucking in a childish way (which I felt totally ashamed of the following morning). I fell straight asleep, not bothering with the sofa-bed, preferring the floor.

On waking I drank a couple of glasses of water. Esther cooked us poached egg on toast. I was disappointed that she could not tell me which one of her hens, Flossie or Dewdrop, had laid the eggs. Whichever it was, they were extremely tasty. After a strong cup of tea I felt surprisingly good and I tried to explain to Esther why I thought this was as she drove me to the police station.

'You know when you are feeling happy and all the endorphins are swimming around, I don't think drink affects you as much.'

Esther was sceptical.

'Where did you hear that?'

'I'm not entirely sure but I think it's true.'

'Hm. And I am not sure endorphins swim.'

'I'm sure they have done some research.'

'They?'

'I think I heard about it on some program or other. Radio 4, I think it was - that science programme.'

'Or that medical programme.'

'It may have been. Did you hear it too?'

She did not reply but smiled - a laughing smile.

'You're making fun of me.'

There was a companionable silence for a few moments presently broken by Esther.

'You realise we might be suspects too?'

'Yes, I was thinking that. Our DNA is likely to be all over the place in that alcove.'

We pulled up outside the police station.

'I wouldn't worry, anyway,' continued Esther, 'it's not likely that there is much of your DNA in that cubbyhole. You're too high and mighty to spend any time there with those overstocks - you leave it to us minions.'

She drove off, the corner of her mouth creased into a cheeky smile. We were going to meet later when I had finished seeing the inspector.

The inspector seemed pleased with what we had done.

'I don't suppose this man would have left his name?'

'It wouldn't make any sense if you planned to murder someone,' I commented as he scanned down the list.

'You are assuming that this was a planned murder - if that is what it was. From my initial discussion with the pathologist it seems that some force must have been involved in order to cause that degree of penetration so it seems likely that, as I suspected, another party was involved - though this helmet appears to have had a particularly long spike. I was about to visit the forensic pathologist. You could come along if you like. He might have a question for you about this pickle thing.'

'I'm not sure if there is any special knowledge I have but I am happy to try and help however I can.'

I was, in truth, intrigued and a little flattered to be involved in this way.

The drive was not a long one and the inspector seemed more intent on discussing his daughter than the case. She had been to university and decided to move back home.

'In my day, as soon as you left home, that was it. You never thought about moving back.'

'I've heard it's quite a common occurrence with the housing market being like it is.'

'But doesn't she want her independence? I know I did at that age.' He sighed.' I suppose you're right. It's just economics in the end.'

At the pathologist's lab I was spared a visit to see the body. Instead I was included in a discussion in the office with the pathologist, a Mr Kirk. He was rotund and bearded with a pleasing eager manner.

'This *Pickelhaube* that you had in your bookshop had an extremely long spike,' he observed.

'Yes, I remember the author who brought it in telling me that it was just about the longest that was ever produced - 13 centimetres I think he said - it belonged to a Saxon Reserve Officer. I just never thought that it might be used in this way.'

'Well it does seem that it was certainly the cause of his downfall though I must say that in some ways he was a little unfortunate. The spike went into Mr Nielsen's windpipe and punctured at least one blood vessel. This caused air to get into the blood stream. It is more common when blood vessels are punctured above the level of the heart as in this case. This is not always dangerous in itself but it appears that Mr Nielsen was one of the twenty per cent or so of the population that has an Atrial Septal Defect.'

'A what?'

'It's a little complicated but I will try to explain. We have to go right back to the beginning of the story - the foetus. When the foetus is developing, the lungs are not developed enough to oxygenate the blood. This function is performed by the placenta and it happens via something called the foramen ovale. Now in most cases this becomes covered by a layer of tissue over the course of time. However in a number of cases this doesn't happen sufficiently for it to become completely sealed. The importance of this is that it allows air in the blood to travel to the right side of the heart causing the lung to contract. If the pressure rises high enough, as seems to have been the case here, and the foramen ovale is not completely sealed, the air bubble can then travel to the left side of the heart to the brain and on to the coronary arteries, resulting in random ischemic damage which if not treated within a few minutes is irreversible.'

'Sorry, I think you've lost me there.'

'Basically, in this case we believe it caused a heart attack.'

'So if it wasn't for this condition he may well have survived.'

'Possibly.'

'You will never get Kirk to commit to anything that he's not absolutely certain of,' added the inspector.

'And what are the chances of him just having fallen against the spike?'

'I would say, extremely unlikely. If he fell or tripped he might have given himself a nasty gash or cut but for this extent of an injury, it would require some force.' Clinton looked at me as if in vindication. 'But that doesn't mean, of course, that the force was applied with the intention of maiming Mr Nielsen. It could've just been a momentary fit of rage.'

Inspector Clinton and I walked to where his car was parked. I tried to clarify the situation with him.

'So it's possible that this could just be seen as an unfortunate accident?'

'If you mean did Nielsen trip over and fall on the spike I think, like Kirk said, that's extremely unlikely. However, if you're asking whether it was planned or intentional, that's another matter. It may have been planned, but equally it may have happened on the spur of the moment. He may have been, for example, a jealous husband or partner who chose that moment to confront him, passions may have been roused and things may have just gone further than intended.'

'Or it could have been a jealous academic?'

He looked at me quizzically. At first I thought he did not understand.

'Because Nielsen was one of the foremost experts on Shakespeare,' I continued, 'he may have been a rival or disagreed with him in some way.'

'Yes, we are still gathering information from that end. Some very strange things go on in that academic world I can tell you. There's petty rivalry and jealousy like you would not believe. Where murder is involved, logic often goes out of the window. Emotion and opportunity are often more relevant. It's perfectly likely that there was no intention to murder or maim beforehand. That's why it's worth checking your lists to see if this man is on there. If he had no intention to hurt Mr Nielsen he would have had no reason not to include his name on the guest list. And, at this stage, there's no absolute certainty that this man, whoever he was, was the person responsible. It could've been another man - or woman. All we have is the word of a small boy.'

'And a precocious one at that.'

'Just because Nielsen and this man with the beard went down there at that moment, it doesn't necessarily mean that the man with the beard was responsible for his death. How long would you say they were gone away from the signing before the body was found?'

'It must've been quite a long time. I would have been at least 10 minutes looking for him in the car park and around the shop.'

'Then it's possible that this man with the beard might be an innocent diversion.'

'Had to be quite important, though, to take him away from the book signing,' I speculated. 'I have rarely known an author who didn't like signing books.'

On the way home I had a sudden pang of guilt that I had not sent our bestseller list to the local paper as I usually did. 'We would certainly be in the paper the following week,' I mused, 'for all the wrong reasons'.

When I arrived back at the bookshop Esther was already ahead of me and was busy editing and magnifying the photos on a PC in between serving customers. I made coffees for us both and watched over her shoulder.

'I took a couple at the beginning of the evening in case we forgot - you know - like we do. There was one I took of the audience to show what a good crowd we had in.'

She clicked on the mouse selecting the most relevant photos. There was one of the author and me.

'Why do I always do that?' I sighed. 'Close my eyes at the wrong moment.'

Esther giggled.

'And stick your belly out.'

I self-consciously took in a deep intake of breath in order to flatten my stomach.

There was one photo of the author in full flow, expounding on some point or other. That would have been the one that we would have chosen to send to the paper.

'I'm quite pleased with that one,' remarked Esther.

'Yes, it's a good one.'

There were four or five customers in shot but no one we did not recognise. Then came the photo of the audience. It was a decent shot though a little fuzzy at the edges. There were about twenty or so of our customers in the photo.

'Apart from the moustache we don't know what he looks like,' Esther said.

'We probably talked to him.'

'Without recognizing the moustache?'

'Perhaps he took it off.'

Esther cackled. It is difficult to have an endearing cackle but somehow Esther managed it.

'I can't see a moustache there but if it was just a small moustache it would be difficult to tell with everybody in this photo.'

Some of the heads of the audience were inclined away from the photo or just the top of their heads were visible. In a couple of cases there were hands obscuring mouths.

'If only he could have warned us I would've taken more note,' she said.

'Well, I suppose the person who we know definitely had most contact with him was Mrs Kay. I wonder if we might have another chat with her? If we show her the photos she might remember something.'

'It has to be worth a try.'

'I just hope we don't receive too much adverse publicity from this.'

'It could work the other way. They say no publicity is bad publicity.'

'I'm not so sure in this case. Would you like to frequent a shop that has had a recent murder?'

'Alleged murder.'

'Alleged murder.'

'I'll have to think about that one.'

'Do you know where Mrs Kay lives?'

'I'll have to look it up. Some manor somewhere, I think.'

7

We were in luck. Mrs Kay said she would be delighted to welcome us as long as we did not mind cats. We had plenty of experience of cats at Aggie's house so I assured her that this would be fine. Esther agreed to accompany me in the late afternoon, while Aggie, who was supposed to be working just for the morning, agreed to look after the shop for the rest of the day.

I had already counted five cats by the time we sat down for tea in the low ceilinged, beamed lounge of her magnificent home that dated back to the 16th century. This was the first time I had occasion to visit her, and was a little unnerved by the fact that she shooed a cat, apparently named Tiger, from off the table which laid out with a selection of cakes and a large pot of tea.

Mrs Kay had money and influence but did not worry too much about what people thought of her, the way she dressed or the state of her house.

Cats were chased off chairs and we were invited to sit down on some ancient looking though (as it turned out), very comfortable armchairs. Esther smoothed the way.

'So good of you to see us.'

'Not at all, such a wicked thing to have happened in your lovely little shop.'

Though she had a tendency to ramble Mrs Kay had been a loyal supporter of our bookshop over the years. Esther took out the magnified photo.

'I have put crosses above the people that we can identify ourselves. That leaves twelve people.'

'Such a shame to spoil a nice photo.'

'It's just a copy. I have it stored on our computer.'

'It is so marvellous what you young people can do on computers.'

I gave an involuntary smirk when I considered Esther was

now in her late thirties which was causing her considerable consternation. She jabbed her elbow into my stomach, a technique she had developed recently that had already caused me a degree of discomfort. It was such a swift deft movement that she had perfected that it was almost imperceptible to the naked eye. So it was that Mrs Kay was ignorant of the cause of my little cry of pain.

'Are you quite all right Elliot?' asked Mrs Kay solicitously.

Esther answered for me.

'Just the strain of all this awful business. Have some more tea, Mr Todd.' She passed me over a cup accompanied by an innocent smile but I could detect all the wickedness behind it.

'I recognise two of them,' said Mrs Kay, 'but unfortunately neither of them is him.'

'Never mind. Do you know the names of the two people you do recognise?'

'Now let me see. I believe one of them is called Barbara - or is it Anne. Do you know, I'm not sure if I do?'

'We can leave it with you if you like, see if anything comes to mind.'

'Could you? My niece is coming round later, you know Samantha. She might know. My memory is so bad nowadays. They call her Sam. Such a lovely girl - she's at university - and she loves books. I don't suppose you have any openings for her at the bookshop - holidays and so on?'

'Yes I know Sam, she did some work experience for us. One of the best we have ever had. I'm afraid there is nothing at the moment but I'll make a mental note in case anything should come up.'

'Tell me, this dreadful business: was it really murder?'

'They are not absolutely sure but it appears that there was a strong likelihood that it was - or at least a disagreement that had an unfortunate outcome.'

'Dreadful. I have told the police all I know.'

'I'm sure.'

'Quite nice that Inspector Clinton, if a little brusque.'

She leaned forward, confidentially.

'And I'm not at all sure if he likes cats.'

'Perhaps he has an allergy.'

'Yes, I know, lots of people do. Too much clean living.'

Esther involuntarily laughed and put her hand to her mouth.

'What?' I could not help saying.

'Everything is sanitised. *You must eat a peck of dirt before you die*. That's what I was told when I was young - but they don't nowadays.'

'That was Swift you know, who said that, in his *Polite Conversation*.'

'How clever of you to know that, Esther. You do have such clever staff Elliot.'

Esther coloured up a little.

'I'm sorry, I didn't mean to sound like a know-it-all. I have just been reading a book about Swift and I just happen to remember it.'

'Nonsense, you shouldn't be ashamed of it: you should be proud of it. There is too much of an anti-intellectual culture in this country. That is something we can learn from the French. They embrace knowledge there while we seem to be embarrassed by it'.

Interesting as this was we were forgetting the point of our visit.

'We have taken up enough of your time and hospitality Mrs Kay, but may I ask, did you have any contact with this man with the moustache apart from when you were having your book signed?'

'No, I can't say I did. In fact, that was the first time I noticed him all evening.'

'This seems to be developing into a familiar theme. I am getting the feeling that this man, whoever he was, didn't appear until the time of the signing and - the death – of Nielsen.'

'A mystery man.'

'Quite.'

'Well I'm so sorry about all the trouble this is causing you. Perhaps the police will come up with something shortly. You don't have any of those camera things?'

'CCTV. No, I'm afraid we don't have any of those installed.'

She looked a little tired and I thought there was nothing more to be gained by staying longer.

'Well, thank you so much Mrs Kay. We must be on our way.'

She smiled sweetly and showed us to the door.

As we walked down the path towards my car I had an uncomfortable feeling in my mouth. I extracted a hair.

'I think that's one of Tiger's,' laughed Esther. 'I had one in my cake too.'

I spat in an undignified way, trying to rid myself of all trace of Tiger. I received another dig in the stomach from Esther. I was becoming a little fed up with this and was about to tell her so, but she had turned back towards the house. Evidently Esther had been trying to direct my attention. Mrs Kay had reappeared in her doorway.

'I meant to say, if you have any more photos you want me to look at I will be more than happy.'

'Unfortunately, that was the only one where we thought the mystery man may have appeared.'

'Oh...' she hesitated trying to work something out. 'I don't suppose my niece would have one? She took several of me with her mobile phone.'

'It's certainly worth a try.'

'Shall I ask her to contact you?'

'Yes, that would be very kind.'

I started up the engine though I was undecided as to whether I was heading back to the bookshop or home.

'What do you think, should we go back and review the evidence?'

'It's my yoga night, but I could skip it if you like.'

'I don't see why you should. All work and all that.'

'If you're sure. I always feel better after my yoga.'

'Then it's best you do it. This can wait. Anyway, you might be able to work it all out during your yoga session.'

'I'm not sure if I can. The whole point is to empty your mind and not try to control your thoughts.'

'Whilst wrapping your leg around your head.'

'Something like that.'

'I think that's what would bother me. I think if I ever managed to wrap my leg around my head my only thought would be whether I could get it back down again afterwards.'

She smiled and shook her head as though she was humouring a child.

I did not go back to the shop. I wanted, rather like Esther was doing with her yoga, to escape from the recent reality of the death of Nielsen. After I had dropped her by her car, I drove home determined that I should indulge in an evening of reading. I did not want anything too taxing. I felt in the mood for something entertaining.

Perversely, my idea of light entertainment as far as reading was concerned was a crime novel, which inevitably meant reading about murder. I thumbed the shelves and picked up a copy of *Strong Poison* by Dorothy L. Sayers. This was the crime novel that introduced Harriet Vane into fiction. I had always enjoyed the romantic sparring of Vane and Wimsey and in a sort of wistful way began to draw a parallel between this and Esther's and my own relationship. I realised I had perhaps been doing this rather a lot lately and it was probably this that drew me to that particular book that evening. I suspected I was searching for a way to explain my own quiet obsession with Esther. However, I quickly realised that by comparing us with Harriet Vane and Lord Peter Wimsey, I was stretching a point and that there were only a few tentative similarities.

When I went to bed at about ten, anxious to make an early start the next morning, I soon fell asleep. However, I had a disturbing dream. Harriet Vane, Esther, myself and Wimsey, the murdered Nielsen and the man with a *goatee* beard became inextricably linked. There was a horrifying image of Nielsen freeing himself from the position where we had found him impaled upon the *Pickelhaube*. He began lunging across the floor with blood pouring from the gaping wound in his neck. He veered in my direction mouthing some words that I could not hear. I began to back away until he came right up close to me. I still could not hear the words he was saying. He came closer still so that I could clearly see the wound in his neck from which the blood continued to weep. He was pointing past me and saying, 'It was her Elliot, she did this to me.' I turned round in the direction he was pointing and saw Esther, but Esther dressed as a man and with a *goatee* beard and with a sort of leering very un-Esther like smile on her face. I awoke suddenly to hear the phone ringing. I glanced at the clock on the bedside table. It was just before twelve. I let it ring a moment before deciding that I should answer it. I was always wary of late night calls as I associated them with bad news, so I answered with some trepidation.

'Hello.'

'Elliot, I'm sorry to catch you so late. Were you asleep?'

It was Esther, the murderer of my dream.

'That's all right, I had only just gone up to bed,' I lied.

'I'm sorry. Do you want me to ring off?'

'No, it's fine.'

'Are you all right? You don't sound brilliant?'

'No, it's OK, really, you carry on.'

'I just wondered if you had seen the photos.'

'What photos?'

'The ones that Samantha sent through by email to the bookshop. You didn't mind me looking did you, you always said …'

'No, not at all, there is nothing private about that email address. No, I haven't checked it this evening. Sounds like they're interesting?'

'Yes, there are a couple of this man with the beard.'

'Brilliant!'

'Sorry, you do sound a bit out of sorts.'

'I just had this … bad dream that's all.'

I did not want to reveal to her the exact details.

'I know, all this must be very upsetting for you,'

'It's upsetting for all of us. How did your yoga go?'

I wanted to change the subject.

'It was good. I feel so much better. You should try it some time.'

'Yes, perhaps I will.'

'Anyway, sorry for bothering you.'

'That's all right.'

'Night Elliot.'

'Night Esther.'

8

Esther was already at the bookshop when I arrived just before eight the following morning. She was hunched over a computer, her eyes fixed to the screen.

'I thought I would make an early start,' she said without greeting me.

I looked over her shoulder. She had on the screen two photos of the mystery man. In her email, Sam had explained that, accompanying her aunt as she did, she witnessed the interruption and the 'stealing away' of the author Nielsen. Neither photo was very clear but one of them showed his head right in the centre of the shot - on the move and slightly blurred, but identifiable. The moustache was in fact joined up at the bottom with a tuft of beard.

'Those *goatees* must be a nightmare to keep in order.'

'Actually, it's not a goatee. A *goatee* is just a little tuft at the bottom. When there is a separate moustache it is called a *Van Dyke*.'

'But this is joined up?'

'Well, in that case it's a *moutee*.'

'How do you know so much about it?'

'I used to go out with someone who had one.'

'Which one?'

'Like the one in the picture.'

'A *moutee* then?'

'Yes. Except most people call them *goatees* in any case.'

'This isn't him?'

'No, it was a long time ago. This one, though, is not bad looking.'

'For a murderer,' I countered.

'But was he?'

'All the evidence points that way. If not, why would he leave the scene of the crime?'

We both stared hard at the photo.

'Do you remember him, Esther?'

'No, but you know how it is, the more I look at it the more I convince myself that perhaps I did see him.'

'I have to admit, I don't remember him at all. It also means that our theory about him just slipping in at the time of the signing is wrong. He was there for a least some of the talk.'

'Well, this is where Clinton will have to get involved. Somebody must have talked to him. It wouldn't be like our customers to have let him get away with standing in a corner on his own.'

'OK, I'll contact him right away.'

I had the inspector's email contact address stored. I wrote a short explanatory note and attached the file containing the photo.

For all the disruption caused by the death of Harry Nielsen the bookshop had only remained closed for one day and trade did not seem to have been affected. Normality was quickly resumed at Ex Libris. We decided to go ahead with our next book talk which was just a fortnight later. There were enquiries from customers who were there on the night of the talk and were curious to follow the progress of the police inquiry. There were also those who wanted to play amateur detective and expound their own (often outlandish) theories. Others had a morbid curiosity to see the 'scene of the crime'. Though the requirement to stay away from the area had been lifted and it was no longer cordoned off, I put a low display stand in front of the stock room to deter sightseers from making their way there. One female student wanted to leave flowers at the point where Nielsen died in the stock room area. I became irritated at this and said I did not think it was appropriate. Seeing the student welling up with tears, Esther pointed out that there had been no such request from the immediate family. Esther suggested that it might be more useful if she gave money to the charity.

'I wonder why she felt so strongly,' I said to Esther.

'Probably her tutor.'

'Unless … no I'm probably being unkind.'

'No, go on.'

'Well, unless he was having some sort of relationship with her. He did have a reputation.'

'I don't suppose we'll ever know.'

The poetry evening came around. This involved a series of readings from members of the local poetry society. It went down well with the forty or so customers who made up the audience. The poets varied in style and quality but there was some intense and moving work. Not for the first time, I reflected on the vast resource of largely unpublished and untapped literature that there was in the world.

I spoke to Chrissie, the chair of the poetry group, over a glass of wine.

'I'm so glad that you were able to get a good turnout for your group. I was worried that the death here might have affected things.'

'Well, perhaps they heard the news of the arrest.'

'What?'

'It was in the paper today.' She looked at me quizzically. 'Sorry, I thought you would know. They have arrested a man.'

'I must have a look.'

I had bought the paper that day but not looked at it. I found it in my office and Chrissie found the page for me where the news of the arrest appeared. There were just a few lines announcing that a man with a *goatee* beard was helping the police with their enquiries. By the time Chrissie and I had re-joined the throng, the word had spread and, unfortunately for the poetry group, the poetry was pushed to one side and the arrest of the man became the main topic of conversation within the bookshop that evening.

Mrs Pargeter made a point of seeking me out.

'I must say I'm extremely relieved.'

'He is only helping them with their enquiries at this stage,' I cautioned.

'But just to think there is someone like that on the loose.'

I could not help finding this amusing. When Mrs Pargeter had left I recounted the conversation to Esther.

'What do you suppose she means by someone like that?'

'Someone who goes around looking for English lecturers to spike on a *Pickelhaube*.'

'I suppose we will be asked to go along and testify.'

'But we didn't actually see him did we - not that we're aware of?'

'No, we just have the photos to go on.'

I could see Esther thinking intently.

'What is it Esther?'

'Nothing, just something in the back of my mind.'

Simon Bonneville came up to us.

'Now we can all sleep safe in our beds.'

Esther and I burst out laughing. Luckily it was Simon, who could take a joke.

'Glad you find all this amusing. Anyway, what I really came to talk to you about was this cricket match.'

'Oh, God yeah, I had forgotten.'

'You're not going to try and wriggle out of it are you?'

'No, of course not.'

Though I had to admit I was in two minds, having not played for so long.

'It's Saturday fifth at two.'

'Fine, I'm not working am I Esther?'

'No, it's Aggie and me.'

'I was wondering if you could contribute some sort of prize for the auction of promises.'

'I'll see what I can find.'

'Splendid. Ah, I've just spotted Victoria, I'll see if I can persuade her to offer me a free back massage or something.'

'You old devil,' I said playfully.

'Not for me, for the auction of promises.'

There was a surprised look on Victoria's face as she was cornered by a determined Simon Bonneville.

'I wonder how they found him?' I said to Esther, returning to the subject of the arrest of the man with the beard.

'I don't suppose there are too many of these *goatee* suspects around.'

'*Moutee*,' I corrected her.

'But wouldn't he have shaved it off if he was worried about being a suspect?'

Suddenly to have a beard and then not to have one, that would raise suspicion in itself.'

'I suppose you're right.'

The customers were beginning to leave now.

'Esther, I know it's not our normal night for going out and I'm sure that this arrest is not as cut and dried as some of our customers have made out, but the Old Vic's showing *The Third Man* tomorrow night. I wondered if you would like to see it and have supper afterwards.'

She thought for a moment.

'I would have to do something with Flossie and Dewdrop before we went out.'

I replied in a mock serious tone.

'Of course, I understand the chickens come first.'

'But I have to admit you know how to reach my soft spot. *The Third Man*, screenplay by one of my favourite writers and one of my very favourite films. I would love to.'

Then she added thoughtfully:

'Another Harry.'

'What? Oh, yes of course, from Harry Nielsen to Harry Lime.'

'For thirty years under the Borgias, they had warfare, terror, murder and bloodshed, but they produced Michelangelo, Leonardo da Vinci and the Renaissance. In Switzerland, they had brotherly love, they had five hundred years of democracy and peace - and what did they produce? The cuckoo clock.'

'How do you remember that? I never get it right.'

'They are just such great lines.'

I was looking forward to seeing *The Third Man* in a cinema as I had only seen it on television or video before. To know that it was one of Esther's favourite films made it all the more special an event. I had first seen it as a child, introduced to it by my mother as a 'thriller', a concept I had not come across before but which I immediately took to. I was captivated by the zither music played by Anton Karrass. As I grew older I watched the film over and over again, each time finding something new and interesting. The film, which came out in 1950, was set in Vienna in the aftermath of the Second World War, divided as it was into four zones, each governed by one of the victorious allies. American western writer Holly Martins arrives seeking an old friend, Harry Lime, who has invited him there to help him with some work. He finds that Lime has been run down and killed by a car. However, Martins becomes suspicious about his death and approaches a Major Calloway to investigate it. Calloway shocks him by revealing that Lime was a racketeer and stole the new wonder drug penicillin from hospitals causing many patients, who might otherwise have been saved, to be maimed or die. Holly falls in love with Lime's girlfriend actress Anna but his love is not reciprocated. Eventually it is discovered that Harry is not dead. The film ends with an exciting chase through the sewers where Martins is responsible for shooting Harry. The final sequence is of Anna walking back from the funeral. Martins is waiting for her but she walks straight past him. His love for her remains unrequited.

We had a drink in the bar afterwards and discussed the various points of the film including the famous closing sequence.

'I can tell you another thing that you might not know,' I lectured Esther, 'that scene at the end where Anna walks past ignoring Holly Martins; Graham Greene wanted Martins to go up and put his arm through hers and they were going to walk off into the sunset together.'

Having enjoyed the novelty of seeing the film in the cinema and with someone who shared my enthusiasm for it, I felt curiously down when I went home. What were the chances of Esther liking that film so much and was it not some sort of proof of our compatibility? However, just because you like the same things as someone else does not mean that they love you or you them. That was the problem for me, the more I spent time with Esther the more I found things I liked about her and a reason to love her. But it did not seem to work in the same way for her and I was not sure if it was that she was still in love with her deceased husband, or that she just did not feel this way towards me. I had thought that our friendship was strengthening and my feelings were at least under control. That evening, I think I had discovered that these feelings were becoming stronger again. The trouble was, I had never quite felt this way about anyone else and I was not sure what to do about it. I spent a restless night wondering whether it would be best if Esther did not work at the bookshop or whether I should take a holiday.

9

The next morning I had a further reason to be deflated. The local news reported that the moustachioed suspect had been released after 24 hours. It was discovered that, not only was he not in the country at the time of Nielsen's death but that at fifteen stone he was completely the wrong build. I was disappointed for I had hoped that we could now move on from Nielsen's death.

'Perhaps it will be one of those great unsolved mysteries,' I suggested to Esther when I delivered the news to her on the steps of the bookshop (we had managed to arrive at exactly the same time).

'I did have a theory...'

'What?'

'No, it's too bizarre.'

'Esther, you can't just leave it hanging in the air like that.'

'Well, it's what you were saying about the *moutee* and shaving it off and so on. What if it really was worn as a disguise?'

'Go on.'

'Well all everybody talks about is the man with the *moutee*. They don't talk about whether he's thin or short or tall or fat - I presume that's why they arrested that fifteen stone man - just happening to forget that he had any other distinguishing features about him. I think it might be this *moutee* that's getting in the way. Just imagine, Elliot, if the *moutee* was false and only worn during that man's visit to the bookshop simply for us to fall into the trap of looking for a man who would never normally sport a *moutee* or beard of any sort.'

'It's an interesting theory. If you think about it, Bonneville's grandson saw the man with the beard go down to the stock room but nobody saw him coming back – notwithstanding your theory about him not being noticed because he ducked behind the shelf units.'

'Of course he might have done minus the *moutee*. If he was

completely clean shaven, nobody would have thought it was the same man.'

We were both silent for a moment as we processed our thoughts.

'What about that man who challenged Nielsen during his talk?'

'The one who did not rate Shakespeare. He was very...'

'Antagonistic?'

'Yes, you're right. It's not the first time someone has challenged one of our authors, but they are usually a bit more polite about it.'

'You didn't speak to him by any chance?'

'No, I noticed him before-hand but I can't remember seeing him talk to anyone. He was stuck in a corner. He does have this sort of moody, brooding air.'

'Does?'

'He's been in before - you know, one of those occasional customers. I can almost remember what he ordered. I know it was something a bit obscure. I seem to remember him making a challenging remark or two when he ordered the book. He's the sort of person who makes you feel ... a bit uncomfortable.'

'You don't think he might have some sort of grudge against Nielsen?'

'It's possible. He's the kind who might have a grudge against most people.'

'I don't suppose you remember his name?'

'Patrick somebody. I don't know. Leave it with me. If I can remember the book he ordered I can trace him back through the orders file.'

10

Not all of our customers had heard the news that the bearded man had been released and assumed that the 'murderer' had been caught, which caused a lot of confusion, explanation and counter explanation until we grew weary of it all.

I had a call from Sam to say they were going to hold a memorial service in the chapel at the university for Harry Nielsen. The burial service had already been held in his home town in Yorkshire. Due to the distance from the university it was thought appropriate to have a separate service for students, staff and the local community. I guessed that the family would have preferred it if the person responsible for the death of Nielsen had been found so that there was some sort of closure.

'You really ought to come,' Sam said. I thought so too. She said she would look out for me but warned me to get there early as it was bound to be busy. I went on my own to the service while Esther looked after the shop.

The memorial service had been arranged for ten-thirty. Sam was correct about it being well attended; though I arrived just after ten, we struggled to get a seat together. All the seating near the back was taken but there were two seats together against the wall about four rows from the front, which we accepted gratefully. It did mean we had a good view of proceedings. By the time the service began the church was full to overflowing. The gathering consisted mainly of students, though at the front of the church there were what I guessed to be Nielsen's family and relations and some of the academic staff.

'Quite a turnout,' I said to Sam.

'Yes, though, without being cynical you have to admit there is a large captive audience with all the students on campus.'

After the first hymn, Harry Nielsen's brother approached the lectern. He spoke in a Yorkshire brogue, unlike his brother who had certainly managed to lose any trace of an accent.

'We were a family of six: me, Harold, as my mum and dad always insisted on calling him.' There was some encouraging laughter from the front pews at this. He smiled briefly and glanced towards his parents on the front row. 'And my two sisters. Maggie was a full- time mum - and me and Alice, well, we worked on the farm. But Harry...' His voice began to crack before he could end the sentence. He seemed to lose his way for a moment. The lady, who was sitting next to him (I presumed his sister), rose from her chair to comfort him.

'No it's all right,' he muttered to her and continued. 'The point I am trying to make is that Harry, he was the clever one. And boy was he clever. There's a rumour that his first word was SHAKESPEARE.' There was general laughter at that and he looked pleased. One could only think of the number of times he had gone over his speech, like the best man at a wedding wondering what was appropriate. It was a sincere speech with a good mixture of humour and pathos that I believed Harry Nielsen would have enjoyed.

Some music from Shakespeare followed: *Under the Greenwood Tree.*

'From *As You Like it,*' the knowledgeable Sam informed me. I felt slightly ashamed that I had read Thomas Hardy's book of the same name and had not appreciated the source of the inspiration for the title.

A striking, slim, dark haired lady in a smart suit, who I guessed to be in her late thirties, took the stand.

'Who's that, Sam?' I whispered.

'That's Miranda Reeves, a work colleague of Nielsen's. She's a Shakespeare specialist too.'

She moved the microphone a little closer to her, composed herself and began to speak.

'Harry Nielsen was a fellow lecturer and tutor. He had an encyclopedic knowledge of Shakespeare and broke new ground with some of his research. Sometimes I was lucky enough to share in it or contribute to it. He will, as they say, be a hard act to follow. I did not really know what to speak about today though I thought it might be appropriate to read a passage of Shakespeare in his memory. So here goes'.

She coughed to clear her throat and took a sip of water.

All the world's a stage,
And all the men and women merely players;
They have their exits and their entrances,
And one man in his time plays many parts,
His acts being seven ages. At first, the infant,
Mewling and puking in the nurse's arms.
Then the whining schoolboy, with his satchel
And shining morning face, creeping like snail
Unwillingly to school. And then the lover,
Sighing like furnace, with a woeful ballad
Made to his mistress' eyebrow. Then a soldier,
Full of strange oaths and, bearded like the pard,
Jealous in honour, sudden and quick in quarrel,
Seeking the bubble reputation
Even in the cannon's mouth. And then the justice,
In fair round belly with good capon lined,
With eyes severe and beard of formal cut,
Full of wise saws and modern instances;
And so he plays his part. The sixth age shifts
Into the lean and slippered pantaloon
With spectacles on nose and pouch on side;
His youthful hose, well saved, a world too wide
For his shrunk shank, and his big manly voice,
Turning again toward childish treble, pipes
And whistles in his sound. Last scene of all,
That ends this strange eventful history,
Is second childishness and mere oblivion,
Sans teeth, sans eyes, sans taste, sans everything.

'It is a great shame that Harry Nielsen was denied the right to experience the full seven ages of man.'

She concluded with a 'thank you' and returned to her seat.

There were further eulogies from members of the family followed by an address from the Chaplain. The service ended with a Shakespeare song. The congregation divided into those who drifted off back to lectures or work or home and those who queued to offer their condolences.

I joined the queue. I was curious to learn something about the family, though I was slightly nervous about my position as the owner of the shop where his death took place, for if he had not come to give his talk at the bookshop and the spiked helmet had not been in the position it was, he may have escaped his dreadful fate. Though I hesitated, the feeling grew within me that it was an obligation and a duty that I should meet them. I said goodbye to Sam, who was rushing off to a lecture, and waited several minutes until the queue had died down to the last few people. Nielsen's mother was at the head of the family group.

'I am so sorry, I am the owner of the bookshop where Harry came to do his talk.'

I could not bear to be blunt and mention the incident of his death.

'Mr Todd, isn't it?' she said through tear-stained eyes.

'Yes, in some ways I feel responsible for what happened.'

'Don't be,' she said. 'I understand he thought highly of your bookshop. There was nothing you could have done to prevent it.'

I had received absolution from the matriarch of the family, and, I had to admit to feeling better for it.

'His talk was a very good one, you would have been proud of it,' I said, honestly.

She began to cry and I felt my own eyes begin to water. I shook her hand and she gave me a brief hug.

'Will you come back to the house?'

'I'm afraid it will not be for very long, I need to get back to the shop, but yes I would be very pleased to.'

I followed the Nielsen family car as I had not been to Harry's house before. We embarked on a journey of ten miles or so, crossing a wooded valley and then an open stretch of moorland before arriving at a small village. His house was a large Victorian villa set in the lea of a hill. It had a long gravel drive but, even so, it was full of cars and I parked on the grass verge on the road.

The centre of the house was a large seating/dining area where

I guessed two rooms had been made into one. His interests were self-evident as within this room were several bookcases containing a fine collection of books. Pride of place was given to several collections of Shakespeare plays and sonnets and an even larger collection of books of criticism and biographies about Shakespeare. I noticed books by G. Wilson Knight and Stanley Wells, among others. An edition of *Characters of Shakespeare's Plays* by William Hazlitt dated 1817 particularly stood out to my collector's eye.

An elderly lady was questioning Mrs Nielsen.

'Harry never married?'

'No, I know he had several close women friends over the years.'

'Why do you think that was?'

'Do you know, I think it was because he was married to his work. I don't think he found room to have a committed relationship as well – it just sort of got in the way.'

'He had a girlfriend when he was at university,' his brother put in. 'That lasted for years. There was talk of them marrying but that all seemed to go a bit sour. I can never remember him having a steady relationship after that again.'

Perhaps that will be me, I thought.

'The academic world is something I'm not too familiar with but I suppose with all the teaching you perhaps don't have much time to mix with people of your own age,' his mother continued.

'Did you keep in touch?'

'Not an awful lot. We all used to get together at Christmas. That was the main time when we used to catch up with each other.'

I wondered idly what would happen to the books though thought it insensitive to ask.

There were sandwiches and cups of tea, beer and wine.

I asked someone where the toilet was and was directed to the bathroom upstairs. The wall of the bathroom was covered with erotic photos by Helmut Newton. *It definitely has the feel of a bachelor house*, I thought.

When I returned downstairs I noticed Nielsen's colleague, Miranda Reeves, who had made an address at the memorial service. I introduced myself.

'That piece you read from Shakespeare, its Jacques isn't it?'

'Poor melancholy Jacques.'

'*As You Like It* ?'

In fact I knew very well, especially since I had had to read a piece from it.

'Yes, Act II, Scene VII.'

I explained how Nielsen had asked me to read the humorous passage on the night of his talk at the bookshop.

'A brilliant concept,' I offered, 'splitting life into seven ages like that.'

She had coloured up a little. I wondered if she was embarrassed. I suppose she had taken a bit of risk with the piece that she had chosen from Shakespeare with that bit about 'mewling and puking' at the beginning of the piece, though it had allowed her to make her point about him not being allowed to reach the seventh age.

'It is a brilliant concept,' she agreed, 'though, as with so much of Shakespeare, it was not his own. You can trace its origins back to Petronius and Aristotle though they tended to talk about three or four ages of man rather than seven which is more of a medieval concept and associated with Henry the Fifth – sorry I'm being boring. I have slipped into academic mode.'

'Not at all. It must be wonderful having all that knowledge at your fingertips.'

'Sometimes I wonder if it is a burden and has closed me off to some of the other wonders of the world.'

'Well, maybe, but there can't be many things more rarefied than inhabiting the world of Shakespeare. And you're talking to a book anorak here so it would be difficult to make me bored with all this stuff. What you were saying about Shakespeare borrowing this concept doesn't make it any less a powerful speech.'

'Of course, he developed them and improved them, often into works of genius, of which I think that speech is an example. It's an unusual play, though, *As You Like It*; the critics have always been divided by it. Samuel Johnson and George Bernard Shaw didn't like it and Tolstoy thought it was immoral.'

'I know that Tolstoy was not a great lover of Shakespeare but why immoral?'

'I suppose it's all that sexual ambiguity with Rosalind dressing up as a boy and some critics have identified homoerotic themes in the play. Though you could say the same thing about several other of Shakespeare's plays.'

'What do you think?'

'I think some of the themes are better developed in later plays like *Measure for Measure* but I think it's a fun play – it's certainly performed a lot - and I do love the character of Rosalind.'

Her mobile phone made a noise.

'I'm sorry, I have to go now but it's been lovely to meet you. Perhaps we can talk again some time.'

Others were beginning to leave. I went and had another look at the books while waiting for the right moment to make my departure. I thought I had used the G. Wilson Knight book at university and was curious about how it would appear to me after such a long interval. The strange thing, though, was that it was gone. There was a gap on the shelves between the book by Stanley Wells and the one by William Hazlitt where I had originally found it.

Unusual that someone else was looking at it as well, I thought.

I said goodbye to the mother and Harry's brother and thanked them for inviting me back after the memorial service. When I returned to the bookshop, Esther had news for me.

'I remembered the book ordered by the man who had a go at Nielsen during the talk. It was *Who Wrote Shakespeare,* not a surprising choice when you think of it. His name is Patrick Williams.'

'Have we got his details?'

'We have an address but no phone number.'

She retrieved his record from the computer.

'La Strade Terrace.'

'I know where that is, not far from the railway station. I sometimes go home that way.'

'There is another book waiting to be posted to him on Thomas à Kempis.'

'Perhaps I could take it with me and drop it off on the way home.'

11

La Strade Terrace was a row of squat Victorian houses originally built for railway workers. The houses had no garden at the front and faced directly onto the pavement.

I rang the bell of number nine. When I did not get an answer after a few moments I tried the knocker. A net curtain twitched and a few moments later the door was opened by an emaciated woman dressed in a housecoat who could have been anywhere between fifty and seventy.

'Can I help you?' she said warily, opening the door a short way. I detected a Yorkshire accent.

'I'm from the bookshop. I happened to be passing this way and thought I might drop Patrick's book off.'

'Patrick's not here. He's at the library.'

'He seems to be a great reader.'

'Books are his obsession.'

'Mine, too, as you would expect.'

She gave me a thin smile.

'Look, I have just poured a cup of tea, would you like one?'

'If it's no trouble?'

We went into a small sitting room. Every wall from floor to ceiling was stuffed with books and there were books on the floor.

'All the other rooms are the same,' she commented as a train roared past. It felt as though the train was just a few yards from the other side of the wall.

'I presume you're Patrick's mother?'

'Yes, sorry, I should have introduced myself, I'm Kathleen.'

We shook hands.

'For my sins,' she added.

'Patrick was at one of our author talks recently.'

I did not mention Nielsen's death.

'He expresses his opinions very forcibly,' I added.

'That's Patrick. Would you like a biscuit?'

'No, thank you.'

'He's actually a very shy person - I know to my great cost - that is why he is still living with his mother. But when he feels strongly about something - doesn't matter where you are - could be talking to the Queen herself - he will give you his opinion.'

'That's not such a bad thing.'

'I know, but sometimes he can be perhaps a little too serious - people take him the wrong way.'

'Sounds like it may have caused you some problems?'

'There has been a time or two – let's say - when I could have done without it.'

At that moment she looked as though all the weight of the world was on her shoulders.

'He has had a difficult life, you know. Didn't really know his father. He left us when Patrick was so young. God knows where he is - he never kept in touch. I think he missed that father figure. Don't you think it's important?'

'Yes, I do. I remember so many things I did with my father.'

'Patrick has never been able to socialise. Small talk has never been his thing. There was a girlfriend once but it didn't work out. Wasn't her fault. She was a nice girl, really. But Patrick has such intensity, everything is black and white with him and nothing in-between. He sees betrayal everywhere. Then he gets into a real temper and can sulk for days.'

She gave a heavy sigh.

'Anyway, let's just say, with this girl, it had its consequences. The truth is Mr Todd, after Janet - that was her name - he felt so bad he had a breakdown. He had to go into the local sanitorium. Then there was care in the community. It's been better for him really though I must admit I feel the strain at times.'

'I'm sure he appreciates what you do for him.'

'I hope so - though I do wonder sometimes.'

She laughed.

'But underneath it all he's a good lad really. I suppose I would say that. But there's plenty worse than him.'

'Does he have a job?'

'Yes, he does. He has a job in the library. That's where he is now?'

'Sorry, I misunderstood. I thought he was there borrowing books.'

'That, too. He spends most of his life there.'

'He's a librarian, then?'

'Of sorts. I suppose you would call him a librarian's assistant, nothing special. The truth is with his brain he could do anything.'

'I'm sure.'

'He was an accountant once but he got fed up with that. He can't cope with the pressure - you know - of organising and meeting people. He's so sensitive to people's comments. You get on a topic he's interested in though, he'll talk till the cows come home.'

She sat looking wistful for a moment.

'I suppose you must have heard about the unfortunate happening at our bookshop.'

'Yes, I didn't like to mention it. It must have been awful for you.'

'Yes, I remember the moment when Patrick put the author on the spot with a difficult question at the talk before it happened. Did he mention it to you?'

'I don't remember him saying anything – though all the days seem to roll into one at the moment.'

'I know the police have been trying to get in contact with everyone who was there that night. Do you know if they have been in touch with Patrick yet? It obviously takes them a long time to get round everyone.'

'Not that I know of, but then that's just the sort of thing he would keep from me. That's how he is.'

I finished the last mouthful of my tea.

'I had better be going, Mrs Williams. I have already taken up too much of your time. Tell Patrick he can pay for his book next time he is in the shop.'

When I got home I had it in my mind to ring Esther to let her know how I had got on, but shortly after I had arrived my mother rang with one of her marathon phone calls. We had not spoken for a while (of which she reminded me) and she had a catalogue of things to tell me, particularly about the achievements of my brother Dominic and his family. Then she became a little maudlin about my father and I knew this was the signal for her to come down to stay for a few days.

'I don't like to ask Dominic, he's so busy,' she said pointedly.

As though I am not, I thought a little resentfully.

She was not aware of the murder at the bookshop. I decided I would let her know when she visited. There was a kind of unwritten rule between myself and my mother that she would come for a long weekend, three or four days, which seemed to be just long enough for both of us.

After the phone call, I felt I needed some quick food and cooked myself an omelette. It was not until I was tucked up in bed that I remembered I had not rung Esther. Never mind, I thought, it would do in the morning.

12

Esther had already begun cataloguing a small pile of books before I arrived at the shop the following morning. It was still a few minutes before opening time and I was glad of the opportunity to be able to speak to her before any customers arrived. I launched into my news.

'I found out something really interesting yesterday evening. That Patrick Williams, he's not right up here.' I pointed to my head. 'He has spent some time in a nuthouse.'

She continued cataloguing the book without looking up. This news had not hit the mark in the way I had intended it to.

'Which means what?' she said without looking up from her book?

'Well, you know, if he's been in an asylum, it may be that he is not too stable and this might have caused him to…'

'Murder Nielsen.'

She did look up towards me now, but in a challenging way.

'You think one thing naturally leads to the other?'

'Not naturally. It just seems more likely.'

She became visibly angry.

'Why?' she shouted. 'Why should it be more likely?'

'It just is. I didn't think I needed to explain.'

I immediately regretted saying this. She banged the large book shut that she was cataloguing.

'I am so disappointed in you, Elliot. I thought you were a humane and thoughtful person, not given to cheap prejudice and stereotyping. One in four people has a mental health problem of some sort in this country at some time in their lives. I suppose you think they are all potential murderers?'

'I didn't mean it like that I …'

'Let's just hope you never make it to be a judge.'

She stomped off with an armful of books and began putting them away aggressively on the shelves. She did not speak to me for the rest of the day except when it was absolutely necessary. This was the first time I had ever known Esther in a rage at me like this and I did not enjoy the feeling. I had also wanted to share my worries with her about my mother but felt that I was not able to now. It was as though she was a different person.

Even so, I decided I would check the guest list for the night of the talk with Nielsen. Patrick William's name was not among them. It meant that Inspector Clinton did not have his details so I emailed them to him. I explained that he was the one who had questioned Nielsen on the night of the talk and mentioned my conversation with his mother. I also alluded to his mental health problem though I tried not to make a big issue of it. After my conversation with Esther I felt as though I was being something of a sneak. In the afternoon I had to see two publishers' representatives and did not have much opportunity to speak to Esther. She said goodbye to me as she rushed out of the door at closing time but she lacked her usual warmth.

Twice after I had arrived home, I picked up the phone to ring Esther, only to put it down again. I was unsure what to say. An apology, an attempt at an explanation? Would it just make the situation worse? On the third occasion I made the call. There was no reply. I did not leave an answer phone message. I rang twice more an hour later. I began watching a documentary on polar bears but did not really take any of it in. While I was in the middle of making myself a coffee the phone rang. It was Esther.

'Elliot, I need to speak to you in person. Can we meet up?'

'My place or yours?'

I said it with the wrong emphasis, as though we were meeting for a date, even though I had not intended to. The more I tried to be careful, it seemed, the more crass I sounded. However, thankfully, she did not seem to notice.

'I think neutral territory would be best. There is a pub at Newtown, The Pure Drop.'

'I know.'

'About half-an-hour?'

'OK, I'll see you then.'

I felt deeply concerned as I drove the short distance to Newtown. I was convinced that Esther was going to resign from the bookshop and did not know how I was going to manage without her. Apart from the fact that I had strong feelings of affection for her, I had become used to her company and felt my life had become enriched by having her around. Her talent for organisation had also taken much of the burden of running the bookshop off me.

I approached the pub with an uneasy feeling. I felt as though I was prepared to say anything, like an infatuated lover, to keep her at the bookshop, but I also knew that once someone's mind was made up, especially when that someone was Esther, what was broken could not easily be unbroken. By the time I walked through the entrance my stomach had become tied up in knots.

She was already there at a table in the corner. She had a pint of bitter waiting for me.

'Look, Esther…' I began as soon as I sat down.

But she interrupted me.

'No, Elliot, let me speak. I will have my say and then you can have yours.'

'The fact is,' she continued, 'I did overreact. I realise that.'

'But I was being crass.'

'You were possibly a little bit insensitive. And after all we were only recently talking about a madman off the street murdering Nielsen.'

'That was different. We were just trying to explain how it might be a random act of violence rather than a planned murder.'

'Let me speak and then you can have your say.'

'Sorry.'

'And I was also saying how Patrick Williams was a morose and a difficult character. The fact is, there was a reason why I overreacted.' She looked down into her drink. 'I was in an asylum myself once.'

'Oh, Esther, I'm so foolish.'

'No, look, the last thing I want is sympathy. I needed to go into an asylum. For a while, shortly after David's death, I completely lost my mind.'

She began rubbing the palms of her hands in an uncharacteristically nervous way.

'I didn't feel that way immediately. With all the funeral arrangements and the paperwork to sort through there was plenty to do after his death. Also, I know this sounds strange, but I had to support other people. David with all his singing

72

performances was very popular. I had to answer lots of letters from people who were upset, who had seen him in some obscure performance on the other side of the country or the world and, of course, there was family and friends to comfort. They loved him too.

'I suppose it was a couple of weeks later when it was all over, when I was at last on my own that it started. In some ways I was looking forward to being on my own after all the activity and emotion around the funeral. I thought it would give me time to think things through and get things sorted out in my head. But it didn't work out that way. My brain went into overdrive and I couldn't switch off. I spent days when I couldn't remember sleeping at all. I went to bed and just lay there thinking all night through until the morning without consciously falling asleep. I constantly went over things in an obsessive way. This went on night after night. I suppose my brain just could not take it anymore and became overloaded. That's when I began hearing the voices. I knew I needed help. At first these voices used to come and go, then one evening they were there all the time in my head. Whatever I did I couldn't get rid of them. I could not bear the thought of another night in my house. I phoned the local Samaritans. After talking to them I realized I needed professional help.'

'What a terrible experience. I'm so sorry.'

'I feel guilty that I didn't mention it at the interview. I suppose legally you could sack me for withholding information or something.'

'I have a feeling in employment law you might have a right to withhold it anyway.'

'In any case, I think I should have told you.'

She gave me a weak uncertain smile.

'So, look, if you want to sack me for my outburst, I quite understand.'

'Oh, Esther, I was so worried that you were coming here to tell me that you didn't want to work for me any more. You have been so brilliant since you joined the bookshop.'

'And I have enjoyed the experience so much.'

She did, however, pause for a good long while.

'There is something else, though.' She took a breath. 'A few months after David died I met someone. I felt I needed physical release.'

'It is perfectly understandable.'

'Well I went with this man and it was horrible. I felt guilt and shame. The last thing I felt was any sort of enjoyment or comfort. I was actually physically sick afterwards. Now I just feel that I never want to be in a relationship again. I am resigned to being a spinster - with my chickens.'

'There are worse things to be. There is so much pressure on us to conform. You must do what works for you.'

I could not believe the words I was saying. I was telling the woman, on whom I had a deep crush, not to consider a physical relationship.

'I'm sorry to unburden myself on you like this. I didn't want to tell any of my girlfriends because none of them knew about this. With you it's like I am on neutral ground.'

'I'm happy if I can help.'

'I'm so glad we had this chat. That feeling of working with books, it is a hard one to beat as far as I am concerned. I can't promise that I will always agree with you Elliot but I promise you that I will always work hard and give it my all.'

'That's exactly the way I would want it.'

'Friends again then?'

'Friends.'

We clinched our declaration with a shake of hands across the table.

We simultaneously both let out a long sigh and both laughed at having the same reaction.

'Back to business.' Esther said, 'This Patrick Williams, then, you think he could be a likely suspect?'

I recounted my conversation with his mother.

'He certainly seems an odd cove. I think we have gone as far as we can and need to let the police handle it now.'

*

I returned home feeling much happier than when I had left for the pub earlier that evening. Esther's breakdown following the death of her husband further emphasised her loss and how difficult it would be for her to move on, and what a long process it would likely be. However, at the same time I felt as though a great weight had been lifted from my mind. I was especially pleased that Esther was eager to stay working at the bookshop.

I thought I would check my messages before I went to bed. There was one from Simon Bonneville.

'Bonneville here. Just reminding you about that cricket match. I know you've had a lot on your plate recently but need you to confirm if it's OK for you to play cricket this Saturday.'

I rang him straight away. He answered the phone in a subdued manner. It was very 'un-Simon-like'.

'Is everything all right, Simon?' I asked.

'Oh, yes. It's just, after I phoned you, I began thinking about the goings on at your bookshop. It seems to be such a long process establishing who was responsible. I don't think I ever said, but I was mortified when I heard that chap had been killed. Just to think, if that *Pickelhaube* thing hadn't been around, he might have been safe.'

'You're not making me feel any better, Simon.'

'I know, but it can hardly be your fault that someone decided to go and impale themselves. After all, it's not a public area is it?'

'I know, that's true, it's one thing in my favour.'

'Besides, I'm the one who suggested that author to you?'

'So, I can blame you?'

'I wouldn't go quite as far as that. Shame though, he seemed a pleasant chap. He certainly knew how to put on the charm. Knowledgeable too – knew his stuff.'

'Actually, I was a bit worried about your grandson. He hasn't suffered any ill effects from discovering the body has he?'

'Funny you should say that, I'd been worrying about that myself. But no, he seems as right as rain, never seems to have mentioned it. His parents are on the ball. I think they would know if there was something amiss. I think it was for him a bit like a game. And, talking of games,' and now the tone of his voice lightened, 'the thing I really wanted to talk to you about was that cricket match.'

'As you know, I haven't played for years but I wouldn't mind giving it a go.'

'I'll let you open if you like.'

'No chance, put me somewhere in the middle, make sure the shine is off the ball and all the fast men have done their stuff.'

'I don't know if there are any fast men, they are mostly old codgers like me. Mind you, it might be good to have a few young "Turks" to liven things up a bit.'

'And there's always the village blacksmith.'

'What? Oh, yes. Very good, I know what you mean. 'Do you think you might be able to turn your arm over for a couple or three overs?'

'I am happy to give it a try.'

'Splendid. I will see you at twoish.'

I put the phone down and decided that I needed to check to see if my cricket trousers still fitted or if they had been attacked by moths. However, before I got any further the phone rang.

'Sorry, Simon here again. I forgot to say, do you remember I said there was an auction of promises? Just a reminder to bring something for the prize?'

I had forgotten all about it but remembered that I had a second-hand book on the notorious 'bodyline tour' to Australia which would do nicely.

I found my trousers stuffed in the bottom of my cricket bag in the garage. In fact everything in there had a musty smell. The trousers were, mercifully, free of holes and I thought could be rescued with a wash. I tried them on to check that they still fitted. Luckily they were tied together with a loose pajama-like chord which meant that there was plenty of play in the waist, but I resolved there and then to go on a two day diet. There was also only one glove. The pads were OK though the bat was looking a bit tired and battered. It was, however, certainly not worth buying another one. This might, after all, be the only match I played that season – or ever again.

I would have no practice before this match, which was particularly concerning as I had not played for so long and I was not likely to get the opportunity the following day. I fetched down a long mirror and placed it at one end of the hall, propped on a chair. Then I began bowling my slow imaginary balls into the mirror for several minutes. Having bowled the entire opposition side out in a manner that would have done justice to Billy Liar, I went to bed.

'Gosh, I feel hungry this morning,' pronounced Esther almost as soon as she entered the door of the bookshop the next day. 'I think it is the thought of it being Friday. We deserve a little treat for making it to the end of the week – a pastry of some sort. Do you fancy something?'

'You are doing it on purpose aren't you?'

'What?'

'Well, you know I have this cricket match tomorrow. I could hardly get into my cricket whites, even though they have an expandable waist.'

However, the main thought going through my head was that I was so pleased that my old relationship with Esther was back.

'I think your problems are hardly going to be solved by cutting out the odd pastry.'

She gave a pitying look in the direction of my stomach.

She bought two tasty looking pastries from the local bakery and made it clear that there was no obligation for me to have one as she could have the other one the following day. Further weakened by the smell of delicious, hot, strong coffee, I cracked, accepted the pastry and gobbled it down feeling a mixture of pleasure and self-loathing that I had been unable to keep up my resolve for less than twelve hours.

I searched for and quickly found the book that I had in mind for the auction, resplendent with pictures of the aristocratic Jardine and the powerhouse of a bowler and ex-coal miner, Harold Larwood. The bodyline series caused such controversy with England's use of what was euphemistically called 'leg theory', that the two governments of Great Britain and Australia came close to severing diplomatic relations. There was a particularly dramatic picture of the Australian batsman Woodfull being knocked to the ground by one of Larwood's vicious deliveries. By coincidence, Simon Bonneville rang as I had the book in my hand. Esther took the call.

'He sounds very out of breath,' Esther warned me.

'I am in a spot of bother,' said Simon. 'I've been told that I need all this auction of promises business sorted today. Apparently it's not good enough just to turn up with them at the match.'

'Funnily enough, I've just picked my contribution off the shelf.'

'I can come and get it if you like?'

I knew he would but his voice lacked his usual conviction.

'Look, you have enough to do. Why don't I pop it along after work? It won't take me a moment.'

'That's very good of you. Tell you what, why don't you have a bite of supper?'

'Well...'

'Go on, we haven't seen you here for ages. I'll need a bit of company after flying around like a blue-arsed fly.'

'OK, then.'

'Shall we say about seven-thirty?'

I should have known better. I had never been to Simon Bonneville's house without imbibing more alcohol than was good for me. I resolved to be strong.

Later that morning I received a nudge in the ribs from Esther.

'Look who is outside.'

We had a couple of cafe tables outside, along with a stall of some of our less expensive second-hand books. Patrick Williams was sitting at one of the tables with his nose in a book. I went over to him.

'Would you like a drink?' I asked.

He looked up as though bothered that he was being disturbed. 'Perhaps a coffee?'

I went and fetched it for him and was back in a few moments.

'Here's your coffee. Found anything good?'

'Is it OK if I have a look through it first? I am not sure if I want to buy anything yet.'

He hardly looked at me. I could tell he did not really want me there but I remembered what his mum said about taking part in a conversation when the subject interested him.

'No, of course, that's what bookshops are for – browsers' paradise.'

He went back to his book. I would have to try a bit harder. I felt, if his mother was right, I just had to get him going on a subject he was interested in.

'Weren't you at the Shakespeare evening a few weeks ago? I seem to remember you asked one or two interesting questions.'

'What?' he said a little grumpily, and then, as if thinking about what I had said for the first time, he turned away from his books and looked at me.

'I find all this reverence for Shakespeare a bit hard to take. I'm not the first. Tolstoy didn't like his plays much...'

'So I understand.'

'And Wittgenstein found them difficult to read and unrealistic.' He put his book down before continuing. 'I also think that there's a very strong possibility that Shakespeare was not the author of the plays attributed to him. Despite the fact that I think many of them are overrated, they do show a craft and complexity that just doesn't fit in with Shakespeare's education and background.'

'Who do you think wrote them, Sir Francis Bacon?'

'No, I know he was an early candidate and I know a lot of people, and Freud was one of them, think it could have been Edward de Vere. Personally, I don't think you have to look any further than Christopher Marlowe. Look at the facts. He spent six-and-a-half years at Cambridge University even though he was born into the same social class as Shakespeare. His father was a cobbler while Shakespeare's was a glove-maker. But his education gave him a knowledge and depth on historical subjects which Shakespeare could not possibly have obtained at his Grammar School – if indeed he even went there. He and Shakespeare were also almost exactly the same age - born within a couple of months of each other. We also know that he was mixed up with the spying game. I believe that his death in 1593 in a tavern was faked to protect him. Thomas Walsingham was probably the mastermind behind it. Don't get me wrong, I don't think he became Shakespeare, but I think that Shakespeare was the front man for Marlowe. Consider this, Marlowe dies on the 30th May. Thirteen days later the very first work linked to the name of Shakespeare, *Venus and Adonis*, is registered with the

Stationers' Company with no one named as its author. Before his supposed death Marlowe was also a pioneer of blank verse which was also used to great effect in some of the later plays attributed to Shakespeare.'

'But what about de Vere, I thought he had a greater claim?'

'The trouble with his claim is that it depends too much on clever work on codes and ciphers. Marlowe was a proven writer of great worth before his death. Look at *Doctor Faustus* – you can see the quality of the writing in this play alone.'

He began to turn back to his book.

'You argue very convincingly, as you did that night.'

'Ah, well, I've read a lot about it.'

He had not mentioned the murder in the bookshop. He was obviously not into conversational niceties.

'Did you know Harry Nielsen?' I blurted in desperation trying to get him to talk again and keep him from his book.

'I hadn't seen him for a long time.'

'Had you seen him speaking before?'

'No, I mean a real long time. We were at school together.'

'Where?'

'In Yorkshire.'

'At secondary school?'

'Yes, we were in the same class, the top form. I am not bragging, but we were the ones who won most of the prizes, especially the English prizes. He went on to do 'A' Levels and university and I didn't.'

'Do you think he recognised you on the night of the talk?'

'No, I don't think so. And if he did, he didn't show it.'

'Why did you not go to university?'

'It's all down to money, really. My dad left us when I was a child. And I don't know whether I would have been able to stand all that mixing.'

'That must have been upsetting for you.'

'I know I'm not the only one. It happens all the time. Single parents, only children. But when I was sixteen my mum was worrying about money and she didn't seem to care about whether I had any more education. She said you've got good 'O' levels already and she kept talking about jobs in banks and accountancy, so in the end that's what I did, became an accountant. There's nothing wrong with those jobs but my soul was in English. There hasn't been a day in my life when I haven't read a book.'

'And when you saw Harry Nielsen you saw what you might have been?'

'I suppose so. I'm not sure I could have flown that high. But look, he gets paid – did get paid - for something he actually enjoyed.'

'You're not in accountancy now, though.'

'No, one day I flipped.' He hesitated before going on. 'I couldn't stand the thought of one more day with those figures. But it paid pretty well. We own our house outright and we don't need to worry as long as we have enough to pay the rates and for food and so on.'

'When you... flipped. That must have been difficult.'

'Yes, I lost my mind.'

'Years of frustration?'

'I suppose. You can tell I don't have the happiest temperament. And there was this girl. I am not very proud of the way I behaved. I suppose I took it out on her a bit. I'm not very good socially. Since I left school my life has really been work and my mum. There weren't many opportunities to meet people at my accountancy firm. It doesn't make for good socialising, all those figures. I suppose I envy someone like you.'

'Me?'

'With your bookshop. Not a bad way to make a living.'

'Though not the most lucrative I'm afraid.'

'Oh, that reminds me, I think I owe you for a book.'

'Sorry, I wasn't trying to suggest ... Just see Esther inside when you're ready.'

Our conversation had ended. He turned back to his book.

14

Simon Bonneville's house was next to the church at Little Churling. It was an old rectory with umpteen rooms and a large garden, with a lawn almost big enough to play a cricket match on. I reflected as I drove along the gravel drive to the house that I might get a chance to have a quick practice before supper, my only opportunity before the match the following day.

The five miles or so to his house had flown by as I reflected once more on my curious conversation with Patrick Williams. I had, in fact, got much more than I had bargained for with the discovery that he had known Harry Nielsen at school.

'There could be grounds there for resentment,' said Esther after Williams had left and I had told her about our conversation. 'Almost like sibling rivalry. We also know that he would not be afraid of getting into an argument with Nielsen – or anyone, for that matter.'

'I know, but why would he tell me about all this if he wanted to hide something.'

'He probably reckons that the police will find out about his knowing Nielsen, anyway.'

'So, better not to appear like you're hiding anything. I see what you mean. Oh, I forgot to ask him if he had been interviewed by the police yet.'

'I think you should tell them what you have found out.'

'Do you? This should all come up in any questions they ask anyway, shouldn't it?'

'I don't think I would leave anything to chance. It only takes a few seconds to email.'

So I did email a very brief summary of our conversation though I was beginning to feel more and more like an informer.

When I arrived at Simon's house, Miriam greeted me with a kiss on the cheek.

'He's out the back on the verandah,' she said. 'He's been swearing and carrying on a bit but I think he's just about finished now.'

'That's boeuf bourguignon isn't it,' I said as we passed by the kitchen. I could not mistake its delectable smell.

On the verandah were laid out a bewildering variety of objects for the auction of promises, ranging from a bouquet of flowers to a large vacuum cleaner.

'Hello, Elliot. Luckily, a lot of them are just promises on bits of paper, car washes, massages and the like, otherwise I wouldn't have room for them all.'

I handed my own over.

'I feel mine is a little insignificant among all these splendours.'

'Nonsense, what can be more splendid than a book.' He glanced at it briefly. 'And this is a splendid book.'

What I particularly liked about Simon was that he was one of those people who you always felt better for being with. I invariably felt cheered by his company.

He had a label ready for the book. He wrote on it and attached it with some ribbon.

'I've just got two more to do and then I've finished.'

I looked out onto the lawn.

'I was wondering if you might have a chance to throw a few balls to me before dinner. I haven't been able to get any practice in.'

'Might do, yes, might well do,' he said distractedly as he concentrated on the last two labels.

Miriam came out to the edge of the verandah.

'It's ready now boys.'

'Give us five minutes can you Miriam?'

'It'd better be a genuine five minutes. I'm not letting the vegetables spoil.'

'Of course, of course.'

He finished the last label and jogged towards the house.

'Five minutes is better than nothing,' I thought.

But rather than returning with a cricket bat and ball as I had hoped, he emerged with a bottle and two glasses.

'Quick snifter before we start.'

'I'll just have half...'

But it was too late. He had already poured two large glasses.

'Here's to tomorrow. May it be a glorious occasion!'

'Cheers.'

The wine tasted amazing, as always. Simon was not short of money and had a great interest in wine.

'What is it Simon?'

'It's a Pouilly-Fumé.'

We received our final call to eat from Miriam. Simon led me to the dining room. There was salmon and a side salad for starters.

'I thought you said a bit of supper, Simon. This is a feast.'

'Oh, it's just a stew and a few bits and pieces,' said Miriam.

'When Miriam gets something into her head you can't stop her. Another glass of white?'

'No thanks, Simon. I've got be careful, I'm driving.'

'You can always stay, you know, and pop back in the morning before the match. You'd be very welcome.'

'That's very kind, Simon, but as I haven't played for a long time, it might not be such a good idea.'

The salmon finished, Miriam brought in the main course and the vegetables she had been worrying about.

'Now, I have a special red for the main course, you must just have one glass of that,' said Simon. 'It's a Grand Cru Burgundy, Clos de Vougeot, a vineyard enclosed by Cistercian monks in the 14th century.'

'Ah, those monks knew how to make their wines.'

'You have to be careful though. It's been divided up between 82 owners. Some of it is frankly not very good. You need to go to the owners in the upper and middle parts to get the best stuff. And, as I think you'll appreciate, this is very decent.'

'OK, just one and then that's it.'

It was indeed wonderful, as was the whole evening. Something else that I liked about Simon was that he always made you feel comfortable and at your ease, just as though you were part of the family. He regaled me with a funny story of his youth in Argentina where he had been brought up.

Miriam brought in a cheese board that would have done justice to a banquet. The brie was beginning to run over the side. Simon knew my weakness for it.

'Better catch that before it ends up on the table, Elliot.'

I ate some and came back for more. I eyed the bottle of wine.

'Offer still stands about staying. There's a bed already made up.'

For the second time that day my resolve was broken and I gave in to temptation. There was no going back now. A second bottle was opened. Miriam made excuses and left us to it. We wandered into the next room, which contained a three-quarter size snooker table, and made a poor attempt at playing a game. Simon persuaded me to have a special cigar. I reflected in my increasingly inebriated state that here was part of the problem; everything Simon offered you was 'special'. I wondered if he had not used that word, whether I would be able to resist the temptations he put in front of me. We decided that we would be unable to finish the game that evening as neither of us seemed remotely capable of potting any balls and we wandered outside. Simon insisted that I help him finish the last dregs of the second bottle.

Miriam appeared again and offered us some coffee. I thought at last that I was to begin my rehabilitation. I told myself if I drank plenty of water I should be all right. However, Simon had decided that the coffee needed an accompaniment and shouted, 'Don't forget the brandy dear,' just as Miriam left the room.

Two brandies and two coffees later as the grandfather clock in the hall chimed one, we decided that we had had enough. Simon showed me unsteadily to my bedroom.

I did not wake until ten the following morning. I felt parched and dry. I had forgotten to drink any water and fallen straight to sleep as soon as I went to bed. When I bent down to pick up my clothes, which I found scattered on the floor, my head began to throb.

I went downstairs and found Simon munching his way through a large cooked breakfast.

'Might have overdone it last night. Some breakfast will set you straight.'

He was right, too. Orange juice, sausages, bacon, tomatoes, mushrooms, black pudding, fried egg, toast and endless cups of tea worked wonders on my abused body.

In a moment of subconscious foresight, I had packed my cricket bag in the car the day before in readiness, so I was spared the bother of having to rush home before the match, which delighted Simon.

'Pleased about that. You can help me load the prizes into the car.'

I smiled weakly and said 'of course', though, in fact, the constant bending and lifting up and down, brought on my hangover headache again. The last thing I felt like doing was playing cricket though I knew I could not back out now. I only had myself to blame. Had I learnt nothing in all my years of association with Simon Bonneville?

Simon provided me with a razor and some shaving foam and I felt that I took a further step forward on the road to recovery when I took a nice long hot bath. While I was lying there with the water as hot as I could bear I felt that perhaps I was not feeling too bad after all. However, as I bent forward for my towel the tell-tale hangover signs made themselves known again. I thought I would be OK if they did not make me run anywhere on the cricket field. Perhaps they would let me field in the slips, though, thinking about it, my alcohol induced reactions would no doubt be so slow that I would be an embarrassment. Perhaps I could find a place at third man near the boundary and hope the ball would not come to me.

Now Simon knocked on my bathroom door.

'Sorry old chap, we have to be going in a few minutes. We need to get there a bit early to set everything up.'

I hurried along and changed straight into my cricket things. My clothes from the night before smelled of smoke, something I could not remember experiencing for a long time. I folded them and took them along with me in case I should need them after the match.

Before I left Miriam handed me a large glass of liquid.

'Here, have this, Simon swears by it.'

It was true, Simon seemed to be suffering far less from the effects of the previous night than I was.

I drank down the concoction which tasted predominately of banana and orange, and thanked her for her hospitality.

The cricket ground at Little Churling was charming. At nearly 300 feet above sea level its climate was less favourable to cricket than many of the surrounding venues that were less elevated. However, when the sun shone, as it did that day, and set as it was against a backdrop of surrounding hills with cows and sheep grazing the grassland, there was no better place to be.

When we arrived at the cricket ground just after one we found it a hive of activity with tents and stalls on their way to being set up. Next to the ancient cricket pavilion, inscribed with the date 1885, which marked the founding of the cricket club, was a marquee.

'That's where we are,' Simon said.

I helped with some trestle tables which we carried from the pavilion. Everybody seemed to know Simon, who made a point of introducing me as his good friend. He seemed to engender a good atmosphere and get the best out of people, wherever he went. Partly because of this and partly, I suspected, because of Miriam's fabulous reviving concoction, rather than wishing that I was not there I was now feeling that staying to play cricket might be not be such a bad option after all.

Once we had set up the tables to Simon's satisfaction, we felt able to relax for a few moments. The first of the away team members arrived. There were more introductions followed by the arrival of some of the home team. While we were waiting for them all to get changed, we went and had a look at the wicket.

'Looks pretty good,' I said, 'not too much grass.'

'A few cracks. You might be able to make use of those, especially if we bat first.'

Simon was the captain for the day.

'What are you going to do if you win the toss?'

'Same as I always do. I subscribe to the great man's view: *When you win the toss - bat. If you are in doubt, think about it, then bat. If you have very big doubts, consult a colleague - then bat.*'

The great man was W.G. Grace, the doctor, who is considered by many to be the most important figure in the development of the game of cricket.

Simon did win the toss and as he had indicated he would, he put us in to bat. As I had requested, I was placed in the middle order at number five. I went out to umpire until the first wicket went down. I wanted to get some indication of the pace of the wicket, as it was so long since I had batted. Within two overs, with the ball still shiny, there was a tame edge to the slips and we lost our first wicket. Another player swapped umpiring roles with me and I went off to get padded up.

I felt a little queasy, partly at the thought of going out to bat and partly because of my drinking activities from the night before. However, any hopes that I had of not being required to bat at all began to vanish when another wicket fell in the eighth over. It was not long before I was walking out to the middle when a further wicket fell two overs later.

Confidence is probably more important a factor in cricket than any other sport and it is particularly so in a batsman where you are only given one chance of making a mistake or an ill-judged shot. I tried to adopt an air of confidence as I strode to the wicket though inside I felt vulnerable.

I took my guard and gave myself a few moments to take a look around the field to see in which position the players were placed and where the gaps were. I felt very rusty and feeling under the weather as I did, thought it better to die by the sword rather than go out to a timid shot. So when the first ball was delivered I played a beautiful classic off drive. The only problem was that it did not connect with the ball. In fact the bat and the ball were some distance away from each other. The bowler received, I thought, undeserved applause from his players in the field as the error was all in my inadequate shot rather than the rather nondescript ball that had been bowled. I realised, even in my parlous state, that I had played that first ball far too early and when the second ball came I played it a lot later, though this time far too late; a Chinese cut raced off behind the wickets to the boundary for four. I received some ironic clapping but then proceeded over the next few balls 'to get my eye in'. My feet began to move closer to the pitch of the ball and on several occasions I found the middle of the bat. With a generous helping of luck I made a brisk 21 and received a round of applause as I left the field to a good catch in the outfield. Then came a 'ringer', an ex-county player who showed us how it should be done. Simon who came in at number nine entertained us with two splendid sixes over the long on boundary. Largely because of the efforts of the ex-county player we reached a very respectable 239 off our 40 overs.

By virtue of the fact that it was a charity cricket match, there was an extended tea interval so that everybody had an opportunity to visit some of the stalls around the cricket field. Cricket teas very rarely disappoint and this was no exception. Apart from the usual fare of sandwiches, exotic crisps, sausage rolls and malt loaf there was a cream tea with jam and scones.

We sat around on rugs on the grass.

'Do you know, Simon?' I said. 'I have just realised, I don't think we mentioned Nielsen's death once last night. And I don't think I thought of it once, either.'

'You must be getting used to it, I suppose.' He slurped some tea before he continued. 'It is bizarre, though, that the police haven't come up with anything. Perhaps, like our footballing friends, we have to *think outside the box*.'

Though I was talking in an aside to Simon, I could see a couple of players next to us prick their ears up.

'I have a theory,' he continued.' No, you'll probably think it's too silly.'

'No, go on.'

'Well, what if this chap had an accomplice.'

'Yes.'

'Well, he might have gone down there, done the dirty deed, hidden among the boxes – there's enough mess down there...'

'Thank you, Simon.'

'Waited for a call on his mobile from his accomplice to say everything's OK – or the accomplice might have created a diversion. You don't remember anything - a loud noise, someone fainting?'

'No.'

Joe, the fast bowler chipped in.

'A stink bomb going off.'

'Or perhaps he didn't have an accomplice. Perhaps he hid at the back of the stock room, waited until everyone had gone and slipped out later when no one was looking, or, even in the middle of the night when everyone had gone.'

'What about the alarm system – I mean if he slipped out in the middle of the night - it would go off.'

'He might know the code.'

'How?'

'He might have waited outside and seen you punch it in – or taken a photo and then blown it up on the camera until he could see the code. I think they do something similar with those hole-in-the-wall machines. You don't even know they are collecting your information. Or he might be an ex-alarm engineer and he might know some tricks.'

'You're making it sound like *Mission Impossible*.'

'Or he could've waited right until the morning when you came in bleary eyed – not sure where you were yet and what time of day it was after a few drinks the night before.'

'I only had one.'

'Anyway, the principle's the same, you would be bleary eyed in the morning and probably would not have noticed anyone going out.'

A few of the players next to me had caught the gist of the conversation. The incident had become common knowledge locally with the reports in the local paper.

'What about if he is still there?' someone commented. 'You haven't heard anyone snoring?'

There was general laughter at my expense.

'I don't suppose there is anywhere he could have got out at the back?' said Joe.

'No, there's just a brick wall.'

'Or above.'

'There is a skylight but it's about twenty feet up. He would have had to have been Spiderman to get up there.'

'He's my suspect,' someone said. There was more laughter.

I explained Esther's theory that there would be no need to hide or escape from the back of the shop as it would have been quite easy for the culprit to duck low behind the units and make their escape.

'Whatever, it remains a mystery,' said Simon. 'Damn funny business. Anyway, we had better get back to it, see what we can do in the field.'

The opposition side made a promising start and our bowling was a little wayward, exhibiting all the excesses associated with a long tea. After twenty overs they had half our score and had only lost two wickets. When Simon chucked the ball to me I thought his captaincy smacked of desperation. I bowled what I believed were a couple of overs of mesmerising spin, taking the wicket of the key player, though his downfall was probably more to do with the innocent looking nature of my bowling and a rush of overconfidence as he eyed a six on the leg-side boundary and holed out, mistiming his shot and falling several yards short. During the next over, I took a running catch which seemed to initiate a general collapse in the batting side. I began to feel happy about my contribution and was pleased that I had agreed to play. They were all out for 180 making us comfortable winners. The result, though, truly did not matter too much that day as the main purpose was to have a bit of fun and raise money for charity. In any case, the opposing side achieved a kind of parity by easily winning the tug-of-war that followed. A large number of locals and friends of the cricket club began to turn up. Then came the auction of promises, hosted by Simon. He talked up the prizes and persuaded several people to give up their money in a good cause. My book went for £50.

A bar was opened and the barbecue that had been started just as we left the field was pronounced ready. I was uncertain how I could face the thought of further food. Then Esther and Aggie arrived. I had quite forgotten that they had promised to come. Simon praised my contribution with bat and ball and I attempted to be modest.

'I came with Aggie,' said Esther. 'I can drive your car home and then Aggie can drop me off if you want to have a drink.'

It was the last thing I really needed but Simon was already pushing a beer into my hand.

'Go on,' said Aggie, 'it will do you good.'

Carried away by the party atmosphere that had been developing since we had left the field, I gave in to temptation, yet again. When I went to bed that night I felt as though I had put on at least a stone and become the most ardent follower of the god Dionysus. 'I will be good tomorrow,' I resolved to myself.

15

As the days went by there was a feeling of unreality about the death in the bookshop and it became difficult to believe that it had really happened. The mystery man appeared to have vanished into thin air and if it was not for the evidence of the photo it would have been easy to believe that he did not exist at all. Other lines of enquiry, such as the involvement of Patrick Williams or otherwise, did not seem to be bearing fruit, at least not as far as we were aware. We settled back into our ordinary bookshop routine which was not, however, that ordinary. We were lucky enough to be visited by a Booker Prize winning author for which we had advance bookings for over a hundred people, requiring us to resort to hiring a local hall. I also made a purchase of books from the son of an ornithologist who had died. As well as books on birds he had a magnificent collection of other natural history books in excellent condition, many of them with beautiful colour plates.

The death of Nielsen had not quite slipped out of memory but it had been put onto the back burner. My working relationship with Esther developed and our social relationship mellowed. My early expectations of wanting something more receded (though I knew if I ever delved deep enough there was a spark waiting to be ignited). Those who were close enough to us just accepted it as it was and drew their own conclusions. Everyone seemed content with it. All that is except for one person, my mother, Elizabeth.

She made one of her periodic visits to stay with me for three or four days in early June. She immediately took to Esther and appeared at the bookshop each day of her stay. My mother was a great reader herself, particularly of biographies, and always insisted on buying a pile of books when she visited, so that by the time she was ready to take the train back home, she had an impossible number to transport. Some remained with me in a box in my house to deliver next time I was over. I suspected that this was in part a ruse; a way of suggesting that I did not go to see her enough and to encourage more frequent visits.

All my mother's little mannerisms that I considered irksome did not seem to irritate Esther at all. I apologised to Esther for my mother's behaviour over our weekly dinner the day after she had gone home.

'No need to apologise,' said Esther. 'She's charming.'

'But rather overbearing don't you think?'

'She's just interested in you as a good mother should be. Look, if you want my advice when she comes to stay you should make more of a fuss of her and give her some more of your time.'

'But how can I spend more time with her? She follows me around as it is. She is in the bookshop almost every day.'

'But, don't you see, that's the point, you should be taking her to the cinema, taking her out to dinner, letting her know that you have something planned for her rather than leaving it up to her to trot around after you making her own amusement. If you did that I am sure you would feel much less constrained. Besides,' she added, 'you're lucky to have a mother. I lost mine ten years ago.'

'I know you're right, we don't appreciate them until they're gone. You still have your father though, don't you?'

'Yes.'

'And do you spoil him?'

'When I can. He is very independent – like your mother – but, unlike your mother, he would never think of coming to see me. He has his own little world of golf, gardening and the parish council. He's too busy to bother with me. So I have the other problem: finding when he has enough spare time for me to go and visit him.'

'I bet he enjoys it when you do.'

'He loves to show me off to his local cronies.'

'Do you have any brothers and sisters?'

'A brother and a sister, so we do share him around a bit. I shouldn't say this but I think he finds Cat a bit too bossy and Rupert, my brother, is on the other side of the world.'

'Cat?'

'Sorry, Catriona.'

'As in Stevenson's book?'

'Yes, my mother was a great Stevenson fan.'

'Me too.'

'What about you?'

'I have a more successful brother.'

'In what way?'

'In every way. He's a lawyer, he's married and he has two lovely children.'

'Why is that more successful? You might not be wealthy but you have a lovely bookshop and know lots of interesting people.'

'I meant not successful by my mother's definition.'

My mother, given Esther's friendliness towards her, completely got the wrong end of the stick about our relationship. She rang me a few days after her visit to thank me for her stay and to remind me to bring the books she had bought.

'There are some books there that I simply must read as soon as possible.'

'As soon as I get an opportunity I will be right over with them,' I assured her.

Then she moved the conversation on.

'And how is the lovely Esther?'

'Absolutely fine, I think she really enjoys working here. And she's very good at her job, just what the bookshop needs.'

'And how are you two getting on?'

'I just told you.'

'No, the two of you together.'

'Fine, we work very well together.'

I knew this was not what she meant.

'I've seen the way you look at her and the glint in her eye.'

I sighed.

'Look, we are just good friends that's all.'

'Whatever you say my dear.'

I shuddered to think how she would be if she knew my real feelings for Esther. She was not beyond ringing Esther and telling her. I decided to stick to my line about just being good friends, which of course was the reality of the case.

*

As I pulled into the driveway when I visited my mother the weekend following the telephone conversation with her, I had the same strange tingly feeling I always felt when returning to home, the house where my mum and dad had lived for so long and which was so much part of my childhood. Even though my father had now been dead more than ten years, I still half expected to see him when I walked through the door. He was not an expressive person like my mother but I found his quiet intelligence re-assuring. I had expected my mother to move once he had died but she had remained where she was and touchingly kept several of my dad's things around the house.

'I speak to him every day,' she had told me on numerous occasions.

It was a modest red brick house but with a large garden which held many happy memories for me. It also had a particular smell which was unique to that house and to my childhood.

Thinking back to my youth I regretted that I had not been kinder and more thoughtful, especially as a teenager, though I supposed I was no different to many others. I particularly felt guilty that I had not spent more time with my dad. But it was my mother who was alive now and, as Esther was right to remind me, I needed to appreciate her more. However, I also knew that if my behaviour was influenced constantly by guilt and the way I thought I should behave, my relationship with my mother would not be a genuine one.

I did not receive a reply after ringing the bell twice so I tried the door. It was open.

'Hello, Mum,' I shouted and made my way through the kitchen to the sitting room. For a moment I had that uncomfortable feeling that something was wrong but then I saw a note on the table.

'Back shortly, Mum.'

I looked through the window into the garden and saw an image of myself playing in short trousers while my dad mowed the lawn.

At what point, I wondered, do your parents stop being invincible and become vulnerable and mortal? This got me to thinking about children. I had never really had any strong desire to have children without really rationalising why. I suppose I had thought of them as an encumbrance on my freedom. However, I knew also I was denying any offspring those same feelings that I was feeling now about my parents. There were some negative feelings but also many positive ones.

Esther did not have children. I had, I supposed, presumed that she did not want any, otherwise, now as she edged towards her fortieth year, she would have had them. But, if I thought a bit deeper, it may be that she would have had them but for her husband's illness. Why had I not thought of that before? This may of course be influencing her outlook on life. She may be feeling that she has missed out. It might even be that the brief relationship she had with the man after her husband died was in response to this but in the end she could not go through with it. Perhaps it influenced her attitude to me? Even at forty it was not too late to have children. Perhaps she would think more kindly of a relationship with me if I had proclaimed myself in favour of parenthood. But to change my feelings about children in order to get Esther to think positively of me smacked of duplicity.

At that moment, my mother returned.

'So sorry, Elliot, I just had to pop down to the village shop. I was out of butter.'

'You know, in the ten years since your father died,' said my mother as she tucked into the steak she had cooked, 'I have become used to being on my own but I do miss the company.'

'Maybe you can come for a longer stay next time you are over,' I said with considerably mixed feelings.

I slept in my old room. The wallpaper was now some plain pattern but I could remember when it had striking images of racing cars, motorbikes and steam trains.

*

97

'I've been thinking about what you said about staying a bit longer,' my mother said before I left in the morning. 'Perhaps I could come at the beginning of the autumn when all the good books come out.'

16

It was on Midsummer's Day that I received a call from Sam.

'How are you?' I said. I expected she was going to order some course books or possibly ask me about a job in the bookshop over the holidays. If it was the latter I wanted to let her down gently - long gone were the days when I had enough resources to 'find a job for someone.' Her next remark, however, threw me.

'Did you know the *First Folio* has gone missing?'

'Missing?'

'Yes. A facsimile copy was left in its place but some visiting professor noticed that something was not quite right.'

'That's such a shame.'

It was indeed. The university had one of the few copies on display outside the British Library and the USA (which had acquired the majority of copies through an endowment from Henry Folger, the oil millionaire).

'But don't you think it's a bit odd: Nielsen gets murdered and then this priceless artefact disappears?'

'I'm not sure that there is any necessary connection. It's probably just a tragic coincidence. Though of course, Nielsen's death and the attention it got could have reminded someone how valuable it was.'

'The *Folio* was Nielsen's whole life's work,' she continued. 'He was one of the few people who had access to it. It shouldn't have been easy to steal.'

'I remember his enthusiasm on the night of his talk. It must be a great loss for the university and the town.'

Of course, that was true of Nielsen as well as the *Folio*.

There was an uncomfortable silence. I felt I was required to say something.

'I presume it's been reported to the police.'

'I'm sure the university authorities have done that. I'm just not sure whether the police take this sort of thing seriously though

- it just being a dusty old tome.'

Sam had never been backward in coming forward.

'It's difficult to know what else can be done,' was my lame response.

'I just wondered whether they should ask a private detective to get involved or whether they should consult someone like you with your knowledge of old books.'

'I consider myself a lover of books rather than an expert on them. And I'm certainly no Shakespeare expert.'

'I think you're being too modest. Working in your bookshop was one of the most rewarding experiences I have ever had.'

'You were young and impressionable - you still are young and impressionable.'

She laughed. We went on to talk about the courses she was studying and she ordered a couple of books.

Of course I was flattered by what she said about the experience she had gained working in the bookshop and her confidence in me.

'But the way she was talking,' I explained to Esther later, 'it was as though she wanted me to do something about this *Folio* business.'

'Which, of course, you can't?'

One of the irritating things about Esther was that she was forever challenging my 'comfort zone.' I was quite happy there. The clue was in the first word, 'comfort', I enjoyed the comfortableness of it. Somehow she never quite grasped this. Now it seemed that she was in conspiracy with Sam.

'But surely the police...'

'Pah!'

She had become very cynical and scathing about our boys in blue.

'OK, then, what do you suggest I do?'

'Try to establish a connection.'

'Or not. The police have still not managed to find the original suspect for the murder of Nielsen.'

'My point exactly.'

When I arrived home that evening I felt duty bound at least to conduct some research on the *First Folio* and on Shakespeare.

Nielsen's book was informative and stylishly written. However, it was as much an entertainment as a piece of historical fact, so I looked at other authors' offerings that I had in my possession as well as making use of the internet. I discovered that the *Folio* took two years to be produced and cost £1 which made it expensive for the time when a single play would cost only 6d. It would have been a substantial risk for the two men, John Hemminge and Henry Condell, who were primarily responsible (along with the printer William Jaggard) for its coming into being. In the introduction to the *Folio* Heminge and Condell declared that they *acted without ambition of self-profit, or fame, only to keepe the memory of so worthy a Friend, & Fellow alieue, as was our Shakespeare.* It was in fact very successful; second, third and fourth editions were produced.

It made me then want to re-visit the plays and I turned to an old text of the complete Shakespeare and thumbed my way through. I felt like looking for a bit of comedy to lighten my mood. I turned to *As You Like It*. This was, of course, the play that included Jaques, which I had read from on the night of Nielsen's death. I was just reading the opening lines, the address from Orlando to Adam, when I received a phone call I was not expecting.

'Hello, Elliot, it's Miriam.'

It was the first time I could remember receiving a phone call from Miriam. I thought it must be about Simon.

'Is Simon all right?' I could not help myself saying.

She could hear the concern in my voice.

'It's all right, he's not hurt or anything.'

'Thank God for that!'

'But there is a problem. They have taken him away for questioning.'

'Who have?'

'The police.'

I could not immediately see where she was going with this. I knew that Simon had dealings in business over the years and wondered if it was to do with tax or VAT.

'What's he supposed to have done?' I continued.

'Oh, Elliot, they have taken him in for questioning about the death of Mr Nielsen in the bookshop.'

'What?'

'They have found some DNA evidence or something.'

'I'm sure it's only routine.'

'But why now? He was questioned at the start like everyone else. Why single him out now?'

'I don't know, Miriam, but you know they are probably just being methodical and looking at the case from every angle. Look, why don't I come around for a while?'

'No, Elliot, that's kind of you, but honestly I'm fine.'

'Are you sure?'

'Yes, really.'

'Would you mind ringing when he comes back home?'

'Yes, of course.'

'Let me know if you change your mind about me coming round – it's no trouble, whatever time of night – and let me know if there is anything else I can help with.'

This was unexpected. I sat down and tried to take it in. For a moment I contemplated the unthinkable. What if Simon, behind all his bonhomie and easy manners was responsible for Nielsen's death? Though Simon was a friend there were great gaps in my knowledge of his past. Perhaps, like Patrick Williams, he had known him in his youth and bore a grudge that he had been harbouring all these years, and then he had discovered the perfect cover for the murder when he realised that he was coming to the bookshop for the talk. The talk with Nielsen had been arranged before the military talk that had taken place before it, and had not Simon been instrumental in arranging the military talk in the first place? If I was being the "devil's advocate" I might say that he had cleverly stayed in the background when I went to greet to Nielsen. He had even suggested to me that I could store the helmets for a while until the author could collect them. He may have subtly masterminded the whole thing. No, it was preposterous! How could I think such thoughts? I rang Esther.

She was surprised too.

'I'm sure they are just reviewing the evidence. If you think about it, there is a lot of good reason to think that his DNA should be there. The *Pickelhaube* author, (Langer wasn't it?), was a friend of his and, knowing Simon, I'm sure he couldn't have resisted handling the helmet at some stage.'

Later on that evening I received a call from Simon.

'Simon, so pleased to hear from you.'

'It's all right, Miriam was worrying a bit like she does. They were just eliminating me from their enquiries. I told them I knew Langer well and had handled his stuff. I think they were satisfied. Just doing their job when you think about it. If they find some evidence they have to follow it through in some way. I think poor Miriam thought she would never see me again.'

When I put the phone down I felt a little guilty for ever having imagined, even for a moment, that Simon could be guilty of any such crime.

However, this was not quite the end of it. I was called on by the inspector the following morning. Once again we sat in my tiny cramped office. He was there, he said, 'just to review the evidence.' We went through the day's events in a perfunctory sort of way, then he turned to the author who had given the talk on the helmets the week before.

'How well did you know...' he looked at his sheet of paper, 'Mr Langer?'

'Not at all, until I met him. He was introduced to me by Simon Bonneville.'

'Who as you have stated is a friend of yours?'

'Yes.'

'And this Mr Langer is a friend of Mr Bonneville?'

'Yes.'

'But even though you're both friends of Simon Bonneville you didn't know each other?'

'Simon is not a childhood friend. Our friendship has been formed through the bookshop over the years,' (like many of my friendships, I thought), 'so I suppose it has a particular slant. I suppose I see him mainly through his visits to the bookshop.'

'So you would not, for example, visit him at his house or he yours?'

My overnight stay before the charity cricket match was still fresh in my mind.

'Well, I have been to supper on occasion. I had supper and

stayed with him recently when we had a charity cricket match in his village.'

I felt uncomfortable having my personal relationships picked over by the police like this. Was it really any of their business? I was also aware that the inspector already knew about my visiting Simon from Simon himself; I needed to make sure I got my story straight.

'As far as I can remember he has never visited me at home, though I do hope to return the favour some time.'

'And are you interested in military matters, like Mr Bonneville?'

'No, far from it. I suppose in many ways it's quite surprising we are friends as our views are very different.'

He raised an eyebrow. I felt I was being disloyal, which had not been my intention.

'But I find him very kind and generous. He would do anything for you. And despite our differences we seem to get on very well.'

I had not been made to examine our friendship like this before. How curious life could be that it was a police interview that was making me do this.

'You say that Mr Bonneville was responsible for asking Mr Langer to do this military talk, even though you are not interested in military matters?'

'It's not that I am uninterested in them but it's not something I seek out. As far as history goes I suppose I'm more interested in the broader sweep of history – movements and cultural and social changes, that sort of thing.'

What a strange conversation this was turning out to be. Where would it all lead?

'So what attracted you to putting on a talk for this man?'

'Well, I have to think commercially as well as with my heart, and it's true that military books sell quite well for us. I suppose, also, I was swayed by Simon. If he was enthusiastic, I thought there was a good chance that other people would be.'

'And when the display was brought in, the spiky helmet and so on, did Simon Bonneville help with that?'

At last I could see where I thought this was leading. I wanted to say yes, he handled the helmet display so, therefore, it was natural that you would find his DNA, but if he had asked Simon and he had said that he didn't, it would sound like there was a conspiracy going on. I decided to fudge it.

'Yes I think he did. I think I remember him helping but to be honest there was a lot going on and I'm not absolutely sure how much he was involved. I know that he, Mr Langer, visited him at his house beforehand.'

My fudge was probably in any case the truth as I understood it and I did want to tell the truth didn't I?

There were a few more questions about the timing of the comings and goings of various people.

'Did you get the information I sent out about Patrick Williams?'

'Yes, thank you.'

He was obviously not going to reveal any more.

Then he added. 'If you think of anything else, please don't hesitate to contact me.'

'It sounds like the investigations are proving difficult?' I ventured as he stood up to go.

'I can't pretend that they haven't been. We're going over the ground again, making sure there's nothing that we've missed, trying to keep an open mind. I'll let you know if we need to speak to you again. DNA evidence has not been as revealing as we'd hoped. I must admit I am 'baffled' by the lack of progress. Though the moustachioed man appeared briefly in a blurred photo and had been positively witnessed by Bonneville's grandson and Mrs Kay, apart from Sam, no one else seems to have noticed his appearance or spoken to him.'

When the inspector had gone, I went and found Esther. I described the interview to her.

'It sounds to me they are a bit desperate and trying to pursue every avenue however unlikely,' she said.

I went to look at some second-hand books in the afternoon, which had been described by the seller as a 'good mixture, a bit of everything.' They were, in fact, from our point of view a poor selection, consisting mainly of celebrity biographies. I came away without buying anything. As it had already gone five, I went straight home rather than returning to the bookshop.

Esther rang soon after I got in the door.

'I know you'll not like this but I have been thinking about that phone call from Sam and arranged a meeting at the university with Miranda Reeves. You remember, she was at Nielsen's memorial service?'

'Yes, I do.' I remembered our interesting conversation at Nielsen's house, which made me less bothered by Esther's interference than she might have supposed.

'Well you also probably know that she was Nielsen's associate at the Faculty. I told her you had a wide knowledge of old books and knew lots about Shakespeare so you had better bone up on it.'

'When's the appointment for?'

'Tomorrow.'

'It's lucky then that I am about to do that at this very moment. I will go on one condition.'

'What.'

'You have got to come with me.'

I had effectively been told that I was to make the visit to the university to see Miranda Reeves and that I did not have any choice in the matter. I ruefully thought that I might as well be married to Esther. I rang Aggie who was happy to cover the bookshop for the day. Esther rang back saying that she had booked the tickets on-line for the eight-thirty train and would pick me up on the way.

I turned to my books on Shakespeare. I decided I'd better leave the reading of *As You Like It* for another time and concentrate on reading as much as I could about the *First Folio*. I did not see my bed until one o'clock the following morning, more than once cursing the interference of Esther.

17

The fast train that we'd taken became the slow train as the slow train had been cancelled. However, we made good use of our time. I was able to read some of a new local book for a talk on organic gardening we were having the following week and Esther was reading a book called, appropriately enough, *The Shakespeare Murders*, an ageing second-hand tome.

'It was written by the same chap who wrote *England Their England*, you know the...'

'The cricket match,' I interrupted. 'A. G. Macdonell.'

It was one of my favourite books.

'Only he wrote this under the name of Neil Gordon.'

'Now that I did not know. You know Esther, you really are coming on.'

Fortunately my book protected me from another one of Esther's elbow jabs.

'In this book the murder is solved by quotes from Shakespeare.'

'Interesting - though absolutely of no relevance to this case.'

'But, as you say, interesting.'

'Ah, *knowledge for its own sake - that is the last snare of morality*.'

'Is that a Shakespeare quote?'

'No, Nietzsche, *Beyond Good and Evil*.'

It was, in fact, just about the only sentence I remembered from the whole of that book but I was happy if I could impress Esther.

The delay to our train had made us late for our appointment. As we hurried on foot, Esther complained about the steep ascent to the university while I in turn complained about the impracticality of her high heels, an expensive label purchased from a local charity shop, though critically, half a size too small.

Despite my marathon reading session the night before, I still really had no firm idea about how to proceed once we arrived there. I had seen most of Shakespeare's plays and handled countless volumes of dusty old one volume editions which, because of their widespread availability, usually commanded a very low market value - but that was about as far as my knowledge of Shakespeare went. However, an interview with Miranda Reeves, had, according to Esther, been surprisingly easy to arrange via the Vice Chancellor. I wondered if the fact that I had met her at the memorial service had smoothed our path.

We met in her spacious office on the second floor of the English Faculty. Since I had met her at the memorial service she had been given a rather severe haircut. Her dark close-cut hair and smart dark trouser suit accentuated her thin boyish features.

'It's good to meet you again,' she said.

'I'm sorry to hear about the theft of the *Folio*,' I said, 'a great loss to the university.'

'Indeed.'

'As must have been the death of Mr Nielsen,' added Esther.

'I'm sure he has been much missed,' I said, thinking back to his enthusiastic talk at the bookshop.

'Yes, he had a thorough knowledge of the *Folio* even if I didn't always agree with his conclusions.'

I looked at her face, though no emotion appeared to accompany her criticism.

'I suppose there is a lot of controversy about the *Folio*. I know they can't even decide which of the paintings represent him.'

There were several framed pictures on the wall of her office, some familiar, which I presumed were of Shakespeare.

'That's correct.'

She stood up and walked across to one of the portraits which I recognised.

'The Chandos portrait is thought to have been the inspiration for the portrait on the front of the *First Folio*, an engraving by Martin Droeshout, but there is no certainty about it. We are not even sure who painted it. Some say it was Shakespeare's friend Richard Burbage, others that it is by John Taylor. Whatever, it is not the most attractive with his head appearing to sink right into his neck. It may be of Shakespeare but no one is sure - and then there's the question of the Cobbe portrait.'

I remembered something about this in the news but was not clear about it. I realised the whole basis of my being there was my knowledge of Shakespeare so, in moments of ignorance adopted a policy of nodding wisely at key moments.

'Can you remind us who Cobbe is?' interjected Esther who was less shy about admitting her ignorance than me.

'The owner of the painting, Alex Cobbe. It had been in his family since the 1700's but it was not until he saw the Janssen Portrait at the National Portrait Gallery a few years ago that he made a connection.'

'Janssen?' I said timidly as I could not remember hearing that name.

'The Janssen portrait was for many years thought to be possibly that of Shakespeare.'

'Until…'

'Until it was discovered that the Janssen portrait was altered to make it more like the Droeshout engraving with the balding hairline, no doubt to make it seem more authentic. Also, the date and the age were added later.'

'Now I'm confused,' I admitted.

'Well it was simply that when Cobbe saw the Janssen portrait and how similar it was to his own, it made Cobbe think that it might be worth testing his out for its authenticity.'

Reeves took a sip of tea that had been provided for us in a bright Clarice Cliff style tea pot with matching cups.

'Cobbe contacted the Shakespeare Birthplace Trust. They researched it for three years and then concluded that Shakespeare was the subject of the portrait.'

'Good.'

'Except, not everybody agrees.'

'There are always sceptics.'

'Some of these are quite notable and think that Henry Wriothesley, the Third Earl of Southampton - Shakespeare's patron - is a more likely subject, but then there are other Southampton portraits.'

She walked over to a wide bookcase and reached up for a large book. She opened it up and showed us a picture.

'This is also in the Cobbe collection.'

There was a portrait of a woman clasping, as I thought, her right hand against her breast and the end of a long tress of hair that came down across the front of her neck.

'A woman.'

'So it was thought for many years. Now it is thought to be that of Southampton himself.'

I looked again, this time trying to imagine the woman as a man. I could see that, perhaps, it could be a young man with still boyish looks. She laughed at my quizzical look.

'So, you see, things are not always what they seem. As we were discussing at the memorial service, sexual ambiguity is a theme of some of Shakespeare's plays, complicated by the fact that, as I'm sure you are aware, all the parts in Shakespeare's time were acted by men.'

'What do you think about all these competing claims to authorship?'

I was thinking of Patrick Williams.

'I think they are *argumentum ex silentio*.'

'What?'

'They are arguing from silence, or ignorance some might say. They look at inconsistencies in his spelling of his name. But he was typical of his time. People were inconsistent in their spellings of words and of their own names – that's just how it was. Dr Johnson didn't finish his Dictionary until 1755. These anti-Stratfordians drive me mad. It's all circumstantial evidence and they come up with extraordinary theories and are always talking about encrypted codes. It is basically a form of snobbery. They refuse to believe that someone with as little education as Shakespeare could come up with such brilliant pieces of drama. Well, though he didn't go to university his education at a grammar school would have been pretty good in lots of ways. There was a national curriculum. He would have been educated in Latin grammar, the classics and rhetoric. The point is that a genius like Shakespeare's requires something more than just a good university education, it requires you to take facts and invest them with an emotion and intelligence that cannot be taught. We know he got a lot of historical things wrong and that he stole a lot of his ideas. Some of the words in Richard the Second, for example, exactly resemble those in *Holinshed's Chronicles* word for word.'

'*Talent imitates, genius steals*, don't they say?' put in Esther.

'But when he did use other peoples' work he added so much more and made it more than the sum of its parts. And he wasn't the only example. Ben Johnson didn't go to university either.'

'So you don't think there's much evidence for someone else having written Shakespeare's plays?'

'No, this is a bit like holocaust deniers denying the murder of the Jews. There is so much contemporary evidence, people referring to Shakespeare the actor, documentary evidence and people like Ben Johnson and others. In fact Johnson criticised Shakespeare almost as much as he praised him.

'Where I do think there is a case to answer is the fact that there is some doubt over his authorship, or the extent of his authorship of one or two plays, usually less well known ones like *Two Noble Kinsmen* which was not included in the *First Folio* and is often left out of modern compilations of his plays. It is now believed that John Fletcher and Shakespeare shared the authorship about 50/50.

'You can even get a masters in Shakespeare authorship studies at a supposedly prestigious university. It's all nonsense. As you can tell, I feel strongly about it... in the end it doesn't matter a jot. The most important thing is the genius of the plays themselves, whoever wrote them.'

There was no doubting Miranda Reeves's passion for Shakespeare and the intellectual rigour with which she defended him.

We returned to our seats and our cups of tea.

'I suppose you must particularly miss being able to share your knowledge with Nielsen?' I ventured.

'We were work colleagues and after a number of years one establishes a close working relationship. It is a sad loss.'

'Were you both working on the *Folio*?'

'The two of us were granted access. We would be accompanied by another member of staff, usually a porter. Anybody else would have to come through us.'

'How often would you need access?' asked Esther

'Most of the time we would work from a facsimile copy so access was not often necessary. However, the *Folios* are not all exactly the same as they were corrected as they were printed so it's when trying to establish these differences that it's most likely the *Folios* would be consulted.'

'Yes, I remember Mr Nielsen talking about that when he gave his talk.'

'How many times would you have accessed the *Folio* in the last year?' asked Esther.

'From memory, I don't know - maybe half-a-dozen times. I probably have a record of the dates in my diary if you need them.'

'The porter who accompanied you, was it always the same one?'

'As far as I remember, it was always Mr Grindley.'

Esther wrote it down in her notebook. She appeared very calm and professional. I thought she would make a good police inspector. I made a mental note to remember to tell her that.

'Would you say Nielsen was easy to work with?'

'Most of the time.'

'What about when he wasn't easy?'

'He could be stubborn.'

'About what sort of things?'

'Work things I suppose I mean. He didn't like admitting he was wrong.'

'Which of us does?'

She hesitated as though she was about to say something but seemed to change her mind.

'Yes, you're right,' she gave a little laugh, 'which of us does?'

'I'm sorry I have to ask this. Did this lead to any unpleasantness between you?'

I saw Esther's eyes flicker. I knew I was taking a risk asking this and was expecting an adverse reaction. However, Reeves looked into my eyes and smiled.

'What sort of thing did you have in mind?'

'I don't know. Let us say a professional grudge, the sort of thing that can happen when ideas get exchanged freely, so that there is confusion over whose ideas belong to whom.'

'You're right, that can be a grey area. But I think we managed to overcome anything of that sort - one way or another.'

When we had finished the interview we went to the nearest common room and had a coffee.

'What did you make of that?'

'A bit on the cool side towards Nielsen to begin with but I suppose she didn't say anything that she didn't think was accurate. It was brave of you asking that question about a possible grudge.'

'I suppose it would be less realistic if she was gushing over him. We can't criticise her for telling the truth.'

'She stands to gain by Nielsen's death. No doubt she'll take over Nielsen's post.'

'I suppose that's true but she already had a growing reputation of her own and would have been able to achieve a similar status at another university in any case. I certainly don't think that murdering Nielsen, if that is what you are suggesting, would be her only means of promotion or the most desirable one.'

'Apart from the fact that she's the wrong sex.'

'That, too.'

'Unless she had an accomplice.'

Esther was thoughtful for a moment and squeezed her bottom lip together with her thumb and forefinger, an affectation of hers when thinking hard.

'You know the person who I'd really like to talk to? Mr Grindley.'

'We might as well make good use of our time while we're here.'

'I suppose we had better arrange it through the Vice Chancellor again. It's better if we have his authority.'

We walked over to the administrative buildings, which were situated at one end of the square that occupied the centre of the university campus. The Vice Chancellor was not available. We decided to leave it until after lunch and thought it worthwhile to spend some time looking around the university. We went to the old chapel where the *Folio* would normally have been on display. Inside the glass case was an insignificant looking notice: *The Shakespeare First Folio is currently unavailable for display.*

'An understatement if ever there was one,' commented Esther. Outside there was a perfectly manicured green lawn, edged with a gravel path and solid looking wooden benches. We selected the nearest one and sat there soaking up the summer sunshine. Esther took a neatly folded brown paper bag out of her copious handbag. Inside was a luscious looking sandwich.

'Glad I brought this. I'm starving.'

She took a big bite and looked at me sideways. I could smell fresh brown bread, salad and pesto. She gave a satisfied 'mm.'

'Where's yours?' she said as she munched away.

'Oh, I'm not hungry,' I lied. I had only had an orange juice for breakfast and a coffee on the train. I knew I just had to hold my nerve.

'You're hopeless.' She delved once more into her handbag, bringing out another neat little package which she flung across to me.

'One day you'll get yourself organised.'

For all her apparent toughness, Esther had an unerring caring instinct.

'Thanks Esther,' I said with the genuine feeling of a hungry man. 'You're a real friend.'

With the effects of the sumptuous sandwich and the sunshine we both began to feel a little sleepy.

'Budge up.'she said, propelling me to the other end of the bench. Then she lay down with her head on my lap and her feet over the edge of the bench.

'Power nap - wake me up in half-an-hour.'

She closed her eyes.

'O sleep, O gentle sleep, Nature's soft nurse.'

I couldn't help myself - I caressed the top of her head. She flicked my hand away.

This was the nature of our relationship. There was a charming innocence about it which I had come to accept and enjoy for its own sake, though inside my own head there was a desire for another more physical relationship.

'King Henry Fourth, Part II,' she mouthed with her eyes closed.

'Very good, Esther.'

I tried to blot out of my mind the more intimate relationship I longed for and sat there contentedly dipping further into my book on organic gardening. If this was the extent of our relationship - well - I could think of nothing better at that moment. As I sat there looking down on her pretty face and feeling her breath against my arm, another piece of verse came into my head.

'*Her breath is more sweete than a gentle south-west wind,*' I spouted. 'I bet you won't get that one Esther.'

But a gentle snore indicated that she was already fast asleep.

18

Once Esther had awoken (with a sudden start, though she soon recovered herself), we tried the Vice Chancellor's office again. This time we were lucky and able to arrange an impromptu interview with the porter, Grindley, in a back room of the Porters' Lodge.

'I can give you ten minutes before I start my rounds. What is it you wanted to ask me about?'

Grindley was a stockily built man in his late forties with a pock-marked face. He had a certain presence and a kind of rough charm. For a big man he also appeared surprisingly nimble as he rearranged the chairs in the room for us.

I asked the questions while Esther sat beside me with her notebook.

'I understand that you would accompany either Mr Nielsen or Miss Reeves when they wanted to look at the *Folio*?'

'That's right, Sir. Always a pleasure. Makes my mouth go a bit dry I don't mind admitting, all that history and such like.'

'And you accompanied both Mr Nielsen and Miss Reeves?'

'That's correct.'

'Did they visit about the same number of times?'

'About the same I would say. Although… well, perhaps I should not say.'

'Go on.'

'I'm not saying anything against Miss Reeves but she was a bit more, you know, strict. Mr Nielsen liked it that I was interested. He would say to me things like, "Just to think that we are in the presence of this great piece of work printed just after Mr Shakespeare's death." And he would even show me places where they had made mistakes and told me how there were different things in different books - that sort of thing.'

'And Miss Reeves would not do that?'

'No, as I said, she was more of the strict kind and there was that time after Nielsen's death when she sent me away - though I supposed I could understand it even if it felt a little weird.'

'Go on.'

'Well, I'm afraid I was rather upset by Mr Nielsen's death and I did go on about it rather. Well, this time we went to visit the *Folio* and she said to me, "You know Mr Grindley, Mr Nielsen's death has rather upset me too and I would like to pay my respects to Mr Nielsen in a quiet way with the piece of work that meant most to him. I can get closer to Mr Nielsen here than in any church or chapel." Then she made a little choking sound like she was upset. It was quite a moving speech and not her usual way of talking.'

'Death affects us all in strange ways.'

'I said I would go and wait outside. She said thank you but first could I go and fetch a candle as she would like to light one for Mr Nielsen. It was an unusual request and a bit of a nuisance as it would take a good five or six minutes to fetch one, but seeing as how she was, I said I didn't mind.'

'And you took the candle to her?'

'She was waiting at the door when I got there. She thanked me and asked if I would wait outside for a few minutes. She was as good as her word and met me outside I would say about ten minutes later.'

'You said Nielsen and Reeves were a bit different from each other. I don't want you to tell tales out of school but is there any other way you would say they were different?'

'It's not really for me to say. They seemed to get on all right overall but I suppose, when you think about it, nowadays there is competition everywhere. I suppose it's no different in the academic world than everywhere else.'

'Can you give any specific examples?'

'Well, I don't know of any examples exactly but sometimes you would just get a feeling that things were not entirely right between them. But we're all human I suppose.'

Once out of earshot of the Porters' Lodge I turned to Esther.

'What did you make of all that?'

'It seems like he is definitely trying to suggest something about

Miranda Reeves.'

'Suggesting, but refusing to say anything definite.'

'I presume he's said all this to the police?'

'And no doubt, they have questioned Miranda Reeves.'

'Why didn't Miranda Reeves mention that bit about lighting the candle?'

'I suppose she didn't feel it was important or perhaps felt it was none of our business.'

Having a few minutes to spare we browsed in a second-hand bookshop which was en route to the station. I was always keen to look at other bookshops. There was a worn copy of *England Their England* which Esther snapped up for £3.

'Still a good bargain,' I said, 'despite the condition.'

On the train journey back I had to suffer Esther giggling most of the way. When she got to the part in the book where the cricket match took place. I tried to get involved.

'Is the village blacksmith bowling yet?' I entreated her.

She shook her head and continued reading and giggling.

I was jealous. My own tome on organic gardening was a little dry by comparison.

19

The day after our visit to the university I followed up our second-hand book enquiry. Some of our more valuable sales were through website enquiries and sales over the last few weeks were down. I knew that this was partly because we needed to add some more interesting stock. There was one large collection of books at an old vicarage in a nearby village which I was particularly interested in. I phoned my client, a Mrs Dupre, the daughter of the owner of the house who had recently died, and it was agreed that I should visit that afternoon.

It was an attractive old house with spacious rooms and high ceilings. The owners had resisted any attempt to sanitise the interior and give it a modern shell, keeping many of its original features. As I followed Mrs Dupre along the hall I admired the exposed elm floorboards. I was shown into the first of the reception rooms which was lined with dark wooden shelving from floor to ceiling and filled with books. There was a particularly fine selection of titles about Egypt, many of them dating from the nineteenth century. This was the first of many rooms each containing an extensive selection of books. Overall it was an impressive collection. After we had discussed the price it was agreed that I should return there the following day and take the first load.

I arrived early next morning and approached my task with relish. It was when I was knee-deep in the collection of books on Egypt that I received a call on my mobile.

'Mr Todd?'

'Yes?'

'I have the book.'

'I'm sorry?'

This sort of thing often happened. Someone had been talking to me about a book a month before and would ring expecting that I would instantly recall the conversation. No doubt the bookshop number was busy and they had resorted to the mobile which appeared on our website.

'I have the *Folio*.'

'The *Folio*?' I repeated. My brain had not yet come to life.

'The *First Folio*.'

'I am so pleased it has been found.'

I did not recognise the voice but I reasoned it was someone from the faculty or maybe an assistant to the Vice Chancellor. It was kind of them to ring and put me in the picture. I was a little flattered that they had rung to inform me.

'You must all be mightily relieved?' I continued.

'I don't think you understand. I am in possession of the *Folio*.'

And then at once, of course, I did. I was talking to the thief.

'You stole it?'

'I have it in my possession.'

A nicety of expression, I thought. *Possession, stolen. What was the difference?*

'Why,' I asked, 'are you phoning me and not the university?'

'You are a collector.'

'Ha!' I could not help laughing.

'Do you know how much that thing is worth?'

'Several million quid.'

The most expensive book I had ever sold was a little over £300. I waited for him to continue.

'As I said, it came into my possession. I don't want to be in the limelight. You can have that and claim your reward.'

There was a £20,000 reward that had been put out by the university for the unearthing of the *Folio*.

'I just want ten thousand. You could get the same and the publicity.'

'Why don't you want the glory?'

'I should think that was obvious.'

But it was not obvious to me.

'So you are the thief?' I ventured.

I wanted to establish the situation. It was possible he might have found the *Folio* abandoned.

He did not answer my question.

'I will ring you again in a couple of days.'

He hung up. I looked up incoming calls and saw that the identity of the last number had been withheld. It was all a little surreal. I sat down among the sea of books that I had been loading into boxes.

I rang Esther at the bookshop.

'So do you think he really is the thief?' Esther said.

'He kept using this phrase *in possession*.'

'Perhaps he came across it somewhere? In which case he could legitimately claim the reward.'

'But he says he doesn't want it all. He wants to share it with me.'

'Maybe he's not the thief but has done something else. Perhaps he is an ex-lag and has form – or he's Nielsen's murderer.'

'Or maybe he was ringing from prison?'

'Or - how about this? He has tried to dispose of it, found it was too hot to handle so he comes to you and tries to dump it.'

'But he could still go direct to the university and claim a reward and pretend he had found it.'

After a moment's thought, I continued.

'So, what do I do?'

'Sleep on it.'

This was easier said than done. I felt uneasy about the fact that I had been singled out to be contacted and I spent a restless night. His knowledge of me was a little unnerving.

The next morning I arrived early at the bookshop to put in some extra time cataloguing and was waiting for Esther when she came into the shop just before nine.

'Having slept on it I have decided to go to the police.' I told Esther.'

'I was thinking about this. Why don't you go to that woman at the faculty first? If there is anything in it for you, you damn well deserve it.'

'That is the kindest thing, Esther, you have said to me for a long time.' I gulped with unexpected emotion but recovered myself. 'If I didn't know you better, Esther, I would think you had lain awake thinking about a life of crime.'

Esther did not laugh and had on that stony face she wore when she was being deadly serious. I knew better than to continue with my merry banter.

'But it is a practical and logical step - I can see that', I continued. I left a message on Miranda Reeves's answerphone saying that there had been an urgent development with regard to the *Folio* that I would like to discuss with her. She in turn left a message on my office answerphone saying that she could see me the following day at six in the evening - Esther's yoga night.

'In any case,' said Esther when I discussed it with her, 'I think it might be better if you saw her alone. She might be more relaxed with you on her own and might feel less intimidated - you know without the presence of another woman. If she gives you an opportunity to talk, you talk - and don't forget to listen.'

The following day I walked past the medieval church and the Victorian Gothic architecture of the building that fronted the main entrance to the university before finding my way to the red brick building that housed the faculty of English. I climbed the steps up to Miranda Reeves's room on the second floor. I knocked on the door which was slightly open. There was no reply so I gingerly walked in. The office was roomy and imposing, more like a manager's office in a large corporation than one belonging to an academic, I thought, probably reflecting her status. I paced up and down the floor and took another look at the Shakespeare portraits. On an adjacent wall were some other portraits that I had not noticed the first time. My attention was taken by a portrait in profile of Radclyffe Hall, the author of the lesbian classic *Well of Loneliness*. As I examined the portrait Miranda Reeves rushed in, a little out of breath.

'Sorry to keep you, Mr Todd.'

She took her place behind the desk.

'You said you had some important information about the *Folio*.'

'Yes, I had an anonymous phone call. I can't decide what to do about it. I thought I would ask you first.'

'Thank you for considering me.' She sat down. 'Now, what's this all about?'

'The gist of it is that the phone caller said he has the *Folio* and wanted to offer me the opportunity of sharing the reward. He didn't say whether he had stolen it - he kept using this phrase

122

that he was *in possession* of it - but I can only assume that he had stolen it.'

She sank back in her chair and put her hands into an upside down v-shape to her mouth.

'Of course it could be a prank.'

I considered this.

'A student prank?'

'Yes. We have had similar things before - not quite these high stakes.'

'It would take a degree of nerve.'

'Yes.'

'I was thinking of going to the police.'

She thought for a good long moment.

'You could leave it with me for a day or two and see what I could find out.'

I was intrigued.

'Do you know any students that might be responsible?'

'Sometimes you hear things. I don't know - I suppose it is unlikely that someone is going to suddenly admit it to me. Perhaps you're right and we should go to the police. In fact why don't I ring them for you right now?

She called from the phone on her desk. She explained the situation exactly as I had described it to her. A meeting was arranged between the inspector and me for the following day.

After she had made the phone call she offered me some tea. My first instinct was to leave, having accomplished what I had come there for - a decision on whether to go to the police - but what Esther had said about not forgetting to take the chance to talk if there was an opportunity, stuck in my mind, so I said, 'Yes, please, I would love to.'

There was a corner in the room with a kettle and a sink and the brightly coloured tea-set that she had used last time I had been there. I spoke to her as she busied herself preparing the tea.

'Such a shame about the *Folio* going missing. It must be fascinating working with it.'

'Yes, I'm very lucky. I can truly say I am in love with Shakespeare.'

She swung round to face me and smiled.

'Look, why don't we forget about tea. Do you fancy something a little stronger? I have a bottle of malt in my flat. I've had quite a day with the students and could do with it.'

I shuddered a little bit at the thought of the malt. I did not consider myself an alcoholic but I had a history of not being able to control myself in the presence of a good bottle of whisky. However, in company, I told myself, it would be different. And I heard Esther's voice inside my head: 'Go on, you don't know what you might find out.'

We turned into a central walkway that connected the colleges and the main square.

'Do you ever get fed up with Shakespeare?' I asked her as we walked along. 'Don't you ever think that you have just had enough of him? I know you said to me that you worried that it cut you off from other things.'

'Do you know, I think the truth is I don't think I ever do. At least I never think about it in that way - of being fed up with him - so I expect that proves that I don't. I suppose when I spoke to you I was feeling a little down, given the situation.'

'Thirty-eight odd plays is quite a rich canon in any case.'

'And all the sonnets. And I do teach and research contemporaries of Shakespeare, such as Marlowe and Ben Jonson and his ilk. We do forget that there are some other great Jacobean plays out there. You know if Shakespeare had died at the same time as Marlowe, Marlowe would have definitely been considered the greater playwright. Shakespeare was rather looked down on by some of his contemporaries. Robert Greene described him as *an upstart crow beautified with our feathers*. Most of the playwrights were, like Greene, university educated. There were no doubt big gaps in his education and knowledge but in the end very few could write anything nearly as good. I'm sorry, there I am going on again.'

'No, it's fascinating. I think you have answered my original question more than once.'

Once we arrived at the flat she poured us both a whisky.

She clinked my glass.

'Cheers, it's a single malt. I don't usually have such good stuff.'

She waved her glass in the air. 'A Christmas present. Now seems as good a time to use it as any.'

She put on a CD. 'This is Aris Christofellis. He has a beautiful voice and sings songs from Shakespeare. This first one is from *Hamlet* and is called *How should I your true love know*?'

'Was it his recording at the memorial service?'

'Yes, I believe it was.' She waved me towards a comfortable looking armchair. 'Please sit down.'

I took a sip of the whisky. It tasted great. I ignored the warning in the back of my head.

'Good whisky.'

'Thank you.'

There was, as I would have expected, a row of book lined shelves.

'Makes me feel at home I said - all these books.'

There was a small pile on the coffee table in front of us, including a weighty facsimile copy of *The Folio*, similar to the one that Nielsen had brought to the talk. There were also a few paperbacks including a copy of Jeanette Winterson's *Oranges Are Not the Only Fruit*.

Aris Christofellis began a new Shakespeare song, *Hark! Hark! The Lark*.

'This is from *Cymbeline*. You know Shakespeare was the first to really make songs an integral part of the play. He really is an underrated songster.'

'Should we be thinking of his plays as musicals instead?'

She smiled.

'I think that would be going a bit far.'

She refilled my glass and poured another for herself. This woman could really drink! We talked more about Shakespeare. Her knowledge was truly encyclopaedic. She provided all sorts of insights that I had no knowledge of. I was enjoying her company on a personal level while the rational side of me - which had not totally deserted me - told me that I could see that she was certainly a match for Nielsen and that a professional jealously could have developed in a competitive atmosphere. I wondered if there was anything in what Grindley had said. I realised that I had not asked her anything about Nielsen and felt

I was neglecting my main purpose for being there.

'Are they going to replace Harry Nielsen?' I asked.

'I'm sure they will but you know the cogs within the wheels of the university turn very slowly.'

'Which no doubt means a lot of extra work for you?'

'Of course, but I have some very able assistants to call on. But you are right, it will be a lot of extra work. And the truth is, Harry Nielsen will be a very difficult act to follow. There are not many of his calibre around.'

'I imagine you made quite a team.'

She gave me an awkward smile.

'I think we did. I suppose we were a little bit competitive - though I don't think that is such a bad thing.'

'No, I'm sure you're right. It's in every walk of life and can be a very good thing - as long as everything is kept in proportion.'

'You know, Harry could be very nice but at times he could be a little shit – I'm sorry I have probably had a bit too much to drink - I know it's not nice to talk ill of the dead.'

'You are just being honest. Nothing changes because someone has died.'

She was a little flushed and held her forehead with her hand. I could see her eyes were beginning to water.

'Perhaps I should sign up for one of your classes,' I said, trying to lighten the conversation. 'I'm sure I could learn an awful lot.'

Her face brightened.

'You would be very welcome and I am sure you would make an excellent student. We also have some fun. Shakespeare was no angel and he did have his detractors. A playwright called Thomas Dekker created this lecherous playwright in a play called *Satiromastix* which was based on Shakespeare. He was called Sir Adam Prickshaft.'

I laughed. I was at that most pleasant stage of intoxication feeling just light headed enough that I felt happy and alive, and yet still perfectly in control of my thoughts and speech. It was so easy though, to go beyond this level and proceed to the dangerous next stage, where drink becomes an object in itself. It was important that I stay in control and remember our conversation, though I had to admit that any suspicions I had about Miranda Reeves were vanishing into the background. I was now thinking of Miranda Reeves as a potential friend, or at the very least, a potential customer. Perhaps she would become a regular attendee at our book talks and encourage her students to come along? Moreover, I could give her students special rates and perhaps hold joint events with the university.

She was also attractive. She had touched me on the hand more than once as she expounded on Shakespeare but she was probably, I reasoned, just a tactile person and there was that picture of Radclyffe Hall and the book by Jeanette Winterson in her office that made me think that she was not interested in men in any case. And here to me was the strangest thing of all: even if she was a full blooded heterosexual, I felt a strange sort of loyalty to Esther.

'Are you all right Mr... Elliot?'

I broke out from my reverie.

'I'm sorry, I was just thinking about something.'

'You looked so sad for a moment.'

'It was nothing, just something at the bookshop.'

I patted her hand.

'I think it is wonderful to feel so strongly about your work.'

'But sometimes taking something too seriously can have tragic consequences.'

'It must be like a personal loss now that the *Folio* has gone missing'

She gave me another awkward smile.

'What about Radclyffe Hall - I saw her picture in your office.'

I rather blurted it out. I realised that I had probably by now had a little too much to drink. She paused for a moment as if getting her bearings. My question had come out of the blue and I could see the whisky was having an effect on her as well as me.

'*The Well of Loneliness* was a very important book because it presented lesbianism as natural when for so long it had occupied a shabby corner.'

She hiccupped and spilt her drink slightly.

'There was nothing sexually explicit in it but that didn't stop the book from being banned and all copies ordered to be destroyed.'

She hiccupped again.

'That's what comes of drinking on an empty stomach,' she said. 'I should have eaten something.'

'If I were a gentleman I would have suggested that we have something to eat during our discussion. Trouble is, I need to go. My train leaves shortly.'

Part of me wanted to stay but I was afraid of where things would go if I did. I did not want my enquiries to be compromised in any way and there was the image of Esther hovering in the background.

'That's a shame. I was going to ask your opinion about this new book I am writing about Shakespeare, sex and love.'

'I'm sorry, I really have to go.'

'I have enjoyed our talk. Perhaps next time I can offer you a meal?'

'Yes, thank you, I think I would like that.'

Her movements were a little unsteady as she saw me to the door and shook my hand. I gave her a quick kiss on the cheek.

My walk was a sobering one in more ways than one. I had enjoyed Miranda Reeve's company for all its slight awkwardness though I wondered whether I should have stayed longer in order to try and gain more information. All in all, I felt that we had both been veering towards an inebriated state where nothing more would have been gained or remembered. I lost my way for a moment and found myself going in completely the wrong direction. The university was a labyrinthine place and many of the buildings looked the same. Consequently, I found myself running the last half mile in order to catch the train. I made it just before it pulled out of the station.

I bought some fish and chips on the way home. I had not realised how hungry I was. At that moment they tasted like the best food there had ever been - such can be the effect of excessive alcohol consumption. By the time I arrived home, after a three mile walk, it was dark. I picked up the phone to hear that there were two messages. The first message was a caller deciding after a short silence not to leave a message. The second message was from Esther asking how I had got on with Miranda Reeves. I suspected that both messages were from Esther. I felt tired and dehydrated. I drank a glass of water and went to bed, deciding that as I had not discovered anything earth shattering from Miranda Reeves, I would not phone Esther but speak to her in the morning at work. Unusually for me I encountered blissful sleep and when I woke the next morning, thankfully, I had only a little trace of a hangover. Grateful for the security and comfort of my own bed, I was pleased that I had left Miranda Reeves's flat when I did.

20

Esther did not seem quite herself when I arrived at work in the morning just after nine. She normally greeted me with a cheerful *hello* but she spoke to me without looking up from her work.

'We have an urgent order to get to a local school. Do you think you can help me?'

There were two sides of a printed order. She gave me one of them.

'This is great Esther, a large order like this - gets the day off to a good start.'

She gave a 'humph' and buried her head in the order.

'Don't you want to know how I got on?'

'It sounds like you are going to tell me.'

'What's up?'

'Nothing,' was her terse reply.

'Look Esther, this is not like you.'

She sighed.

'I'm sorry, I'm tired. I didn't sleep very well.'

'I'm sorry.'

'Don't be, it's not your fault.'

Her words did not ease the situation, though. There was a further silence. After a few moments she threw her pen down.

'No, actually it was partly your fault. I tried ringing you. You weren't there. I thought you might let me know.'

'Yes, I admit I did pick up your message but as I was back late I thought I would talk to you this morning.'

'So you did come home then.'

'Yes, of course I came home. I was just late that's all.'

'I know we are not a couple or anything but we are friends. I was worried.'

'I'm sorry. You're right, I should've let you know.'

She was still silent so I continued.

'Look, anyway the gist of it is that we decided to phone the police.'

'We?'

'Yes. After a discussion, we decided it was the best thing. Actually, she was not so keen at first and she was going to leave it a day or so and see what she could find out. I suppose I persuaded her that it was best, though I was not sure myself until that moment.'

'And that took all evening.'

'No, I did what you said. You said, "If she gives you an opportunity to talk you should take it", so when she invited me back to her flat for a drink I thought I should accept the offer.'

She gave a low sarcastic laugh.

'Did I do something wrong?'

'It's a free country, you can do whatever you want.'

'Look, we talked about all sorts of things – she's very clever...'

'I don't doubt it.'

'Yes - and I admit she is attractive.'

'If you like that boyish look.'

'Well it's not her fault if she…'

'Has no tits.'

'I have never liked the use of that word.'

As soon as I said this I realised that it was an unwise elaboration of the point I'd already made. To make matters worse, with a kind of reflex my eyes flickered in the direction of Esther's breasts.

Esther stared at me, menacingly.

I felt embarrassed and turned away.

'And she has no bottom.'

I thought my only way was to carry on regardless.

'Look, I can't deny I really like her. I was wondering whether we could invite her round.'

'Don't drag me into it.'

'Yes, and perhaps Aggie. It might be fun. She knows so much about Shakespeare.'

'I don't think Aggie wants to play gooseberry any more than I want to.'

'Look,' I was getting exasperated now. 'I think she is probably a lesbian anyway. She has a picture of Radclyffe Hall hanging in her office.'

She ignored this last comment.

'Anyway, I've finished those orders while you've been talking. I am just going to take the mail down to the post.'

'And by the way,' she said before leaving, 'Miranda Reeves rang the shop this morning to say what a lovely evening you had but that she thought you might be a little worse for wear and she was worried to know if you had arrived home safely.'

So why did you ask me if I came home? I thought to myself.

Esther's trip to the Post Office gave me a few moments to think about what was behind her bad mood that morning. This kind of sustained invective towards me was unusual from Esther. We joked and laughed a lot in a mock serious way but this was part of the fun of our relationship. Could it be that Esther was really jealous of Miranda Reeves? And if she was, did that mean that she cared about me in a way that went beyond our normal friendship? If so, I had to think about it as a positive development that she had fallen out with me. Of course there could be a number of other reasons for her mood that I was not aware of. Whatever the cause, by the time she returned, her mood had brightened and she seemed more like her old self.

'Time for coffee,' she said. This was her responsibility. I made the tea in the afternoon. It was five minutes past ten.

'Oh, damn!'

'What?'

'I was supposed to meet Clinton at ten. Miranda Reeves arranged it with him last night.'

I rang Clinton to make my apologies. Luckily the inspector was running late. I arrived at the police station just after ten-thirty. In the car I had a little time to ruminate some more over Esther's earlier behaviour. I did not know whether to be worried or pleased about it. My insensitivity about mental illness on an earlier occasion had caused our first real argument but this felt different. As then, though I was increasingly reliant on her practical skills, my biggest fear was losing Esther's support. And with everything that had happened recently, the murder, the disappearance of the *Folio* and now the mysterious phone call, I felt in great need of that support. I switched on the radio and got lost for a moment in a programme on Machiavelli.

The meeting with Clinton, in fact, was very short and business-like. It was decided that if the mysterious caller rang again about the *Folio* we would agree to his terms with the intention of not keeping them. No doubt Machiavelli would have been proud of this strategy. If I would agree to a meeting there would be a discreet but large police presence which would monitor my every move. Though I was obviously being placed in some danger I felt comfortable with the thought of police protection.

When I arrived back, the bookshop was busy with customers. I did not have time to talk properly to Esther until after the lunch break.

'Could I accompany you?' Esther asked this when I had explained the scenario. I was pleased about this change in mood. This wish to be involved was, I was finding, typical of Esther and, of course, made me like her all the more. However, I did not think it was a sensible idea.

'I think it might complicate things, though I suspect it might be possible to accompany the police. We will have to ask. Anyway, the meet-up will probably never happen. No doubt it's a student prank and they are probably already having a good laugh at my expense in the bar.'

I went home that evening with the intention of spending some more time reading about Shakespeare. There was a part finished biography from the night when I swatted up before visiting Miranda Reeves. My meeting with her and her enthusiasm for her subject had inspired me to learn more.

One thing that was becoming clear about Shakespeare was that there was so much that was not known about him. This did not prevent, however, an enormous amount of wild speculation, especially about the time when he 'disappeared' and nothing was known about him, and there also appeared to be an obsession with the significance of the fact that he left his wife, as we had discussed that night at Aggie's, his 'second best bed'. Did this mark him out as callous, uncaring, chauvinistic and unloving or was he simply following a convention of the times when the best bed was left for visiting guests? Or was the person we knew as Shakespeare not the author of the plays at all? However much speculation there was, much of the information was of interest in itself, for what it revealed about attitudes in which Shakespeare lived, and of course there was the wonder of the plays themselves. I began to be drawn into the world of Shakespeare and to appreciate how someone like Miranda Reeves or Harry Nielsen could make it the greater part of their life's work.

Though the brilliance of the writing (for the most part) was not in doubt, there were other elements which began to attract my interest, such as the skill of actors like Richard Burbage (also a talented painter). Shakespeare was thought to write plays with Burbage in mind and it appears that he had tremendous versatility ranging from the young Hamlet to Lear (who was 80 in the play) when he was still under 40. There were also other plays such as *The Spanish Tragedy* by Thomas Kydd (one of the few playwrights who, like Shakespeare, did not go to university but went to a grammar school) and was immensely popular in its time. And it seemed that Shakespeare learnt a good deal from other playwrights such as Christopher Marlowe. I thought back to Miranda Reeves observation that if Shakespeare had died around the time that Marlowe did, Marlowe would have been thought the greater of the two playwrights. His life was full of mystery and intrigue. He was involved in a fight where he stuck a sword through a man. There is also good evidence that he supplemented his income by spying for the government. His death was shrouded in mystery. He was arrested on the 18 May 1593, it was believed in connection with charges of blasphemy. He was brought before the Privy Council for questioning and told to report to them daily. Ten days later Marlowe was stabbed in the eye by Ingram Frizer and died. He had spent all day in a house in Deptford with Frizer and two other men. There was much speculation about whether this was an assassination connected with his spying activities. I could not help relating it to the stabbing of Nielsen by means of the *Pickelhaube* and wondered if the true facts of his demise would remain unsolved, as had Marlowe's death, 400 years before. It seemed that, despite all the advances in detection, there would always be unsolved crimes.

It was while I was speculating on this that the phone rang. I was comfortable in my Jacobean reverie and reluctantly went to answer it. I knew it was an uncharitable thought but I was secretly hoping that it was Esther and not my mother.

However, it was neither of them.

'I said I would ring again. Are you interested in the reward?'

It was the anonymous caller.

'Yes, I think I am but it still puzzles me why you aren't interested in it yourself.'

'I explained it to you.'

'But…'

'Are you interested or not?'

'OK. Yes.'

'We haven't got much time. These are the co-ordinates, then I will give you the instructions.'

So much for my intention of keeping him on the phone. The whole conversation took no more than about 30 seconds. I was to be there at eight the following morning. I rang Inspector Clinton straight away but frustratingly could not get through. I had to be satisfied with leaving a message.

I looked up the coordinates on my local Ordnance Survey map. They were for an aerodrome about 20 miles away. The *Folio* was to be left in a filing cabinet in the corner of the main hangar, and that was also where I was to leave the money. I had to admit to feeling a degree of excitement about my involvement in this, especially as I had the backing and security of the police behind me.

'Make sure you bring the money and don't try anything clever,' were his last words.

I almost laughed at the clichéd language but then I thought, what else would he say?

The inspector did eventually ring back, just as I was contemplating going to bed. He seemed in a jovial mood and appeared pleased that the anonymous caller had rung. He told me not to worry and that everything would be in place for the morning. Before I lefy home I would receive an early visit from a plain clothes policeman delivery a bogus package of money. Even if the man was armed there would be marksmen aiming their guns at him, placed at appropriate points. This was not a hostage situation involving terrorists and the sum the man was asking for was derisory compared with the value of the *Folio*. The risk to myself would be minimal. However, I could not help feeling a little nervous at the prospect of the meeting. I was sure Marlowe had not expected to end his day dying from a stab wound in the eye after his meeting in a tavern in Deptford – if that was indeed what had happened.

21

The plain clothes policeman arrived at six-thirty the following morning and I set off for my appointment in good time. I turned on the radio to listen to Radio 4 but that morning the discussion on the natural history of the 'remarkable' Baobab tree was not enough to keep my attention. I switched to a classical music channel and was grateful for the calming influence of Vaughan Williams's *The Lark Ascending*.

In my mirror I saw a car following me. Was it the person I was meeting, or the police car, or just another car? I was tempted to slow down to a crawl or quickly accelerate to see what the other car would do, though I thought in the end nothing was to be gained by this. It all seemed a little unreal. It was a glorious morning and the sun gleamed through the canopy of trees, whose leaves touched and entwined high above, across the long straight road.

At that moment my mobile on the passenger seat beside me made a noise indicating a text message. I was approaching a crossroads and stopped for a moment. 'Good luck, Esther x'. I wanted it to say 'I love you.' In my heightened state at that moment I sighed for the want of her love.

Before I continued on my way, taking the left turning at the crossroads, I checked my rear view mirror and saw that the same car was still following, it seemed at about the same distance as before, so I presumed it had slowed down. There was another long straight road and as the trees began to thin out I caught sight of a squat control tower, a disused hangar and sad looking strips of concrete encroached upon by grass and weeds. I turned into the aerodrome entrance and parked by the control tower as I had been instructed. I left my car and walked across the open concrete ground that led to the hangar carrying the package in a plastic bag. For the first time I began to feel an element of fear rather than nervousness. With each step away from the car I felt an increase in my vulnerability. Where among all this open ground, I wondered, were the police positioned? I stopped for a moment and looked around. There was no building other than the control tower or the hangar for miles around. The nearest trees were at least half-a-mile. Could it be that they were that far away among the trees with long range binoculars and, if so, how long would it take them to reach me if there was any trouble? Perhaps they were not here at all and had to attend an emergency call.

It is strange how the mind leaps to all sorts of improbable possibilities in such threatening circumstances. Was this a biological or evolutionary function intended to somehow sharpen your wits and make the adrenalin pump through the body? If it was, I felt I could do without it at that moment. I nervously felt in my pocket for my phone and any sign of a further text message or phone call, perhaps saying 'operation cancelled.' I had imagined the police at my shoulder, guns at the ready, but at that moment I felt completely alone.

Just continue with the instructions, I told myself, *The police must surely know what they are doing.*

I walked through the half-open door of the hangar. It was not entirely empty. There were some pallets stacked in one corner and what appeared to be a number of sealed bags of potatoes. In another corner was a rusting filing cabinet standing bizarrely on its own. I walked slowly over to it, conscious of the echoes of my footsteps. The cabinet drawer screeched as I drew it back. Sure enough as indicated in the instructions I had been given, at the back was a large bulky parcel wrapped in brown paper. For a moment I felt a sense of awe that I was in the presence of such an important piece of our heritage. I placed the manuscript in the bag and put it down at my feet. I took out the padded envelope containing the money and placed it at the back of the drawer where the *Folio* had been. I hesitatingly pushed the drawer closed.

I had expected something at this point, the sudden appearance of the man, a shout, a telephone call - something. I felt uneasy standing in the corner of the hangar. I turned quickly on my heel and walked back to the entrance. I had a sudden premonition of a shot in my back and turned around. I continued walking but backwards towards the door, illogically perhaps thinking it would be best if I faced my potential assailant. Once through the door I walked quickly back towards my car. The thought crossed my mind that this was not really the dangerous part. The danger may well come later when the thief, whoever he was, discovered that he had not got what he wanted.

I was about to climb into my car when a man suddenly appeared from behind the tower. I jumped. It was the inspector, followed swiftly by two policemen armed with guns.

'I'm glad to see you here,' I said handing over the package containing the book to the Inspector.

'You drive,' said Clinton.

He got into the passenger seat. The two officers remained and as I pulled off I noticed a third emerge from behind the hangar.

'No sign of a pick up yet. You OK?'

He looked concerned. I guessed he could detect my uneasiness.

'Yeah, I must admit I was a little scared.'

Though now, in the car, with the inspector and the knowledge that armed police were around I felt safe again.

I drove to the edge of the airfield and was instructed to turn right and then almost immediately left into a track that led beyond a small copse of trees to where a police car was parked.

The inspector handed me back the package.

'You had better check it out.'

Suddenly I had acquired the status of a Shakespeare expert again though I knew my knowledge was severely limited in this area and that I would probably have to defer to someone with more expertise. However, I was conscious at that moment of the possibility that I was in the presence of one of the surviving rare copies of a piece of English history. I undid the packaging and revealed the large tome clad in its leather binding.

'So this is what all the fuss is about?' commented the inspector.

'All 900 pages of it. Almost the entire cannon of his plays.'

I did not want the importance of the *Folio* and Shakespeare's achievements to be in any way diminished by the inspector.

'It's certainly the right size and the leather binding would appear to be genuinely old.' I turned over some of the pages and paid particular attention to the preliminary pages. 'However, I'm not sure. It appears to have been rebound, which is not a crime in itself and may have been necessary, but these pages are far too regular for my liking. My suspicion is that this is a fake. But I think you should seek a real expert's opinion.'

I had gone through this process before, believing I had found a first edition of a rare book only to discover that it was in fact a later edition or in such bad condition as to render it valueless. However, I could not help feeling a little disappointed that I was probably not now handling a piece of genuine history.

'Of course, you have the very person who can confirm this at the university in Miranda Reeves - or if you want a further opinion, Christie's or one of the other auction houses.'

Before I returned to the bookshop I phoned Esther and explained what had happened. I did not want to get in her bad books again.

'That's disappointing', she said, 'but well done. Perhaps this will be the end of it now. Perhaps those students have had their laugh.'

'I hope so, though I'm not looking forward to an appearance on YouTube.'

It was after lunchtime when I arrived back at the bookshop. Esther gave me a little hug and a peck on the cheek.

'Well done. Were you scared?'

'A little,' I said.

I decided to work late and put back in some of the time I had lost as a result of my mysterious appointment. There was a small but interesting collection of children's books I had recently acquired and I was eager to catalogue them and assess their value. It was funny, I thought, how sometimes cataloguing could be a joy and sometimes a chore.

That evening it was the former and I found a number of books including a signed early edition of *Peter Pan* illustrated by Arthur Rackham that I had high hopes of selling at over £1,000, the most I had ever asked for a book. It was while I was musing over the description that I should give for this particular title that I received a phone call on my mobile.

I immediately recognised the voice.

'I did not appreciate what you did bringing those goons with you.'

It was the '*Folio* man' with more of his clichéd conversation.

'Well I did not appreciate being given a fake *Folio*.' I was conscious how childish this sounded but I was annoyed at being fooled. 'Have you got the real *Folio* or not?'

Then, to my total surprise, he put the phone down.

I rang Esther.

'Short and sweet. What now, bricks through the window, late night death threats?'

'Well, you know I was thinking about that. It would be rather strange wouldn't it, getting annoyed about the fact that the person you had deceived did not fall for it - I mean him deceiving us about the *Folio*. There must be something like honour among thieves.'

'But you're not a thief.'

'But we did try to deceive him too.'

'You know it could be anybody, a student - anything.'

'Well, when you think about it, a student is quite likely, when you think that it was stolen from the university.'

'And if it had worked, £10,000 would have paid for a lot of beers in the student bar.'

'Let alone student texts.'

'Unless our thief, whoever it was, didn't know. Maybe that is what he meant by possession. Maybe he found it somewhere or someone gave it to him to dispose of and he thought it was genuine.'

'So why did he not argue with me when I challenged him. Why did he just put the phone down on me? And, if he did have the real thing and was only testing us out, why on earth did he not say so?'

'Perhaps it was the first time he realised that it might not be genuine?'

'Which would make him very naïve.'

I felt better after that conversation. Somehow it all seemed less dangerous and menacing. The student theory - perhaps a prank - sounded quite a likely one to me and though I cannot say any fear of reprisals disappeared (for if the thief had my phone number he might also know where to find me), my extra precautions consisted of nothing more than making sure the front door was locked at all times and leaving a light in the hallway. I also kept a cricket bat at the side of the bed. I did in any case like my cricket bat and the smell of linseed oil, which I still insisted on using when most players long ago had resorted to bats with artificial coverings for protection.

As the days went on and nothing more sinister occurred than a few screeching cats and a late night haranguing match between a drunken couple right under my bedroom window, I settled back into running the bookshop. We had two notable authors visiting us in the coming days and I rediscovered the joy of running a bookshop and sparring with Esther.

The week after the author visits, Esther began her two week holiday with her sister and family in northern Spain. It was the first time Esther had been away for this long since she had been at the bookshop and I found that I missed her company enormously. I decided at this time to do some running to take my mind off things. I had been an intermittent runner over the years and it had been a long time since I last ran. I struggled over the first week realising how out of condition I had become. It was hard work and more than once I nearly gave it up. But I had enough experience to know that it would get better. By the end of the second week I started feeling the benefit and began to enjoy it rather than think of it merely as a chore. I vowed to keep it going beyond the summer. I wondered if I could persuade Esther to join me? Aggie came in and filled in wherever she could, though it did mean that I was managing the shop on my own for quite a lot of the time, so I was pleased when Esther returned. She sported a golden tan and looked refreshed.

Then it was Aggie's turn to stay with her sister in The Highlands of Scotland for a couple of weeks, a mammoth undertaking involving her taking the sleeper train. This always seemed to me to give her holiday a little extra edge of excitement. In my usual way I could not help relating it to literature and the exciting fictional train journey taken by Richard Hannay in *The Thirty-*

Nine Steps. I admitted to envy and, as I did every year, vowed that I would make the journey myself one day.

It was during this time that my mother rang requesting to come down again and to stay for longer, as I had suggested when I had visited her.

'There are a few things I need to think about and sort out. How does two weeks sound?'

We agreed that she would come to stay in three weeks' time, after I had taken my own holiday. I was concerned and told Esther so.

'I'm worried that she might be ill,' I told her.

'How old is she?'

'Seventy next birthday.'

'Well that's probably it. She is probably just taking stock. Anyway, as I said before, when she does come you should make more of an effort.'

22

When Aggie returned I took my holiday with my old school friend Cameron who lived in the heart of the Kent countryside. At the same time his wife was taking the opportunity to go and stay with an old school friend of hers, leaving 'the boys' together. I found nothing more boring than just sitting around on a beach so I was delighted when Cameron suggested that we go on a bicycle trip. He had kitted out two robust roadsters, his own and his wife's (which I was to borrow), with panniers.

I took the train into London. I had left myself some time to explore the bookshops in Charing Cross Road. It had been several years since I had last been there. This was the location of Marks and Co. with which Helene Hanff, the New York based author, corresponded over many years. It was turned into a book, *84 Charing Cross Road*, which was mainly a series of letters between her and the owner. It was an unlikely bestseller and was later made into a film starring Anne Bancroft and Anthony Hopkins. This bookshop had long gone, along with many iconic bookshops including Zwemmers and Shipley's Art bookshops, Silver Moon (the women's interest bookshop) and Murder One (the specialist crime bookshop). Their demise had been the result of rent increases and the changing nature of the book environment, and, in particular the influence of the internet, which meant that there was less requirement to seek out these venerable specialist institutions. It seemed to me that with so many great bookshop institutions gone, Charing Cross had lost much of its charm.

I was pleased, though, to see that Foyles Bookshop had been updated and was once again thriving. At one time the largest bookshop in the world, this was a shop that truly had required modernising. It had been stagnating for years and was labyrinthine and Kafkaesque in its layout, with books arranged by publisher. Sales staff had been on a short term contract and poorly paid. They had not been allowed to handle cash, which had involved a frustrating procedure for payment involving queuing three times. When you selected a book, you were given an invoice which you took to a cashier ensconced behind a payment area enclosed in glass before returning with the invoice to collect the book. However, the chaotic layout was, if anything, even more frustrating. I remembered once asking for a book to be told by the member of staff that it was probably in the shop somewhere but that he did not know where and that it would be far quicker if I made the trip to Gower Street (where the bookshop Dillons was at that time situated) where I should be able to find one. Dillons had cleverly taken advantage of this in their advertising and when I went out of the shop I saw an advert on the side of the bus shelter which read, *Foyled Again? Try Dillons.*

Having had my fill of books I made my way towards the fairyland St Pancras Station with its Gothic revival frontage designed by George Gilbert Scott. It was difficult to believe that this magnificent structure had nearly been demolished in the 1960s but for a high profile campaign by the poet John Betjeman. As a station it had been under-used until the advent of the Channel Tunnel and it had now been developed and extended to form the hub of high speed cross channel services. Due reverence had been paid to John Betjeman, with a statue in his memory that I made a point of seeking out. He is depicted looking upwards, no doubt in admiration, at the architecture of the refurbished Barlow roof which, I read, was at the time it was built, the greatest example of a single span roof in the world.

I took the train out of Paddington to Faversham, changing at Victoria. Cameron was waiting for me on the concourse of the station. It had been almost a year since we had met up. We went for a meal at his local pub, The Wheatsheaf, taking with us a series of detailed Ordnance Survey maps and a guide to bed and breakfasts in the area. We looked out a few key places that we would like to visit, though we were determined not to spend too much time making a detailed plan for where we would go each day. The rule was that there were no rules. Like Toad, Ratty and Mole we would set off on the open road with no clear idea where we were going. We were determined, though, not to be, like Toad, seduced by the lure of the motor car.

We had stayed at the pub rather later than we meant to, so rather than set off at the crack of dawn and make the early start that we had promised ourselves, we did not begin our journey until shortly after eleven on a Sunday morning.

We biked until we were hungry, stopped when we wanted to, at the least provocation, as we pedalled along the quietest country lanes we could find, visiting churches, paddling in rivers or just finding a quiet place to read. While Cameron read his history books, I read my selection of novels and travel books. In the middle of the afternoon we phoned one or two bed and breakfasts selected from our trusty bed and breakfast guide and booked our rooms for the night. We tried, if we could, to stay in a pub, feeling that we had earned our beer with our exertions during the day, but if not, we made sure that we were within easy biking distance of one.

After a few days we found that we were within fifteen miles of Canterbury. I had never visited the cathedral so I was eager to do so.

We planned our journey so that we approached from the North West as Cameron said that this would give us the best view. I was not disappointed. The scene was absolutely stunning. The cathedral dominated the skyline. The tower and the main gate looked down on a patchwork of attractive houses interlaced with trees. Magically, the bells began ringing from the huge bell tower as we swung down the road towards the cathedral entrance.

We secured our bikes against some railings and made our way into the cathedral through the city entrance. Cameron, who knew it well, was my guide. We came across the stained glass window of Thomas à Beckett.

'You know all this sainthood was a bit of a sham. He was not well liked by a lot of people. When he was Chancellor he instituted a land tax from all landowners and the churches. It caused a lot of hardship and resentment. He really did do the King's bidding and was actually, as a courtier, a great mate of his. Henry II even sent his son to be with him.'

'Where did it all go wrong?'

'When Beckett was made Archbishop of Canterbury he gave up his position as Chancellor and took all the land associated with Canterbury under his control. Then there were these Constitutions of Clarendon.'

'I've heard of that. That was all to do with Rome, wasn't it?'

'Essentially, yes. Henry wanted to lessen the power and influence of Rome.'

'And Becket didn't agree with it?'

'Well, it wasn't quite that simple. In the end, Becket did say he agreed with it but he refused to go as far as signing it.'

'Sounds very stubborn.'

'Stubborn and grumpy if accounts are to be believed. Anyway, he went before a court at Northampton and was convicted of 'royal contempt' or some such charge but then he escaped to France where Louis the seventh protected him for a couple of years. He nearly persuaded the Pope to excommunicate Henry. Henry was scared by this and there were discussions and a compromise to allow Becket to return to England. The big problem came when the young Henry had a coronation at York rather than Canterbury. Beckett excommunicated the Bishops of York, London and Salisbury who had all taken part. Henry is quoted as saying *will no one rid me of this turbulent priest?* – though the words are disputed – anyway, the upshot is that his words were taken literally. Four knights laid a kind of trap for him by asking him to accompany them to Winchester to account for his actions. It was when he refused that they could say he was going against the King's will and they murdered him. Then all this sainthood business started and not just here – it was all over Europe.'

'I wish I'd had you teaching me at school, you make it all sound so simple – and interesting.'

Shortly after, we were walking around the peaceful cloisters.

'Actually,' I said, picking up on earlier conversation, 'murder has been very much on my mind recently.'

'Not your mother again,' Cameron said in mock seriousness.

I explained to him about the mysterious death at the bookshop.

'And you told me nothing much happened in your neck of the

woods,' he said when I had concluded.

We stocked up with supplies and made our way out of the town centre, striking south on the smallest lanes we could find. Mercifully, the weather remained fine and it still did not get fully dark until about eight. We booked a pub an easy evening ride of ten miles away and late in the afternoon found a perfect spot for a picnic on a bank next to a running stream. It was warm that day and we sat like two children dangling our hot feet in the deliciously cool water. Then we had a go at 'skimming' and paddling across to the furthest reaches of the stream as far as we dare without getting our rolled up trousers too wet, until finally we settled down to our feast on the riverbank.

We carefully laid out our spread of salami, cheese, grapes, crusty bread, olives, tomatoes, chocolate and a bottle St Emilion wine. It all tasted so good.

'This is the life,' I said to Cameron.

'Indeed.'

He cut himself a large slab of cheese.

'You know, I was thinking about the murder in your bookshop.'

'Presumed murder.'

'Well, you know, the great detective...'

'Poirot?'

'Yes, or any of the others, well they would have worked it out up here.'

He pointed to his head

'But they were totally unrealistic.'

'There is one thing that they all agree on, though. There has to be a motive.'

'Agreed.'

'Have you been through all the motives?'

'In a sort of *ad hoc* way as they came up.'

'You know how logical I am.'

'I'm afraid so.'

'So, given all the facts, we should be able to work this out.'

'I have invested a lot of time in trying to do just that.'

'The trouble is you are so close to it you probably can't see the wood for the trees. You need someone objective who can take a look at it dispassionately and work it out.'

'Someone, like you?'

'There's no one else here.'

'All right, if you want to play this game, it's something that occupies my mind a lot.'

He removed a piece of paper from his pannier and found a pen.

'Right, now tell me: who are your main suspects?'

'I don't know if I have any really except this man with the moustache who remains elusive.'

'No one else?'

'There is this slightly odd cove, Patrick Williams.'

'I am sure if an odd cove is the only qualification, you could round up a whole posse of people.'

'He has been in a mental institution but I got wrapped on the knuckles for saying that by Esther.'

'Has there been a history of violence, though, that might be more relevant than just the fact that he was mentally ill?'

'Well, I don't know. I presumed the police would find out about all that stuff – I gave his name to them. There was something that his mother said about an ex-girlfriend. She was not explicit but hinted at some difficulty – I wondered at the time if it could have been something violent.'

I recounted his hostile questioning of Nielsen at the talk.

'Now, that might be more relevant if there was something between Nielsen and this Williams in the past.'

'They were at school together.'

'There you are then. Perhaps it's something more. Perhaps this woman who jilted him was involved with Nielsen? Then we could have a real motive.'

'I never thought of connecting the two things. Perhaps I should try and get another word with his mother. Thanks Cameron. This is a more fruitful conversation than I thought it would be.'

'The little grey cells.' He pointed to his head.

'Who else do we have?' he continued.

'Well, I suppose we have to include Miranda Reeves.'

'You seem reluctant?'

'The truth is, I quite like her.'

'Ah. Well look, let's just ignore the *Folio* for the moment. There may or may not be a connection but if we just take the death of Nielsen, the more serious crime, what would have been her motive for that?'

'Simply that Nielsen was top dog as far as teaching Shakespeare was concerned and she, Reeves, was second top dog. I suppose she stood to inherit that status. But, I'm not convinced by that.'

'Why not?'

'Well, it's not as if she didn't have any status at all. And I'm sure if she wanted promotion she could have moved to another university.'

'But it's a kind of motive.'

'And there was this rather odd conversation we had with the porter, Grindley, about the *Folio* when she was left on her own with it. It was almost as though he was trying to implicate her.'

'For what reason, I wonder? Do you think he might be a suspect?'

'I don't have any concrete motive, just a nagging feeling. After all, he had an opportunity to steal it as much as anyone else.'

'So his motive could be stealing the *Folio* and trying to divert the blame elsewhere. But this still doesn't help us with the main crime of the murder of Nielsen. What possible motive could he have for that?'

'There would have to be something in the past that we aren't aware of.'

'Similar to this Patrick Williams.'

'And this moustachioed man who seems to have vanished into thin air.'

'You can see why the police are having trouble. There has to be something else that has not come to light yet.'

'No point in saving the bottle.'

Cameron poured the last two glasses of St Emilion.

'Damn, this glass is cracked. We'll have to see if we can pick one up somewhere. Maybe the pub will sell us one tonight?'

I liked Cameron. We shared many of the same minor morals. We had both insisted on real wine glasses rather than the more practical plastic ones for our bicycle trip. The wine just didn't taste the same in plastic we agreed. He would no more have plastic glasses than a plastic Christmas tree.

We had one more paddle and then a quiet snooze for an hour or so before we woke and, sleepy from the food and the wine, continued on our way to our bed and breakfast.

The next day we decided to have a good ride out and made it as far as Hythe where we came upon the *World's Smallest Public Railway*, The Romney, Hythe and Dymchuch Railway. Feeling like visitors to Lilliput, we travelled all the way to Dungeness on the tiny line pulled by the Green Goddess steam train built in 1925. The sedate railway was designed, as Cameron informed me, by two millionaire racing drivers of the day, Captain J. E. P. Howey and Count Louis Zborowski.

We spent some time exploring the unusual landscape of Dungeness. Cameron informed me that it was one of the largest expanses of shingle in the world.

'Not the most beautiful place,' I said to Cameron.

'Maybe not beautiful, but I like it. It's also a place of special scientific interest. Do you know, there are over 600 types of plant? And you can't beat it for insects. Some of the insects found here are not found anywhere else in Britain.'

We had lunch at the Brittania Inn, which was close to the station, before heading back.

'I'm not so sure if I would fancy living next to one of those.'

I nodded towards the nuclear power station.

'Well one of them is closed – the Magnox one – but the other one, well it did take years to complete and it was way over budget. But the funny thing is, even that has a positive influence on the wildlife. There is an area which the fisherman call *The Boil* where they pump the waste and sewage from the power station. It is so biologically rich it attracts birds from miles around.'

As we walked further I could see a number of old railway carriages and wooden shack-like buildings.

'Who lives in those?'

'Mainly the fishermen. But you do get some people living here who just want to get away from it all. Apparently they are expensive to buy. It is supposed to be one of the quietest places in Britain. There is this place at the Denge, the old Air Force base here, where they have these acoustic mirrors, an early warning system for detecting aircraft. Apparently it worked OK but then radar came, and that was much more effective.'

'Someone's been enterprising,' I said as we came upon a mature developed garden in front of a rather smart black shack type house.

'That was Derek Jarman's house – you know the film-maker.'

'Of course, I thought the name was familiar. He brought out a book about his garden.'

'Well, I've got to show you this, as a bibliophile.'

I followed him as he skirted the side of the garden and we ended up on one side of the house.

'See, it's John Donne's, *The Sun Rising*.'

In black letters I read the words.

Busy old fool, unruly Sun,
Why dost thou thus
Through windows, and through curtains, call on us?
Must to thy motions lovers' seasons run?
Saucy pedantic wretch, go chide
Late school-boys and sour prentices,
Go tell court-huntsmen that the king will ride,
Call country ants to harvest offices;
Love, all alike, no season knows nor clime,
Nor hours, days, months, which are the rags of time.

We returned to the station. There were a few minutes until the next train so, it being approximately halfway through my holiday break, I decided to ring the bookshop to see how things were going. Esther did greet me enthusiastically enough, but then proceeded to give me a ticking off for ringing in the middle of my holiday

She assured me that everything was OK. If there was a serious problem, she said, she would let me know.

'She's right you know,' Cameron said to me when I related my conversation to him. 'She sounds very capable and I shouldn't worry.'

After we arrived at Dymchurch after our return journey on the train, we set off inland and came across the beautiful little church of St Mary St Ethelburga whose original remains were said to date back to 633. We sat in the pleasant churchyard and I rang a pub to arrange our accommodation. I was thoroughly enjoying this holiday with Cameron.

When we had been shown our rooms in the pub and settled down to our meal in the bar, Cameron returned to the subject of Esther. Though I only saw him infrequently, Cameron was a good friend and in many ways, just about my closest one, the one I could confide in. I confessed to him my feelings about Esther, feelings up to then I had kept to myself.

'What should I do?' I asked him.

'Well, why don't you just tell her how you feel about her and see what her reaction is?'

'The thing is, I sort of know. She's already told me that she is still in love with her dead husband and that she had a brief relationship with someone that made her feel physically sick.'

'You could try making her jealous?'

'Well, in a funny sort of way I think she already is.'

I explained to him her reaction after I had visited Miranda Reeves.

'Well, there you are then, that's your proof.'

'Except I don't think it is. I think she was jealous in a kind of sisterly, motherly sort of way.'

'I don't understand.'

'You know, when a mother thinks a woman is not good enough for her son – that sort of thing. I can remember my mum being a bit like that when I had my first proper girlfriend when I was 17.'

'If you don't mind me saying so, you have put yourself in an awfully difficult situation. I'll tell you what you should do.'

'What?'

'Forget about her completely and just find someone else.'

'But I can't forget about her, I see her nearly every day.'

'Well, just get someone else anyway.'

I went to the toilet. When I came back Cameron was asleep in his chair in the corner of the pub where we had been having our conversation. No doubt a combination of the beer, the intensity of the discussion and the strain of dispensing advice to me had exhausted him.

We spent another three pleasant days meandering back slowly towards Cameron's house. Though we over-indulged a little on beer, the miles that we put behind us each day on our bikes kept us honest and as we neared the end of the journey I felt as though I had become a little fitter. It had been a quiet, contemplative holiday that had allowed me to put things in perspective. I was grateful for my conversations with Cameron even though I did not agree with all the advice he had given me. On the last-but-one day the holiday was cut short when it poured with rain. Finding that we were only 30 miles from Cameron's house we put our heads down, endured the rain and biked for home.

23

Esther was at pains to assure me that there had been no problems
while I was away. There was indeed every appearance that the
shop was in good order and that everything was under control.
When she could see that I was happy with everything she moved
onto another subject.

'Now, there's something else I want to talk to you about. I have
been thinking about all this *Folio* business and the murder...'

'Presumed murder.'

'Of Nielsen. Do you know, I think we've been foolish?'

'I don't doubt it, but I'm sure you have a particular case in
mind.'

'We've let ourselves be diverted by this pretend *Folio* nonsense.'

'Hang on, I put myself in great personal danger.'

'But don't you see? What was the most interesting thing that
Grindley told us?'

'Well, I suppose that Miranda Reeves asked Grindley to leave
her for a while with the *First Folio*.'

'I bet that coincides with the theft.'

'You think she stole it?'

'I don't know, but I swear Grindley had a reason for telling us
that story. He didn't have to tell us.'

'She so loves her Shakespeare - genuinely - you only have to be
with her for five minutes to find that out.'

'And you have been in her company considerably longer.'

I could feel myself colouring up. It was true. I did enjoy Miranda
Reeves's company. I hoped that Esther's judgment was not being
clouded and that she was not taking it out on her through some
sort of personal animosity. I thought briefly of my conversation
with Cameron. But I also knew in reality that though Esther had
said some ungenerous personal things about Miranda Reeves,
she also had an analytical mind. I was sceptical about her theory
but felt as though I could not dismiss it entirely. Part of me also
said, 'Let's prove her innocence.' I also had a theory which I had

been formulating in my mind.

'Of course, Grindley may have been trying to deflect blame from himself.'

'That's a possibility too. We need to confront her so that we can see her reaction.'

'Perhaps we should emulate Hamlet.'

'How would that help?'

'Well, if you remember, Hamlet is told by the ghost that his father was murdered by his uncle, Claudius. In order to determine whether this is right he employs a travelling troupe of players to act out his father's murder in front of Claudius to determine his reaction when his father is killed.'

'So you think we should act out the theft of the *Folio*?'

'At least confront her with the fact that we think she may have been involved in stealing it.'

'And see her reaction?'

'Well it might work - it's got to be worth a try. But we mustn't let her know that is why we are visiting her. We need the element of surprise.'

Miranda Reeves had given me her card the last time that I had visited her. I emailed her thinking I might give something away if I spoke to her on the phone, and also I felt a certain degree of disloyalty regarding our devious intent. I made the excuse that we had come up with some new evidence that required her verification. It took a week but finally we were able to arrange another early evening appointment.

Esther accompanied me. When we arrived at her office the warmth she had formerly shown me was absent.

'I hope this won't take too long,' she said, 'I have to leave in twenty minutes.'

'I'm sorry, we will certainly be as quick as we can.'

'We wanted to ask you about something that Mr Grindley said.' She shifted a little uncomfortably in her chair.

'Mr Grindley told us how, after Nielsen died, you asked him to fetch a candle from his office so that you might have your own little goodbye ceremony.'

'Not to put too fine a point on it,' Esther continued, 'the *Folio* was noticed as stolen a few days later. We wondered if there was any connection.'

Esther held her eyes. I knew that hard look.

'I see.'

She was quiet for a long moment, then it was as if she had made a decision. Her eyes welled up with tears.

'I did something very foolish,' she said at last. She began crying and dabbing at her eyes with a tissue.

'You know Shakespeare is my life. I love that *Folio*. I wouldn't damage it for the world. I thought, if I could just borrow it - for a few days - I could work on it and I must admit the feeling of having it by my side for a few days – it's difficult to explain. It is like being passionately in love with someone.' She looked straight at me, straight into my eyes, appealingly.

'Yes, I do know what you mean. Working with books myself all the time. In some ways it is like a love affair.'

'Then I was unable to return it and it was reported as stolen. What was I to do?'

I sympathised with a nod.

'I wanted to get it back but I needed to do it without anyone knowing I had taken it. I can see now that was wrong but I was too ashamed to think of doing it any other way. I thought if I just made a clean breast of it I would lose my job which means so much to me.'

'But the deception. You phoned the police when Elliot had that mysterious phone call...'

Esther suddenly stopped and as she did the truth struck home. The phone calls had been a hoax but not a student hoax, an elaborate fabrication in order to divert us from the fact that Miranda Reeves had stolen the *Folio* herself. But the phone calls were not from Miranda Reeves.

'I'm sorry, I have to go.'

Still in tears, she rushed past us and out of the door

'What a load of bollocks.'

These were Esther's first words when she entered the car.

I looked at Esther.

'You were completely taken in by her weren't you - I can see by the look on your face.'

I felt on the defensive.

'I obviously can't defend the fact that she stole the *Folio* but I thought... she made quite a convincing case... for borrowing...'

'Not borrowing, stealing it! And convincing!'

She almost shrieked and then mimicked her voice cruelly.

'I can see it was wrong but you understand Mr Bookseller, you love books too.'

'She didn't exactly say that.'

'Not exactly I grant you - but that was the gist of it - and did you see how many times she played with her skirt and her legs in front of you? You're such a soft touch. I wonder how many guilty women there are out there who have manipulated judges with their looks and good figures.'

I began to drive. There was an uncomfortable silence.

'You know, Esther, sometimes you are just too cruel - you can just go too far.'

'Slow down - this is a thirty limit. You always drive too fast when you're annoyed.'

I did not say anything but continued driving at the same speed.

'God, we're just like a married couple.'

I pulled the car over.

'It just doesn't add up Elliot. Why would she make such a secret of it? She might have been worried about seeming foolish but she could hardly have thought it was better than not admitting to the whereabouts of the *Folio*. It might have been a black mark against her but surely it was something she could live with? Think of the trouble she is going to get in now. And to put you through all that business with the fake *Folio*. The amount of deception here is ...' she struggled to find the right word, 'incredible!'

I knew she was right. The deception was the key. I had been taken in by her and did feel a little foolish.

'Do you think we should tell the university?'

'How can we not? God, she really worked on you didn't she?'

'Esther, look, I really didn't notice all that stuff about her skirt. Anyway, as I said, I think she's probably not interested in men.'

'Owning a picture of Radclyffe Hall does not make her a

lesbian. Besides, she might be bi-sexual. Shakespeare is full of sexual confusion and she does purport to love her dear Mr Shakespeare.'

There was a further silence. I knew that much of what Esther said was right but I was not comfortable with this endless tirade against Miranda Reeves, or her unbridled sarcasm.

'Look, Esther, is there something wrong? You don't seem yourself today.'

'It's just that...' she sighed. 'I know it's stupid but it's the anniversary today.'

'Your wedding anniversary?'

'The anniversary of David's death.'

'I'm sorry, I didn't realise.'

'Why should you? '

She began to cry a little. It was not Esther's style to show vulnerability.

'Oh, Esther... '

'It's all right... honestly, I'm fine.'

She wiped her eyes with a tissue.

'Look, Esther I don't know how you feel about this, but what about if I arranged a meal for this evening. I could invite Aggie and Sam, people you know, and we could talk book nonsense, to take your mind off things.'

She thought for a moment.

'That's really sweet of you but in a way it's important I experience this on my own.'

'OK, I understand, but you know I'm around.'

'Yes. Well perhaps we could do it at the weekend, if everybody is free, not to make me feel better especially but just because it would be a nice thing to do - to get us all together.'

She was quiet for a moment looking straight ahead

'There is something else, something I haven't told you, Elliot'

'Only if you want to, Esther. Don't upset yourself.'

'But I need to tell someone. I need to confess.'

'Whatever you think helps.'

'You know,' I said, 'David has only been dead a year.'

'Yes.'

'Well, before he died he became very ill, in the last two years. He was in a wheelchair.'

159

'It must have been very frustrating.'

'For both of us. It didn't matter. The most important thing was to look after him as best as I could. I really did take each day as it came. You know I tried to keep his dignity. He lost control of his bladder, then he was unable to eat by himself. But I didn't mind because I loved him - I love him - it's funny it's sometimes, as I told you, as if he's still here.'

'I know - well I don't know - but I can imagine. I suppose I felt something similar when my dad died.'

'I tried as hard as I could when David was ill but I didn't always succeed. Sometimes I got angry or short tempered. I was not always as helpful as I should have been.'

'You were probably physically exhausted, you shouldn't be so hard on yourself.'

'I know you're right, but I also know that sometimes, I fell short.'

24

Esther decided instead to go away for the weekend and visit David's grave. She had arranged to stay with a girlfriend of hers. She also wanted to meet David's sister who was going to be there.

This sudden change of plan was indicative of her current state of mind. Though I would have described Esther as a lively and intuitive person, she was also logical and there was a calmness about her especially in stressful situations (which had been an extremely useful attribute in recent times).

Her current restlessness and unpredictability was outside the bounds of her normal behaviour. We put the proposed dinner at the weekend on hold. Next year, I decided, I would suggest that she take the day off. I made a note in the back of my current diary. Several times I thought I would ring her to ask her if she was OK but I was also wary of intruding on her space. It did not stop me, though, from worrying about her.

I also thought a good deal about Miranda Reeves. Her confession seemed all too sudden and easy. I wanted to think well of her and as a bibliophile and a shameless acquirer of knowledge (whether it had a use or not), I relished the thought of further discussions about Shakespeare. I reasoned that there had to be something more and that maybe she was protecting someone. Perhaps, unlikely as it may sound, it could be Grindley or, a new idea I had, was that it might be she was in some way protecting Nielsen's past. Though there was no doubt professional rivalry, there had also been a great deal of mutual respect.

Esther was already at the bookshop when I arrived a little after eight on the Monday morning. She appeared calm and refreshed as she chatted about her weekend.

'I've been through the wringer a bit these last few days but now I feel I have come out the other side. Thanks for being so understanding Elliot. I was thinking, some people dread Monday mornings, but I was really looking forward to coming to work.'

Then we went on to discuss Miranda Reeves. We had no way of knowing whether she had revealed her involvement to the university authorities. Esther was insistent.

'We need to know if she went ahead and told the university as we would expect. She must not be allowed to get away without telling them, otherwise we will have to do it.'

'I suppose we could always tell the police.'

'I think that might be going too far at this stage. We need to leave it to the university to decide what steps they want to take.'

'Except they've already been involved. She could be prosecuted for having wasted police time or some such thing. And who was the man who made the phone call to me? I'm still not clear whether that was a student prank or whether it was someone colluding with Reeves.'

We decided that I should send a letter asking her to clarify the position. We thought a letter was more tactful than an email as the one we had was a university one. It was a difficult letter to write as I did not want to appear too threatening and discourage her from replying. But we did need to ensure that she replied. I decided to ask her to reply within two days, otherwise we would be bound to contact the university authorities. It had the tone of one of those threatening letters from the bank or for an overdue bill, but I had little choice but to go ahead with it.

When I had still not received a reply the following Wednesday morning I went down from my office to the shop floor where Esther was unpacking books. It was a busy time as a lot of new titles were beginning to come in for the autumn season and Esther was half-buried among the boxes. I liked this time of year as there was an expectation and a buzz in the air and the days passed quickly. We spoke as she unpacked some of the new arrivals.

'It's disappointing that she hasn't been in touch,' said Esther.

'I really had not expected this. I thought she was bound to get back to us.'

'She might be peeved with us and think it's none of our

business. Perhaps we should make discreet enquiries.'

'Unless she's already left or resigned. The letter may be sitting in a university pigeon hole.'

'How would we know if she has informed the university?'

'There would probably be some sort of announcement.'

'Perhaps they would prefer to keep it quiet - for the reputation of the university.'

'Maybe they will make allowances for Nielsen's death? That sort of thing can really upset people.'

'Perhaps I could do a bit of subtle digging - if you think you could give me the morning off.'

'It's difficult at this time of year but if you really think it will help it would be better sooner rather than later, before it gets too busy. I'll manage with Aggie tomorrow morning.'

The next morning we had a busy day in the bookshop and I found myself along with Aggie spending a lot of time behind the sales counter. There were accounts and cataloguing I had left undone but I did not mind as we were taking money when it mattered. Preoccupied in the bookshop I had quite forgotten about Esther's university trip until she rushed in late in the afternoon. She was excited about something and dragged me away from the counter so that she could talk to me with some degree of privacy. We stood at the bottom of the shop adjacent to the area where Nielsen had been found impaled.

'Miranda Reeves seems to be away at the moment - though I couldn't find out why - but she is expected back.'

'I guess she never picked the letter up.'

'Anyway, though I haven't been able to find out anything much about Miranda Reeves, I've been finding out lots of interesting stuff about the porter. He's not all he seems, our Mr Grindley.'

'How do you mean?'

'He's got form.'

'Esther, really, you have to get out of this habit of talking like that.'

'No, he has. He is an ex-con. He's also been in the army, saved some officer's wife. He was given his position as a sort of reward, despite his shady past.'

'I like a story with a happy ending. I have always believed in redemption.'

'Except it seems old habits die hard. He was found guilty of embezzlement at the university. Apparently he was very free with the petty cash, wines and cigars, that sort of thing.'

'How do you know all this?'

'I've been talking to people. Old Grindley is not loved by everyone. Nielsen wanted him sacked.'

'Esther, we don't know that. It's just speculation.'

'Well, my source didn't think it was speculation.'

'Now you're talking like *deep throat* - it's the Watergate Scandal all over again. I suppose it will be known as *University Gate*.'

I was quite pleased with my joke but she just ignored me and carried on.

'He wanted Grindley to do the right thing, but Miranda Reeves, she defended him, said he should be given another chance. Grindley never forgot that or that Nielsen wanted him dismissed.'

'So he had a grudge against Nielsen. Even though he talked to us as though Nielsen was the kinder of the two. Looks like there is some duplicity here. Do you think he might have made it up about the *Folio*?'

'Elliot what's happened to your grey cells?'

'Sorry, yes of course, she confessed to it - we've had a busy day.'

'That's good.'

'Except, you know, I was never entirely happy about her confession. I did wonder whether she was trying to cover up for somebody.'

'Grindley?'

'Possibly - though I admit it would be difficult to see why - or even, and I know this is a bit of a mad theory, for Nielsen's reputation.'

'You're right, it's a mad theory - except - perhaps it was both their reputations - they were in the same department after all. But, I'm sorry, I know you have a soft spot for her,' I felt myself colouring up again, 'but from what I have seen of Miranda Reeves I don't believe she is altruistic enough to defend someone's reputation, especially when they are no longer around. However, if it was her reputation as well - I could believe that.'

'I wonder where she is?'

'Could be a conference - anything - unless she's gone into hiding. But don't you think the stuff about Grindley is interesting?'

'Yes, if only I could see its relevance.'

'We still have a murder to be solved you know.'

'So you think that he might be somehow involved with Nielsen's murder?'

'I would say it is definitely possible.'

'For trying to get him expelled from the university?'

'I'm sure there have been lesser motives.'

'I don't know. It's all a bit odd. That explanation for stealing the *Folio*. Perhaps that's why she hasn't got back to us because it's not the truth. But then, why would she admit to stealing it?'

'But we don't know that it's not true. There's always a bit of you that wants to defend her, isn't there?'

'Well, like I said, maybe she's covering up for someone.' I felt frustrated. 'We are going round in circles here.'

'Grindley - with his reputation - he might have been a suspect. She might be protecting him.'

'But what would be her motive for protecting him? You don't suppose they are related in some way - blood thicker than water and all that?'

'It seems unlikely, they couldn't look or sound more different - but you never know. I could do a bit more digging.'

'I think you've done quite enough already. Besides haven't you got a bookshop to work in?'

'I know. But what about this: What if he had been blackmailing Reeves?'

'I can see your brain has been working overtime, Esther, but what for?'

'What if it was she who was the murderer?'

'Wrong sex.'

'But she could have been working with an accomplice.'

'She might have a better motive.'

'Which is?'

'Professional jealousy.'

'You mean she was after Nielsen's job, after all?'

'Possibly. But as I said before, she's quite a reputation of her own, and I can vouch for her detailed knowledge of the subject.'

'In effect, she now has Nielsen's job.'

'And finding it hard work.'

'I suppose murder is a bit extreme, especially if you are hiring someone to do it for you.'

'You just don't like her.'

'I just find her … infuriating.'

At that point, we decided to have a cup of tea.

25

The next day was Esther's day off. She did offer to work part of it as she said her visit to the university was not like work at all. However, I told her she should take the day off and rest herself for the oncoming onslaught of customers (that we hoped would arrive) as we moved towards Christmas. I arrived at work at seven, in order to catch up with my paperwork as I knew I would not get a chance later on in the day when I would need to help Aggie in the shop. Aggie was fun to work with, though her customer skills were better than her stock receipting skills and we did not finish unpacking the new stock until closing time. I worked on it until six-thirty and then decided I could take no more of what I already felt had been a long day.

I imagined myself having a relaxing evening, which for me meant a bath, a book and some chocolate.

I had one of those old-fashioned cast iron baths which could hold a dam full of water and was deep enough that I could totally immerse myself. I filled it as full as I dare and as hot as I could take it, before climbing in and letting myself float down among the bubbles of some exotic bath concoction which had Champagne in the title.

Reading in the bath can be a tricky business but over the years I had got it down to a fine art. I stuck a hand towel at strategic length away from me in case of an emergency, a dry flannel was nearby to wipe away any excess condensation from my reading glasses. I had also learnt to keep unerringly still and avoid sudden movements to avoid upending my book in the water. So, prepared, I lay back gingerly with book in hand.

Beginning a new book that you have been looking forward to reading is a particular kind of joy. I also had a superb recording of some English Violin Sonatas playing in the background. As I turned over the title page to begin reading, I felt I was in a kind of blissful bachelor heaven. For the moment, I forgot all about my unrequited love for Esther, the murder of Nielsen, the theft of the *Folio* and the trials and tribulations of the bookshop. Perhaps, I reflected, a bachelor existence was not such a bad thing after all.

Then the phone rang. 'Leave it', I told myself. After all, I might not have been there. I might have been on a walk, working at the shop, at the cinema, anything. I let it ring until it switched over to voice mail. I tried not to feel guilty. Probably my mother. I would ring her back later.

I wallowed in the music for a moment before returning to my book. Then, damn, there was the phone again. I jumped out of the bath and, determined not to miss it now I had made the effort, grabbed my dressing gown and ran dripping down the landing to the phone in my bedroom. *It better not be some damned credit card company or double glazing salesman*, I thought.

'Hello,' I said grumpily.

It was Esther and she was crying.

'Elliot, I've been attacked.'

Esther had been assaulted only a few streets away from her house. I dried and dressed quickly, jumped into the car and drove over to her. When I arrived, I found her sitting at her kitchen table holding a flannel to her face. There was a severe gash on her left cheek.

'He wore a balaclava. He pushed me really hard right against the wall and then cut my face. He said, *No more snooping around do you hear?*'

She tried to laugh but failed and winced with pain. Blood began to ooze from the cut on her face which up to now she had done quite a good job in staunching.

'Look, I'm sorry Esther,' I said, 'but I think you're going to have to go to A and E.'

Five stitches and an hour later, Esther was free to go home. In the meantime, she explained in more detail what had happened to her.

She had spent some time at the university talking to a couple of the porters, as she thought, in confidence. Her most fruitful conversation was with a porter called Stanley. He was the one who had enlightened her about Grindley's past the previous time she had visited. He had been there longer than Grindley and it seemed, had a grievance about being passed over for promotion. Though it meant that some of his information probably lacked a certain objectivity, it did mean that he was happy to talk to a willing listener. She was trying to establish from him a reason why Miranda Reeves might have wanted to support Grindley when he was accused of stealing from the university, while Nielsen did not. If she was hoping for some startling revelation she was disappointed. The best that Stanley could come up with was that he considered that there was some rivalry between Nielsen and Reeves, something that Reeves had already hinted at, and that drove her to take the contrary view to Nielsen. He did add, however, that with Grindley's shady past he would not have been surprised that there were some favours going on. They were interrupted a couple of times during their conversation in the porters' lodge and though Esther tried to be discreet, she suspected that they had been overheard.

'I suppose it has to be Grindley,' I said when she had finished, 'unless it was a thug on the streets and you were just unlucky.'

She shrugged her shoulders.

'Or an accomplice. It has to be, doesn't it?'

'Not what you expect from such a venerable institution.'

'I just can't think of anyone else who would have a motive. It was not as though he tried to steal anything from me.'

The incident had been reported to the police. Esther was to go into the police station to make a statement the following day.

'I just worry that whoever this was might attempt something again.'

As we drove back from the hospital I could tell she was still shaken by the incident. I stopped the car outside her cottage. She was a little reluctant to get out.

'Look Esther, do you want me to stay at yours tonight?'

'Are you sure you don't mind?'

Esther had a half bottle of Jameson's which we shared between us accompanied by egg-fried rice from the local Chinese takeaway. My personal resolution to avoid whisky was steadily being broken down. It was not a natural accompaniment to fried rice but it seemed to work for us that night.

'I'll go to the police first thing in the morning - if that's all right?'

'Of course.' It would mean Esther would be late for work.

'And you think I should say we suspect the porter?'

'Yes. They always ask if you know anyone who has a grudge against you. Esther, do you think that the information from this Stanley chap is reliable?'

'I don't know why it shouldn't be. He might have embellished a few things but given what I have just experienced, what he said seems to make perfect sense. He was not vindictive about him, more wary. He said he was always careful in his company.'

'Meaning?'

'I'm not exactly sure. But I think I understand the sense of what he was saying. You know there are always certain people that you don't want to tell too much to.'

'Like my mother.'

She shrieked with laughter.

'No, not at all like your mother.'

'Anyway,' she continued playfully, 'isn't it about time you rang her? She is due to come any day, isn't she? It must be ages since you did.'

'No I'm sure I only rang her... No, you're right, it must be a couple of weeks.'

'I knew it!'

'But strange she has not rung me to confirm the date.'

'You'll be in trouble.'

'I am always in trouble with my mother. I'm a great disappointment to her.'

'You know that's not true.'

She took a sip of the Jameson's. I thought about when would be the best time to ring my mother and wished Esther had not reminded me of it at that moment.

'You know if we are right and it was Grindley, what was his motive for attacking me?'

'To stop you snooping around.'

I tried to sound like a deep-throated villain but it was not very convincing. Esther laughed.

'Sorry, Elliot, but you will never make a tough guy.'

She squeezed my arm.

'But I mean, what was his real motive? Why did he not want me asking questions?'

'I suppose he didn't want you raking up the past and raising the question of whether he was fit to hold down his job or not. Unless he is the *Folio* thief.'

'I bet that's difficult to say after a few drinks.' I added unnecessarily.

Esther ignored my attempt at humour.

'OK, so he thinks that by scaring me I won't do any more interfering.'

'Yes.'

I did not like the way this was going.

'So, what is it that he doesn't want me to find out? Is it to do with the stealing of the *Folio* or the murder of Nielsen- there must be something more to it than that he just doesn't want me to ask questions about his past. Otherwise it's just too extreme a reaction.'

'His job might be very important to him. He probably wouldn't get another opportunity like that again.'

She was thoughtful and I did not think she was entirely convinced by my answer.

'Look, Esther,' I continued, 'whatever it is, you can't go back there asking any more questions. Besides, it sounds like this Stanley has told you all that he knows. This is where DNA and swabs and the police come in, as I think you once told me a long time ago.'

'Fat lot of good it has done up to now.'

She gave a curious evasive smile and then went across to her bedroom and fetched me a duvet and a couple of pillows from her cupboard.

'Thanks for coming over,' she said and gave me a peck on the cheek.

'You should take some painkillers.'

Her wound was angry looking, an unkind gash, but to my eyes it did not diminish her beauty one little bit.

'I have some here.'

She held up her hand to reveal the capsules enclosed in foil.

*

I had trouble sleeping with everything that had happened and listened to the World Service through the earphones on my pocket radio that I always carried around with me. It was not good news. There had been another devastating earthquake in the Southern Hemisphere. When I did sleep, I dreamed of earthquakes and hurricanes and encounters in dark alleyways.

26

The next day I woke as soon as the sun came up, thankful to be away from the terrors of the night. I opened the back door which led onto the yard. There was a cool breeze but already I could feel a little warmth from the sun. The hens were gently clucking. It was a pleasant scene. Across from the chicken coop was an apple tree laden with fruit. I went across and picked one and munched into the deliciously fresh fruit.

I retreated to the kitchen and made a cup of tea for Esther and myself. I knocked on her bedroom door and eased the door open expecting to find her in bed. However, I was surprised to see her sitting at her dressing table in her dressing gown but naked to the waist, twisting round to look at her back in the mirror.

'I'm sorry,' I said and went to go.

'No, it's OK,' she said. She covered up a little but left her back exposed. 'Look at my bruise.'

'I had one of your delicious apples. Hope you don't... God, that's awful.'

I examined more closely the vicious mass of purple, red and black that covered her right shoulder blade.

'He must have pushed you with some force.'

'It was not... pleasant'

She laughed at her understatement.

'Do you want me to put something on it?'

'There's some arnica over there.'

I picked up the tube from the bedside table and rubbed it into her back while she leant forward.

'Anywhere else?' I said after I gauged I had finished. I received another one of those well aimed jabs in the ribs for my trouble.

Unfortunately, Aggie was unable to cover for Esther in the bookshop while she was at the police station, so I was faced with the task of running the shop on my own, which at times required a lot of multi-tasking and resulted in me missing quite a few phone calls. We did have voice mail but some customers did not choose to leave a message or required an immediate answer. I wondered if one of the calls that I missed was from Esther. She would not necessarily leave a message as she may have wanted to speak to me in person if there were any complicating factors that could not be easily explained in a message.

When she did eventually ring at eleven-thirty I was mightily relieved. The police had taken a long statement and had shown her a good deal of sympathy.

'Why don't you take the afternoon off? I'm managing fine here.'

I had a queue of people at that time and had another phone call on 'call waiting', but I thought I should make the gesture.

'To be honest Elliot, I would rather be doing something. I would feel safer. I will see you in about half-an-hour.'

As soon as the queue had cleared, I rang the university to ask if Miranda Reeves was on campus. I was told that she had several classes that day. I asked if they were being taken by Miranda and not a substitute. They did not know but informed me that she had been seen on the campus. Then I rang the private number I had for her. There was no answer but I left a message on her voice mail asking if I might see her. We needed to know whether she had contacted the university authorities and whether she might be able to throw any light on Grindley and his possible involvement when Esther was attacked.

When Esther arrived back after her visit to the police station, I suggested that she work on cataloguing and answering the phone in the office to avoid the inevitable questions from customers about the cause of her injury. When it came to closing time, she seemed a little hesitant about leaving.

'Esther, don't take this the wrong way, but why don't you come and stay with me for a day or two. As you know, I've plenty of room.'

'I would have to do something about the chickens but I might take you up on the offer. I think I might need a few days just to get my confidence back.'

We decided that she would go back home and feed her chickens and then drive on to my house. I gave her a spare house key which I kept in the safe.

'I'm going to be a bit late,' I said. 'I have to make a home visit about some books but I should be there in a couple of hours.'

In fact, I was telling a white lie. I rang Miranda Reeves again. Still no reply. Somehow, I felt she held the key to this whole business. I decided to drive out to the university and see if I could find her there. I drove as fast as I dared and arrived within about 40 minutes. I went up to her flat and knocked on the door expectantly. There was no reply. I had convinced myself that she would be there, had willed her to be there. I tried at the porters' lodge. All they could tell me was what I already knew, that she had been at the university that day. I wandered across the square thinking that I had been foolish to waste my time like this when I was not certain that I would be able to find her. Of course, there was no reason why she should be waiting for me in her room. There could be a number of other commitments she had. Then I saw Sam. I hailed her. I explained my failed mission.

We went into the student bar. It was tatty and sparsely decorated, a jukebox was blasting away a sad tune in the corner. There was a queue at the bar.

'What are you having?'

'What?'

I was having trouble hearing over the noise.

'She spoke directly into my ear.'

'What would you like to drink?'

'Oh, a pint of something, bitter, not too strong - but let me pay.'

I shoved a screwed up £10 note into her hand. I watched her as she skillfully pushed her shoulder between a queue of people at the front of the bar and almost at once caught the eye of one of the barmen. In a few moments, she was back with two pints of frothing beer.

'I got what I normally have. I hope you like it OK.'

'And change too,' I commented as she shoved some coins into my hand.

'It's a good price - subsidised by the student union.'

She led me over to a corner seat and another group of students that she nodded to. It was a little quieter in the corner though the jukebox was still thumping out its insistent tones.

'It used to be *The Smiths* and *The Police* in my time - *Walking on the Moon, The Charming Man,* that sort of thing.'

'Is there anything I can help you with Elliot?'

'Well, it's a bit delicate, Sam, and I want to be careful and not make accusations that are not true. But the long and the short of it is, well it's Esther - she's been attacked.'

Sam put her hand to her mouth.

'She's OK - a cut to her face - some bruises - though, obviously, a bit shaken up. The thing is...' I took a gulp of beer, 'she came to the university and asked a few questions about Grindley, the porter - found out a few things about him...'

She was there before me.

'And then she was attacked.'

'Yes. We think it was Grindley but we can't be certain.'

'It wouldn't surprise me. There's something very odd about that man. He's been found lurking in student bedrooms, that sort of thing. He gives me the creeps.'

'Any thefts that you know of?'

'Funny you should say that. There's been a spate of things going missing. It gets reported nearly every week in the student rag. Of course, students get the blame. But attacking someone - I would not say it's improbable. There is a nasty side to his character, I'm sure of it. But why would he want to do such a thing?'

'Well, as I say, I can't be certain it was him but I think it might have been to frighten her off. She found out some things about his past that I'm sure he would not like to be generally known.'

I sighed.

'I can't explain all the details but for various reasons I do need to speak to Miranda Reeves.'

'Well, I think she is giving a lecture tomorrow morning at ten. Why not try and catch her after that?'

'Sounds like a good plan. Look, Sam, I know this is an odd question: Miranda Reeves, do you know anything... about her sexuality?'

'Do you mean do I think she is lesbian?'

'Or transgender?' I felt a little uncomfortable about asking but I needed to know.

'You're right, you do ask odd questions! Of course, if she were lesbian, you know that would not be particularly unusual, especially at the university, and it might not excite comment, though thinking about it, that sort of thing does usually get picked up on by students. Universities aren't always the progressive places they might seem. I haven't heard anything. And just because she has rather boyish looks that does not automatically mean she is not heterosexual - some men find that sort of look attractive. I know she is well liked by many of the students - the men as well as the women. She takes part in lots of student events, acting and so on. Why do you ask?'

'It's just a theory I'm following up. The fact is, it would have been convenient if she turned out to be a cross-dresser who likes going out in public in men's clothes. I'm sorry, I'm wasting your time. I think I need to rein myself in and start looking at this in a more conventional light.'

'This is to do with Nielsen, isn't it? There is something else though, and again it might be something or nothing, but there is this student, Katarina Budonovka. Well, it was rumoured she was having an affair with Nielsen - and Tom, this other boy she was going out with, he got jealous and upset. I don't know if it means anything.'

'Do you know this Katarina?'

'She's in my tutor group, in fact she will be at the lecture tomorrow. Actually, so will Tom. That's why she latched on to him, I think, because of his brains. It's funny she always comes in late now. I think it's so Tom will not sit next to her. It got really awkward for a while - you know after this affair with Nielsen was supposed to have started. He would come in and sit next to her and then she would move away - that sort of thing. Look, I'm sorry, I have to go to a meeting about university cuts.'

'I remember we occupied the administrative buildings once, when I was at university. We made the national newspapers and were called a flying circus of Marxists.'

'What was it all about?'

'Do you know, I can't really remember. But I do remember feeling passionately about it at the time.'

'Why don't you come to that lecture tomorrow? Sorry, I must go.'

'Thanks Sam. Bye.'

I made a note of Katarina's name in my address book. I did not trust myself to remember it.

I rang Aggie on my mobile and told her about the attack on Esther. She was horrified.

'Poor Esther, why doesn't she come and stay with me?'

'She's staying at my house, just for a couple of days, but that is a really kind thought and I will let her know that you offered.'

The truth is, I liked the thought of Esther staying with me and did not want to give up her company lightly.

'I wanted to see if I could get to speak to Miranda Reeves at the university. I can't seem to get hold of her on the phone. But I know she is giving a lecture at the university tomorrow. Do you think you could manage a couple of hours first thing tomorrow while I see if I can get to speak to her?'

'Of course, if there's a queue I'll tell them it's your fault.'

Then I rang Esther. I tried her mobile first and then the land line at my house. I could not get a response on either.

'Oh, my God,' I thought, 'what has happened now?'

I rushed home in the car, anxious and wondering why she had not answered the phone. By the time I arrived, I was sick with worry having imagined all kinds of nasty new scenarios. Had Grindley switched his attention to my house or had Esther been caught at her house when she went home to feed the chickens? However, I was encouraged when I saw that her car was in the drive. At least it meant that she had made it to my house. I quickly turned the key in the door.

'Esther?' I called.

There was no answer. I could hear a noise, though. I took a deep breath and went into the sitting room, preparing myself for the worst.

And there was Esther, snoring gently on the sofa with the evening news blasting out on the television. Her head was lolling over the edge of the sofa so I carefully repositioned it with the aid of a cushion. She stirred but did not wake. She must have had little sleep in the last couple of days. Then I went and grabbed a duvet and wrapped it around her. I took away the remains of the meal she had been eating and turned the lights down. My foremost feeling at that moment was one of relief.

When she woke early, on the sofa where she had gone to sleep the evening before, I tried to persuade her to go to one of the spare bedrooms and have a good lie down but she insisted that she had to go and sort the chickens out. I told her briefly about my abortive trip to track down Miranda Reeves but did not volunteer information about my visit to the university to hear her lecture. Luckily, the chickens were very much at the forefront of her mind and she was gone from the house before I knew it.

27

It was a strange feeling attending a university lecture after an interval of twenty years. I arrived early so that I could sit with Sam. We placed ourselves at the back so that we could keep an eye on the students and Sam could tell me when Katarina arrived. Most of the students came in a rush two minutes before the lecture began.

'What does she look like?' I asked Sam.

'Attractive, striking you would say. Small and blonde, but not a natural blonde.'

'Not that that should matter.'

'Not a bit.'

Sam stroked her own dark hair streaked with red.

My eyes blurred with the effort of looking as a hundred or so students came into the theatre. It was obviously a popular lecture. I spotted three unnatural looking blondes who I pointed out to Sam, afraid that I would miss Katarina, but none of them were her. I decided I had missed her when Sam nudged me. An attractive blonde came rushing in late, just after Miranda Reeves had marched in to take her place behind the lectern. She sat at the back in the next row of seats across from us.

Miranda Reeves began her lecture.

'Today's lecture is entitled, Shakespeare in Context. It is my contention that though each new generation of Shakespeare productions finds a parallel or an interpretation that is relevant to contemporary society, we can gain greater understanding of Shakespeare's intended meaning by studying what was going on during Shakespeare's time and, also with reference to how the early plays were originally written, particularly with reference to the *First Folio*.'

I glanced across to Katarina. She was sitting next to another young man who was furiously taking notes, though I presumed that this was not Tom. I wondered if perhaps she had latched onto another talented young academic.

'We need to understand that Shakespeare was not writing these plays in isolation. Shakespeare has acquired what the Shakespearian academic Stanley Wells has called *semi-divine* status and we often refer to the period when he was writing as *Shakespearian*. However, we must recognise that he learnt a lot of his craft from other playwrights and was in competition with them. It is sobering to think that if Shakespeare had died at the same time as Christopher Marlowe there is no doubt that Marlowe would have been considered the greater writer.'

I smiled in recognition of my knowledge of the fact from an earlier conversation with her.

I found the lecture fascinating and when it ended I felt like clapping, though in fact it was succeeded by the sound of a mass of voices taking part in small conversations in unison, and an attempt at a mass exodus. I decided that now I had established that Miranda Reeves was on the campus it was more important for me to seek out Katarina Budonovka while I had knowledge of her whereabouts. She rose immediately the lecture had finished. I followed her out. She was at the head of the queue and I had to run through the crowded foyer to keep her in sight. Eventually, with a little bit of pushing and shoving and several 'excuse me's, I managed to catch up with her.

'I'm sorry to bother you, it's Katarina, isn't it?'

'Yes.'

'My name is Elliot Todd. I am from The *Ex Libris* bookshop. I wondered if you could spare five minutes. It concerns Harry Nielsen.'

She hesitated.

'Yes, as long as it is only five minutes. I have to go and finish an essay.'

'Can I buy you a coffee?'

'OK, there's the JCR through here.'

She found a place for us to sit in the corner.

'How did you enjoy the lecture?'

'It was OK, I guess. But that's not what you came here to ask me, right?'

'No, it's not,' I hesitated not quite sure how to proceed. I took a deep breath.

'OK, I am going to come right out with it. I am going to ask you something personal. I believe you were having an affair with Harry Nielsen.'

Her eyelids flickered.

'And you are not from the police?'

'No, but Harry Nielsen was murdered in my bookshop.'

'I think I should only answer questions from the police.'

Her English was very good though she had a distinctive (quite engaging) accent. I wondered if this had been part of the attraction for Nielsen. She was pretty but her face had a rather fixed, hard look. She rose from her chair.

'Look, what does it matter if I had an affair with Harry?'

Echoes of Anna in *The Third Man* came into my mind. By Katarina's use of Nielsen's first name I suspected I had confirmation of their affair, or at least a close liaison.

'It doesn't matter beyond the fact that it might help us establish the motive for his murder.'

She sat down again.

'Are you sure it was murder?'

'A lot of the evidence appears to point that way.'

'I had no idea I would be involved in anything like this, I just…' She hesitated. 'It was just a sort of fling, that's all.'

'You know that it is against university rules for a lecturer to have an affair with a student?'

She smiled.

'It might be against university rules but that does not make it against the law.'

I had the feeling that this was a rehearsed speech.

'I'm nineteen you know.'

'So, you could be Nielsen's daughter.'

I regretted it the moment I said it.

'I don't think I want to speak to you anymore.' Then she added as a parting shot. 'Anyway, you know it takes two to tango.'

I was annoyed with myself for the way I had handled it. I had not even got as far as asking her about Tom.

'Elliot, are you all right?'

I looked up to see Sam standing over me.

'Oh, hi Sam.'

'You had such a pained look on your face just now. Did you catch up with Katarina?'

'Yes, I was just beating myself up about it. I didn't handle it very well. I managed to sound like the heavy father and she stomped off - and I didn't even get a chance to ask her about this Tom.'

'She's a bit hard-nosed. She's one of those women that doesn't seem to have many girlfriends. Anyway, why don't you speak to Tom himself? He's right over there. He's not hard-nosed. To be honest, I can't understand why they were ever together.'

She pointed over to a slight boy with round glasses sitting at a table in the corner. He appeared shy and awkward looking - one of the last people you would have imagined would have hooked up with Katarina.

'Well, it's what people are like on the inside that counts.'

'Hm.'

'Thanks Sam, I think I'll see if I can have a word.'

I crossed over to his table. He was by himself, which made it easier for me.

'Do you mind if I sit here?'

He barely looked up.

'Sure, go ahead.'

'It's Tom, isn't it?'

He looked up at me and gave me a short appraisal.

'Can I help you with anything?'

'I own the bookshop where Harry Nielsen was killed.'

'Yes, I know your bookshop. I picked up a copy of *The Aeneid* there once.'

'Did you? Was it new or second-hand?'

'I think it was a 1910 edition.'

'Good, I'm glad you found something you wanted.'

'It's a nice bookshop.'

'Thank you.'

'Why did you want to see me?'

'Well, you probably think I have an awful lot of cheek but I wanted to ask you something personal. I am helping the police and the university authorities with enquiries.'

I knew this was perhaps stretching the truth but in essence I thought it was accurate enough.

'We need to check anyone connected with Nielsen or his acquaintances. If you don't want to answer that's your right.'

'What is it you want to know?'

'I'd like to know if you had a relationship with Katarina Budonovka.'

He took a sip of his tea, avoiding my eyes again.

'I was her boyfriend. I loved her. I thought she loved me. That's all over now.'

'I'm sorry. Love can be very hard.'

He could not know with what genuine feeling I said that. He smiled to himself.

'Some of the other students were jealous. They said they couldn't see what she saw in me.'

'Well I understand you're a very clever student.'

'She said she loved me for my brains not just my body and it was better if that side of things waited. She said it was best if we got to know each other first.'

Just for your brains, I thought to myself. But my unkind thoughts were directed at Katarina rather than the seemingly innocent Tom.

'Excuse me for asking this. Did that happen? Did you get to know each other?'

'Yes, she used to come around every week, sometimes more, but she was always tired. She was always saying next time when I have more energy I will make it up to you - but she never did.'

'That must have made you feel very frustrated.'

'It did. That's what ruined it.'

'What happened?'

'I tried to kiss her. She got really annoyed. I said that I thought she was just using me. She used to borrow my English essays.'

'When she got annoyed, what did she say?'

'She said if I was going to be like that she knew someone else who could help her - where she could get better information - and who was more of a man, not just a silly little boy. She went off and never came back. I tried to contact her but she never returned my phone calls or emails. When I saw her in the street she used to ignore me. If I sat next to her in the lecture theatre, like we used to - I would lend her my notes - she would move away to a different seat. Then one of the other students told me about her and Mr Nielsen. I didn't believe it at first. But then I noticed how he looked at her in the classes. I knew it was true.'

'What was true?'

'That she was seeing him and she had definitely finished with me.'

He sighed.

'I'm sorry, it is very tough this love thing.'

'If only I had given that essay to her. I miss her'

'It must be difficult when you see her now.'

'Yes. She just blanks me like I'm not there, like I never existed.'

'Does it make you angry?'

'Yes.'

He hesitated.

'She was the only girlfriend I've ever really had.'

'I know what you are going through. I've been in a similar situation myself.'

'Really?'

'Sometimes I think we would be better off without it - love I mean - it just complicates things. The trouble is we don't always have a choice in the matter, it often chooses us. I was reading this poem the other day. There is a line: *We don't fall in love: it rises through us the way that certain music does.*'

'Is that Shakespeare?'

'No, a very good modern poet.'

'Can I buy you a coffee?'

'No thank you, Tom, I've just had one.'

This interview was going a lot better than my one with Katarina Budonovka. I needed to make the most of it now I had his confidence.

'The trouble is, the other side of love is hate. It is a very thin line.'

'I know.'

'What do you do when you get angry, Tom?'

'Sometimes I kick the wall.'

'Did you ever feel like hurting her - or him? It wouldn't be surprising if you did.'

He avoided my eyes. He could not look at me. He nodded his head. He looked as if he might burst into tears. I felt I could not go any further - not yet anyway.

'Well, thank you Tom.'

I rose from my chair.

'Oh, by the way, do you have any contact with Miranda Reeves?'

He brightened a little and looked up at me again.

'She's my tutor.'

'What's she like as a teacher?'

'She's very good. Very knowledgeable.'

'More knowledgeable than Harry Nielsen?'

'In some ways, she's better. The trouble with Mr Nielsen was I think sometimes, well, he liked showing off.'

'Well. Thanks again, Tom. I hope to see you in the bookshop sometime.'

I really hoped so, though part of me thought that this might not now be possible.

I had intended to go straight back to the shop but I made a short detour to my house. I thought I might find Esther there as I had given her an extra day off to recuperate from her ordeal, and was not disappointed. Even though it was now late in the year, there was not a cloud in the sky and the sun was still giving off some welcome warmth. I found Esther reading on the bench in the garden. I had not phoned beforehand so she was surprised to see me.

'What are you up to, Elliot Todd?'

She always used this phrase when she was in a good mood.

'I think I might have discovered the murderer, but it doesn't make me happy.'

I explained my conversation with Tom.

'I think you are making a lot of assumptions here. You didn't after all ask the question, *Did you murder Nielsen* and get him to admit it?'

'No, but when I asked him if he ever felt like hurting him he nodded and he couldn't look me in the eye.'

'So, you think he was the one with the *moutee* in the photo?'

186

'He could have been witnessing the conversation between Nielsen and this man. The more I think about that *moutee* the more I think that it's probably just an irrelevance. What we do know, though, is that Tom had a motive. Imagine this. He saw this man take Nielsen down to near the stock room. They have a short conversation as Nielsen is aware that he must return to signing his books. However, Tom sees an opportunity to challenge the man who took his girlfriend away.'

'Well, the police will have to deal with it now. Have you contacted them?'

'No, but I will. To be honest, part of me doesn't want to. Nielsen and Katarina Budonovka don't come out of this very well.'

'You mean Nielsen deserved what he got?'

'No, I don't mean that. I don't exactly know what I do mean except that I do have some sympathy for this poor young man and it doesn't give me any great pleasure to turn him in.'

After I had made a phone call to the police I walked to the bookshop. I realised that Tom's confession, if that was what it was, did not explain everything. There was still the attack on Esther to consider and all the business of the *Folio*.

When I arrived at the bookshop, I thanked Aggie for covering and apologised for being longer than expected.

'Not to worry, it's been very quiet. But I've had Sam on the phone twice for you. She sounded excited about something.'

I rang her mobile.

'Oh, Elliot, there's been more drama here. Grindley the porter has died.'

'What? How?'

'Well, it is being described as a tragic accident. Apparently, there was a ladder involved. But I have also heard rumours that there might have been an argument and guess where it took place?'

'You'll have to tell me.'

'In the corridor near Miranda Reeves's apartment.'

After the bookshop closed, I replied to a few emails and then began my walk home. I usually looked forward to my walk and that day welcomed the opportunity of some fresh air and some thinking time to take in all that had happened. I had discovered a route which, though a little longer, for the most part avoided the main roads. It took me over footbridges, along a canal and over a meandering stream until I rejoined the main road and crossed over to the lane that led to my house.

Before I left the High Street, I crossed into the park to find my way along the canal. I stopped briefly to admire the ducks. The park had a large pond that dated back to medieval times and was a playground for an exotic variety of ducks. As I leaned on the fence I noticed a man, dressed in a Burberry type coat with the belt tied in a knot, who was looking vaguely in my direction. I was surprised to see him again ten minutes later when I was walking along the tow-path of the canal. My mobile phone rang. As usual I had a mild moment of panic while I found out which pocket it was in. It was Esther. I am one of those people who cannot stand still while talking on a mobile. I swung round to face the direction I had come and was surprised to see again the man in the Burberry coat. I continued my conversation.

Instead of waiting for him, I turned back to the direction I had been walking and began walking more quickly.

'Listen, Esther, I'll explain later but I have to go.'

But I kept the mobile to my ear until I came to some bushes and a slight bend. I ran twenty or so paces until I came to the first wooden footbridge that crossed a tributary stream to the main river. Instead of crossing the footbridge I slipped down the bank next to it, which was thick with bushes, and crouched beneath the bridge. Sure enough, I heard the man cross the bridge at a brisk pace. I waited about thirty seconds and then climbed the bank and crossed the bridge. He was just in sight. After about another thirty seconds he stopped. I could see him intently scanning the horizon. I went off the path and took refuge behind a tree, just in time as he turned around. He hesitated for a few seconds and then began walking in my direction. I stood behind the tree in perfect stillness while he walked past me and back towards the town. He was tall, very slim looking. How long would I leave it, five minutes? I became impatient after two and regained the pathway and continued at a good pace. I looked behind me several times. The path was clear. The mobile rang again.

'Is it OK to talk? I didn't want to ring but I was worried.'

'I'm OK now but it seems that I was being followed. It looks like I gave him the slip.'

'Who was it?'

'I have no idea. Tall, thin, dressed in a Burberry. I have never seen him before.'

'I think you did the right thing. He probably wants to know where you live.'

'He could probably find out another way. I'm in.... Oh, no I'm not.'

I was going to say I was in the phone book but in fact I was not. Six months ago, one of my lady customers had taken to making phone calls to me in the middle of the night. Esther delighted in reminding me that she had severe behavioural problems.

'Well what is easier than following you home from work?'

'I suppose - and for what purpose? To frighten me?'

'This is all getting too sinister. He's definitely not the one who attacked me if he is thin like you describe.'

'Oh, Esther, I was going to tell you when I got home, Grindley has died.'

'Never!'

'Supposedly an accident - a ladder was involved.'

'But you don't think so?'

'I don't know what to think. I only know what I've just told you.'

Esther had a pot of tea waiting when I arrived home.

'Tea always puts things right,' she reminded me.

We talked more about Grindley.

'You don't think he could have been murdered?'

'I don't know. It just all seems a bit mysterious and now this other man following me home.'

'Except he didn't follow you home. He obviously doesn't know where you live.'

'I suppose it's only a matter of time until he does. I was wondering, Esther, Aggie offered for you to stay at her place for a few days. I wonder if it would be safer.'

'Or perhaps we should both emigrate.'

'I believe the food is excellent in the South of France.'

'We can't keep running away, Elliot. Besides it's probably safer if the two of us are together for the moment.'

28

It was Esther's yoga night that evening. She was obviously feeling a lot better as she was determined to go and brave the inevitable comments that would come her way about the wound on her face.

I had plenty to think about while she was out. There was my conversation with Tom, Grindley's death and now this man following me. However, I did not come to any new conclusion and ended up with a headache with the effort of thinking about it.

Esther had arranged to see, as usual, a girlfriend afterwards and did not arrive until after eleven when I was already in bed.

I had the pleasure of her company as we both walked together to the bookshop the following morning. It was another windswept day and despite recent events there was an air of fun and playfulness between us as we rushed headlong along the tow-path.

'I love the wind in my hair,' Esther announced as she stood astride a style.

'How typically poetical of you Esther.'

She jumped off the style with her hands stretched out in front of her and ran ahead of me.

Despite all that had happened, we arrived at the bookshop in top form ready to welcome the world to our door. However, as I unlocked the door and switched off the alarm, I did a double take as I turned around and saw the mysterious man in the Burberry again, heading straight for the bookshop. Esther noticed him too and looked at me.

'That's him, 'I said in an undertone.

We both waited as he approached us.

'Mr Todd?'

'You've been following me,' was the best I could come up with.

'I have been wanting to speak to you. I believe you left this behind.'

From his pocket, he took out my address book. Irrationally, I patted my jacket pocket to check that it was not there.

Already, I could tell from the man's manner that he was not a "heavy" employed to track me down.

'Oh, thank you. I didn't even know I had lost it.'

Esther giggled, I think with relief.

'Where did you find it?'

'In the JCR. My name is Nick Pearson. I work at the university as a science technician. One of the students told me that you had this bookshop and as I visit my sister here once a week and it is not far away I said I would take it to you. But I don't get home until just after five-thirty and I just missed you the other day. I saw you leaving across the park yesterday but I was unable to catch up with you - you're a fast walker. I thought I would try again this morning. I don't have to be in until later today.'

'I know when I left it. I wrote down a student's name, an unusual name, so I would not forget it when I was in the JCR with Sam - a student that used to work here. Thank you very much – it's very valuable to me. But why did you not leave a note through the door?'

'I wondered if my information was correct after all or if you were the wrong person - that's why I was a bit hesitant just now.'

'You don't know how pleased I am. There are so many important addresses in here. I don't know how I would manage without it.'

'I was worried whether I was doing the right thing, whether it was better to leave it with the JCR in case you rang enquiring about it.'

'No, that's fine. Anyway, I have it now. No harm done.'

Esther had walked away by now and was getting on with the business of opening the shop.

He was hesitating. I wondered if I should give him a reward.

'Why don't you choose a book as a reward, or I could give you a book token to spend.'

'That's kind Mr Todd, but entirely unnecessary. I am just pleased to help. But there is another matter I would like to discuss if you don't mind. It's kind of private.'

I guessed he was perhaps retiring from the university and looking to volunteer at the bookshop. Even though I could not accommodate him I felt obliged to give him my time and consideration. I was also relieved that what appeared to be another strange happening turned out to be as innocuous as someone trying to hand me back my lost property.

'Of course, come up to my office for a moment.'

'It's a nice bookshop you have here, Mr Todd,' he commented as we went up the stairs, 'I'm ashamed to say I have not been here before but I will certainly remedy that in future, looking at the range of volumes that you have on the shelves.'

He sat down in the chair opposite me in the office.

'To begin at the beginning. I don't get particularly well paid, not compared with the lecturers - mind you they are not on a fortune - but they offer me accommodation at the university, I have to say at a very reasonable price.' He sipped some of the coffee Esther had brought us both. I sipped mine. 'It all helps. I am on my own, my wife, you know, we're not together anymore – we're divorced.'

For a moment, there was a great sadness in this unassuming man's eyes. Then he gave a little defiant smile and perked up.

'It's not a bad life really. The students aren't such a bad lot overall.'

Briefly, he was lost in reverie. I was not sure if he was thinking about his wife or his life at the university.

'So, why was it you wanted to see me?'

'I overheard you talking in the bar on the university campus. I often go down for a quick drink in the evening. I feel quite comfortable there. I sit there and nod to the students - a lot of the science students know who I am. I don't go out of my way to listen to other people's conversations but that night I was sitting with my back to you. Well, I could not help overhearing you talking about Miranda Reeves.'

It seemed that perhaps he was not interested in a job at the bookshop after all.

'Do you know her?' I asked.

'A little.' He took another small mouthful of his coffee. I imagined him sipping beer in the student bar in the same way.

I could see how his wife might have become bored or irritated with his mannerisms and conversation but I was also a little intrigued. He appeared to be holding back for dramatic effect. Perhaps there were unseen depths to this man that his wife had not noticed. Didn't he, after all, attempt to chase me down to speak with me?

'She isn't exactly what you call a friend but I know her to nod to and have the occasional word with. She lives next to me in one of the little university flats. Not many of the teaching staff live on the campus but it does seem to suit her. She did say to me once when I saw her in the morning and she was rushing, *I don't know what I would do if I didn't live at the university, I would never be in time for my lectures or tutorials*, or some such phrase. But we don't usually have such conversations.'

He gave a little laugh as though to reinforce the fond memory and then continued.

'Mostly we nod to each other and she is perfectly civil to me.'

Nodding obviously was an important means of communicating in his life. I could not help smiling.

'The point is, something has been puzzling me.'

He took another sip of his coffee.

I await with baited breath, I thought to myself but I was not prepared for what came next.

'I know that she and Mr Nielsen, not to put too fine a point on it, were of an intimate acquaintance.'

'What?'

It took me a moment to translate into plain English.

'You mean they were having an affair?'

There was that well-practised nod again.

'I don't want to go telling tales out of school - or university,' (he gave a little laugh at his own humour), 'but I think the reason they kept it secret was because of university rules. I know that because some years ago we had a little incident - you know I have been there 30 years?' This did not surprise me. 'Well, some years ago there were visiting university research students from the USA.' He was troubled for a moment. 'Or was it Canada?'

'It doesn't matter,' I said a little impatiently, still trying to take in his last revelation about the affair.

'No, it was definitely the USA.' He looked mightily relieved and rewarded himself with another sip of coffee. 'There was one particular lecturer who was a bit flash with the ladies. He thought he was on safe ground with research students as they had postgraduate status but it turned out he wasn't. He had a brief affair with one of them. She became very unhappy when he no longer wanted to continue the relationship. She had a rich daddy in the United States, the head of a big corporation over there - what was it called? I just can't remember for the moment.'

'It's all right, go on.'

'Well, as I said, the head of a big corporation and a major benefactor of the university which she was attached to in the States. He was not very happy with the situation.'

'His poor innocent daughter being jilted by an English university professor.'

'Precisely. Not to put too fine a point on it...'

He had trouble finding the right phrase.

'He made one hell of a stink?' I offered.

'That's it. As a result, they disallowed any relationship between any university lecturer and any fellow staff or students. It was contrary to the interests of the university - or some such phrase. It's a bit difficult as you can imagine because that is where so many people meet - in the workplace. Officially, if a relationship does take place, one or other is asked to leave.'

But, Miranda Reeves and Nielsen? Nobody had as much as hinted at that. In fact, it had seemed unlikely given that there appeared to be a degree of rivalry between them.

'Well, thank you, that is interesting. Thank you very much.'

I shook his hand. I had plenty of work to do and was also keen to discuss this new information with Esther.

'There is something, in some ways even more interesting.'

I somehow doubted it, but I was wrong.

'Well, the reason I know about the relationship between Mr Nielsen and Miss Reeves is because I have seen and heard them - living next door as I do.'

This was a good point. Up to now I had just taken his word that they were having an affair - though I did not want to think too much about the details of what he had seen and heard.

'The funny thing is, it looks like she has started up another relationship.'

'Probably on the rebound.'

He looked at me a little strangely at this but continued.

'The thing is, this is ... a little unusual.'

'Oh?'

I was not quite sure what to expect now.

'I don't want to appear snobbish or anything but she is a good looking intelligent woman.' His directness surprised me. 'And he's a bit of an old sour puss and a bit of a rogue.'

'Who?' I said. 'Who is she is having an affair with?'

'Mr Grindley.'

I was genuinely lost for words.

'Are you sure?'

'I'm not one to gossip but I overheard you asking about Mr Nielsen and the *Folio* and I thought you ought to know.'

After he had left I realised that he was not aware and that I had not told him, about the death of Grindley.

29

Esther was also surprised about the affair between Nielsen and Reeves and did not believe the story of a liaison between Grindley and Reeves.

'You're sure he isn't just a malicious gossip? I'm pretty sure he's wrong about Reeves and Grindley. Why should we believe him about Nielsen and her?'

'He is certainly a gossip. But I'm not sure I would class him as malicious.'

'It is strange, though, that Reeves didn't indicate it in any way to us. In fact, in lots of ways she was quite cool about Nielsen.'

'It's surely an important fact that the police should know.'

'It's not really a fact, though – just gossip.'

'And Grindley? That doesn't sound right at all.'

'And how does all this fit into your theory about Tom?'

'I don't know. The more we get involved in this affair, the more complicated it seems to get.'

Later, I rang Sam.

'Let me ask you something controversial.'

'I'm getting used to it now.'

'Miranda Reeves and Grindley, what would you say If I told you I thought they had been having an affair?'

'You're joking, aren't you?'

'Is it so unlikely?'

'It's apples and pears. She's all posh and academic…and he… Well he isn't…wasn't I should say.'

'But aren't some women attracted by …'

'A bit of rough. ' She thought for a moment. 'No, I can't see it, not with Grindley. There's a bit of nastiness there. What makes you think it's so likely?'

'Miranda Reeves's neighbour in the flat next door, he thought they were having an affair.'

'Well, I suppose he would be in a good position to know. But a porter has lots of responsibilities and Miranda Reeves had pastoral responsibilities for her students - that may be why she was living on campus in the first place. The Head Porter would often have to get involved in little incidents which might involve reporting to her now and again.'

'So, he could have been visiting her room perfectly innocently?'

'I'm only trying to understand it like you are. The only slightly weird thing about Miranda Reeves, I would say, is that in her tutorials she had moments when she could be a little aggressive - mood swings I suppose you would call them. Occasionally she would completely lose it and you wondered if she was entirely sane. The next moment she was as nice as pie.'

'But what about Nielsen and Reeves?'

'Hm. That's an interesting one. I certainly didn't know about it. I can ask around.'

I described my conversation with Sam to Esther.

'Well, even if it isn't true, Grindley was visiting her whatever the reason. Pearson's unlikely to have got that wrong - unless he has a twin.'

'Like Antipholus and Dromio in the *Comedy of Errors*.'

'Is there no situation in life that you won't relate to a Shakespeare play?'

'Therein lies Shakespeare's genius.'

'Now you're beginning to talk like him.'

'No, it would have been much more guttural, hardly recognisable to the modern speaker.'

Not for the first time she ignored what I thought was a perfectly good joke.

'But look, let's assume for a moment it's true. How does it affect anything?'

'It might implicate Reeves in the embezzlement of goods from the university.'

'But why would she need to be involved? She is surely on a reasonable salary? I mean, what does she gain from it?'

'Well, it has to be the *Folio* then.'

'I never believed that cock and bull story about her borrowing it. There has got to be something else behind it.'

When we walked home the wind had calmed down and we strolled at a leisurely pace. There was something else on Esther's mind.

'There is something I wanted to talk to you about Elliot. I want to go home tomorrow.'

'Are you sure? You're very welcome to stay as long as you want.'

'I know, and it is very sweet of you. And I have enjoyed my stay. But I am missing my chickens and my house. I just feel I need to get home. That's where I can be who I am. It's nothing you have done wrong Elliot. We can still do all the things we do together. I just need that distance.'

'I know, you don't have to explain. It's fine, really it is.'

I was not sure I totally understood but I knew if that was how she felt it had to be the right thing for her. She gave me that beautiful warm smile of hers and a peck on the cheek.

'We will have a lovely meal together this evening.'

Our meal was interrupted by a phone call from my mother. She wanted to come and see me for her long planned-for trip.

'Is it OK if I come down this weekend?'

I wasn't sure that I wanted to mention the fact that Esther was there as it would only encourage her speculation. I also remembered what Esther had said to me about appreciating my mother.

'Of course.' Perhaps influenced by the couple of glasses of wine inside me I asked, 'Are you sure everything is all right?'

'What could be wrong?'

'I don't know. Are you sure you're quite well?'

'I went to my doctor the other day. He said I was as fit as a flea and had the body of a 50-year-old.'

'Oh, I'm pleased to hear that. Shall I pick you up from the station?'

'No, I'm going to drive.'

'Drive, you haven't driven this distance for years.'

'Don't be silly, it's no distance at all - and I don't want to be a burden to you.'

'You're not a burden,' I said, while aware that I was not being entirely truthful.

'Anyway, I need my freedom.'

'If you're sure?'

'My mind is quite made up, Elliot. Stop worrying about me.'

'That's perfect,' Esther said to me when I had finished on the phone. 'One woman leaves another one arrives. Did she ask after me?'

'To be honest, I forgot to mention you.'

She looked at me in that penetrating way she had.

'All right, I know it's useless trying to lie to you. The fact is, Esther, my mother is convinced that there is something going on between us.' I put my hands up. 'I assure you I have done nothing to encourage that view. She just sees things that are not there. I'm sorry.'

'Don't worry Elliot, I'm quite flattered really.'

'Are you?'

'Don't look so serious, she just doesn't know our situation that's all. You never know, she might find someone for you while she's here.'

I forced a laugh but it wasn't what I wanted to hear from Esther. Perhaps Cameron was right and I should just give up on all thoughts of being with Esther and look for someone else.

I took Esther's views about my mother on board and, knowing that she was staying a fortnight, arranged a meal and a visit to the theatre in the first week. I had a bit of dilemma regarding Esther. I wanted to include her but did not want my mother to get the wrong idea, so I decided to make sure that I included Aggie as well.

As she usually did, the first day after her arrival my mother visited the bookshop. The extraordinary thing was that two customers arrived in the shop while she was there, Mrs Pomeroy and Mrs Kay, who both remembered her from previous visits. She gave them both coffee at the lone table in the corner and entertained them for the next half-an-hour. While she did so, Nick Pearson arrived. This time he was on book business.

'I told you I would return. Once I find a good place I always stay loyal. Where are your railway books?'

'Just down the bottom of the shop across from the children's section, where those ladies are having coffee.'

Shortly after, Mrs Pomeroy and Mrs Kay thanked my mother for her company. My mother began tidying up the coffee things and seeing Mr Pearson there, offered him a coffee which he gratefully accepted.

'I think we have found a new role for your mother,' Esther said. 'Entertainment Czar.'

'That's very good, Esther. While she's busy there. I think I might take the opportunity of going to the bank.'

'You seemed to make quite an impression with our customers,' I said to my mother that evening over our meal.

'You know what I would really like, Elliot, to visit the university. All the times I've visited you and I have never been and now recently, with it being in the news about the murder of that poor lecturer, it reminded me of what I might have been missing.'

'I won't be able to get any time off tomorrow, I have a busy day I'm afraid.'

'Don't worry, I'll drive down in the afternoon.'

'Are you sure?'

'Of course, I am. I'm not totally decrepit you know.'

'Your mother is showing great independence,' commented Esther when I went into work the following morning and explained about her trip to the university.

'That's what worries me, my mother never does anything without a reason.'

Mum did own a mobile but really only carried it for show and the battery was forever running down. I was unable to contact her as I had hoped before I went home. I tried her several more times after I got in at seven. When it got to eight I became worried and resolved to drive to the university to find her. Just as I was about to leave, the phone rang.

'I'm so glad I have been able to get hold of you, Elliot, the batteries in my mobile have run down and I am having to use a public phone box. The truth is, I am in a slightly embarrassing situation.'

'Embarrassing?'

'Well, I met your friend, you know the one who used to work in the bookshop?'

'Sam?'

'Yes, Sam. Lovely girl. She's so sweet.'

'But why is that embarrassing?'

'Well, she invited me for a drink and then of course I invited her for one back. I'm now over the limit. I totally forgot that I was driving.'

'I knew you would have been better off on the train. I'll come and get you. Where will I find you?'

'In the bar, of course.'

As soon as I put it down the phone rang again. It was Esther.

'I was just wondering how your mother got on?'

I explained the situation complaining rather vehemently about her thoughtlessness.

'Like mother like son, aye.'

I arrived at the university, parked and went straight to the bar where I knew my mother would be. She was not difficult to find. She was sitting centre stage surrounded by several of Sam's friends. Sam came up to me when she saw me.

'Would you like a drink Elliot?'

'We really ought to be going.' Then I thought Sam and the other students deserved a treat of some sort for putting up with my mother. 'OK, Sam but please, I insist on buying it.'

I went over and asked what everyone wanted.

'Then we'll have to go, mother.'

'He's just like his father, so impatient,' she said in an aside to her coterie.

'You might be right about me but I don't think you can accuse my dad of that – he had the patience of a saint.'

I might have added 'to put up with you', but restrained myself. When I returned from the bar several more of Sam's friends had joined her. I made several attempts to suggest that we move on, but Sam insisted that she return the favour of the round. Then I was dragged over to the dartboard to partner Sam in a darts match as she needed some practice for a match she was having the follo/wing day. As it seemed to be impossible to drag my mother away any time soon, I felt I could hardly refuse.

'One round of darts then. Then we must go.'

I had not played for at least a year. I did not manage too badly but I was unable to finish. Luckily Sam was on top form and we won a narrow game.

'Your mum's great, Elliot,' Sam said to me after we had completed the game.

'Really?'

'Yeah, she's so interesting. I wish my parents were more like that. Their world seems to revolve around the television and the supermarket and they don't seem to have an opinion on anything.'

'She'll be on the student council next.'

'Maybe that wouldn't be such a bad thing - a mature representative.'

'I was only joking.'

Why could I not keep my big mouth shut?

'Anyway, it would be impossible. She doesn't live here and only visits occasionally.'

I hoped Sam would not go any further with this. I envisaged weekly trips by my mother to stay with me.

Things were now getting a little bit heated among the group where my mum was sitting. There appeared to be some serious disagreement and my mum was right in the thick of it.

'That's Michael,' pointed out Sam. 'Trust him, he's a real red neck.'

My mum's voice could be heard clearly now.

'Before you engage on sweeping away everything in your brave new world, you have to realise that those rights that you so casually want to do away with were fought for over the centuries, sometimes at great personal cost, and you give them up at your peril.'

There was spontaneous applause from the dozen or so students that now surrounded my mother – all except for one who was bright red in the face and proceeded to walk off in a bit of a lather. I presumed that was Michael.

'How about another drink Elizabeth?' one of the students said.

I could not hang back any longer and rushed up to the group.

'I'm sorry, we really do have to go.'

I picked up my mothers's coat and held it out for her.

'It looks like I will have to go but I will return, as General MacArthur said.'

'We would love to see you,' someone said, 'make sure it's soon.'

Several students proceeded to shake her hand.

'Well that's hopeful,' I said to Sam, 'General MacArthur said that when he was in the Philippines and didn't return for over two years.'

'You're terrible, Elliot,' Sam chided me.

One of the students whose name I did not know turned towards me.

'You know, I've never met anyone like your mother.'

'Nor have I,' I could honestly say.

'What a nice bunch of people,' she said as we walked back to the car park.

'Yes, they are,' I admitted. 'Sam does seem to attract nice friends.'

'Do you think you could give me a lift back in tomorrow to pick up my car?'

'It will have to wait until tomorrow evening, I'm afraid.'

'Oh, that's no good.'

'Why ever not.'

'I suppose you're not to know. There is an important student meeting and they want me there as a kind of senior representative.'

'Well, in that case you'll have to get the train. I'll have to drop you off in the morning, I'm afraid.'

'That's OK, I can find plenty to amuse myself here.'

She went to sleep almost as soon as we reached home, tired out from her long day at the university.

The following day was Esther's day off. I dropped my mother off in the morning to catch the train back to the university. Midway through the afternoon I received a phone call from her.

'How have you been getting on? 'I asked.

'Very well. I think I made some good points at the meeting.

There is something, though, I need to say to you. Esther has invited me to stay at hers for a few days and I've accepted, so I won't be coming home tonight. After that dreadful incident, it might be good for her.'

'But, what about your night things?'

'Well, Esther kindly offered to go and fetch them from you. I understand that she has a key so that she can come and go as she pleases.'

'It's not that...'

I decided not to try and explain.

I asked Esther about it the following day.

'So, this was sudden. Was it her idea or yours?'

She looked a little sheepish.

'Well, we sort of discussed it together.'

'Sounds like I must have upset her.'

'No, I don't think so. I think – you know – she just thought it might be nice for a bit of a change and perhaps give you a bit of a break.'

'Bit of a break. She's only just arrived.'

'Anyway, she seems to be enjoying herself.'

'Good, I am pleased for both of you.'

'I'm just going to have a bit of a tidy up upstairs – bit of a mess up there.'

I felt like Esther was avoiding me.

30

A few days later I was surprised to see Tom turn up in the bookshop. He smiled sheepishly.

'Good to see you,' I said

'I thought I'd have a quick browse.'

'Of course, you're welcome.'

I was desperate to find out what the situation was with him, guessing he must have been questioned by the police by now.

'Look, Tom, before you do, I wondered if we could have a little chat, in private.'

'Of course.'

I took him up to my office.

'I just wanted to know if there was any more news that you had heard on Mr Nielsen and now the death of Mr Grindley.'

'Well, I have to admit I was worried for a while. The police took me into custody and gave me some quite tough questions. I think I may have been considered a suspect.'

'Well, I suppose that they considered you had a possible motive.'

'I think that was it, because of my relationship with Katarina, though I think I've got over that, partly thanks to you.'

'Can I ask what they said to you?'

'What it came down to was they thought I might have got so angry that I went and murdered Mr Nielsen. As it is, it's well known what I did.'

He pulled up his sleeves. There were slash marks across his wrists.

'Oh, Tom, you poor thing. You must have been so upset.'

'It's not as bad as it looks. I didn't try and slash my own wrists. I'm not sure if I'm brave enough to do that. I put them through a plate glass window in a fit of temper. I'd drunk a bottle of whisky, otherwise I don't think I would have done it. I've hardly ever drunk before in my life.'

'Yes, I know only too well what a bottle of that can do.'

'Anyway, they were concerned enough to keep me in hospital for a few days, which was when Nielsen was murdered - so obviously, I couldn't have any part in it. I kept it quiet, said I'd been away with flu. I didn't want to give anyone the satisfaction of knowing what I did. You don't have any jobs going at the moment do you Mr Todd? Only, I was fined by the university for breaking the glass. It's rather expensive.'

'I think that's a bit mean. Surely they know you're a boy of good character.'

I felt the irony of my remarks as I had only days before accused him of being Nielsen's murderer.

'Well thanks for filling me in, Tom. I'd better let you go and look for a book now. And I'm sorry, but we don't have any vacancies at present.'

As soon as he had gone I went and found Esther.

'If Tom's not the murderer, who? And now Grindley's death. I still can't believe that Grindley and Reeves were having an affair, can you?'

Esther shook her head.

'There has to be something else – or someone else. I wonder if, with Grindley's shady past, there is some sort of criminal ring involved. Perhaps he didn't come up with the goods and suffered the consequences of his failure?'

'Surely the police would have discovered something if there had been any criminal connections?'

'And where does Miranda Reeves fit in? I can't believe she has criminal connections. I've got to deliver some play texts to the university in the afternoon. I think I may have another word with our Mr Pearson.

While I was there I picked up some tickets for a production of *Twelfth Night* that had just begun its run at the university. It was after five-thirty by the time I had done that and I wondered if Mr Pearson was in his flat. I was lucky, he was - and he seemed pleased to see me.

'I wondered if I might have a quick chat.'

'Of course, come in.'

He did, however, seem a little nervous.

'It's a nice flat you have here. Just one bedroom, is it?'

'I don't think the university budget would run to two bedrooms. But I do have a sofa bed in case anyone should need to stay over. I did have my cousin over a few times. He comes all the way from Carlisle so it's difficult for him to get here and back in one day.'

I could not help noticing a large double case of books that dominated the room.

'Ah, you have seen my collection of railway books – my secret passion. I have travelled on nearly all the steam railways in this country and a few more abroad. The best way to travel.'

'Yes, I think I agree with you. May I?'

'Of course.'

Though railways were not my absolute area of expertise and passion, I could not resist the opportunity of flicking through a volume on the LNER A4 Pacifics while Mr Pearson chuntered on about the advantages of railway travel over other forms of transport.

'No queuing at airports or your ears popping. A coach is a poor substitute. It makes me sick trying to read on one of those, but on a train.'

'Now, this is a lovely book and that is a lovely train.'

I pointed to the book. My page had fallen open at the Mallard.

'And she could really motor.'

It seemed that his language became more colourful when he was talking about trains, even though he was beginning to mix his metaphors.

'On 3 July 1938, she reached over 125mph. It's still a record for any steam train.'

'Remarkable.'

For a moment, I thought I might be sucked into his world of steams trains, though I was not sure if Esther would approve.

There was a brief silence. I think he knew that there was something else on my mind.

'I was just wondering,' I continued, 'if you heard anything when Mr Grindley was found?'

'The police have already asked me that. Unfortunately, I was out.'

'Where were you?'

'I was at a local historical industrial society meeting on railways. I didn't get back until late. I think it was about eleven though I can't be entirely sure. It was one of those evenings that just flew by. They are thinking of opening one of the local lines to steam again.'

He smiled as he reminisced.

His whereabouts that night were not a surprise to me, given what we had already discussed.

'By the time I got back,' he continued, 'the police were swarming all over the place.'

'Did you speak to Miranda?'

'No, I didn't see her.'

'But I presume they came to see you?'

'Yes, I made a statement.'

'Did you tell them your thoughts about an affair between Reeves and Grindley?'

He looked uncomfortable.

'I didn't really think that it was my place. I thought Miranda should tell them that herself.'

'I still cannot believe those two were having an affair.'

'I might be wrong. I can only tell you what I heard. But to me, well, the evidence seems pretty damming.'

'I hope you don't mind me asking, but did you like Grindley?'

'Well, to be honest I can't say I really had much truck with him and when I did he was friendly enough. I heard stories, though. I'm not sure if he was well liked.'

'What sort of stories?'

'There were a few people who did not trust him. And then all that business when he was supposed to have stolen something. I've heard that there's something in his past.'

When I got home, I told my mother (who had now returned after a few days staying with Esther) about the two tickets I had got for us to see *Twelfth Night* two days later.

'I'm sorry, Elliot, but I have already seen it.'

'You didn't tell me.'

'I have been living in a bit of a whirlwind over the last few days. I meant to but other things just pushed it out. Besides, I'm going home tomorrow.'

'I thought you were here for another four days.'

'I'm sorry, I need a bit of a rest.'

'I thought that is why you came here.'

I rang Esther.

'Do you know what's making her go home early? I haven't upset her in some way have I?'

'No, I don't think so. Well, she hasn't said anything to me. I think she's just a bit tired, that's all.'

I was worried about her long drive back, especially if the reason she was going home was because she was tired. I did not dare ring her mobile in case she decided to answer it while she was driving and that it may cause her to have an accident. I rang her on her home number as soon as work for the day had ended. She told me that she had arrived safely just minutes beforehand.

'Actually, Elliot, there is something I wanted to discuss with you,' she continued, 'but I thought I would rather tell you when I arrived home.'

'What is it?'

'Don't be upset Elliot, but I have another man in my life – apart from you that is, of course.'

She laughed.

'You're getting married?'

'No, not married. I want to see if he's up to scratch first – that's how they do things these days. You know, much as I loved your father, he was not perfect in every way.'

I was not quite sure what she meant by this and had no intention of asking her.

'In fact, you know him.'

I searched through my head for childhood friends of the family but was not prepared for what came.

'It's that nice Mr Pearson.'

Pearson? I knew the name was familiar but could not at once think why.

'I met him at the university.'

I realised now. Nick Pearson, the man who had found my address book. A voice deep inside me screamed 'No!'

'I have to thank you, really, if you had not invited me to stay again, I would not have met him.

'You can't go out with him. He's ...'

I wanted to say 'boring'.

'I'm not sure if he's right for you.'

'I know he's not a professor or anything, but then, neither was your dad, but he is very interesting and kind.'

We surely could not be talking about the same man. Pearson was, after all, a common surname.

'You mean Nick Pearson?'

'Nicholas, that's right.'

'His wife left him,' was all I could think of to say. What on earth had she found interesting about him?

'I know! The poor man! Besides, there is only one way to find out if we get on.'

I did not know what to say.

'Elliot, are you still there.'

'Sorry, mum, I've got to go, there's someone at the door. I will have to ring you back.'

Of course, there was no one at the door; I just needed to take stock and get some air. I took my mobile and walked down the road dialing Esther's number as I did so.

'You knew about this, didn't you?' I accused her when she answered the phone.

'You have to realise, Elliot, Elizabeth is still an attractive woman.'

'Don't speak like that about my mum.'

'I think that's what's blinding you. You must take a step back and be more objective. Look, everybody likes your mum but you seem to be the only one who cannot see it. You're behaving like a child when you're around her, like you're still embarrassed by her.'

'But that's because I am. You're right, she is perfectly capable of reducing me to that little boy in short trousers.'

'I bet that was a sight.'

'What?'

'You in short trousers.'

'But what can I do? She was talking about trying it out.'

She laughed down the phone.

'And, why shouldn't she?'

'Look, please, Esther. I've had enough shocks for one day.'

'There's nothing you can do to stop her. And you mustn't try.'

'What if she wants him to come and stay with her at my house while she's conducting this affair?'

'Well, somebody's got to look after her in her old age.'

'But she's not decrepit or anything. She's quite able to look after herself'

'Obviously.'

'I am not having him sleep over here.'

'Elliot, you have turned into a prude.'

'But he'll bore me to death apart from anything else.'

'There is a rude answer to that which I daren't voice aloud to you.'

'Oh, there is one other thing, I have tickets for *Twelfth Night* tomorrow at the university theatre. I got the tickets for Mum but she has already seen it and now, of course, she's gone home. It is supposed to be a really good production - they have pulled all the stops out, apparently. Sam told me about it.'

'Oh, Elliot, sorry to disappoint you, I can't I'm afraid, I've promised Felicity - you know my Yoga friend - to go to the cinema and then for a meal. I don't really like to let her down.'

'No, that's fine. Another time will do. But I think I will see it in any case. I have never seen a complete production of it before.'

'What about Aggie?'

'I'll try her.'

Aggie was not able to go either as she was already committed to babysitting for Henry, with a friend. I told her about my mother.

'Good for her,' she said.

It seemed that I was the only one who thought that there was anything strange about my mother forming a relationship with this man. There was also a part of me that was saying that while my 70-year-old mother was able to attract boyfriends her son who was more than 30 years younger could not attract a girlfriend.

31

I decided to take the train to the university when I went to the theatre, leaving me free to have a drink with Sam if I wanted to. The new theatre building was situated at the far end of the campus. I was running a little late and rushed in just as the final bell went. I was pleased to see Sam in the queue with some of her friends. I went up to her.

'Are you on your own?' she asked me pityingly.

'Yeah, Esther had another engagement.'

'Why don't you join us afterwards in the bar?'

'Yes, I might. I'm catching the train later.'

The play began with some of Shakespeare's immortal lines.

If music be the food of love, play on;
Give me excess of it, that, surfeiting,
The appetite may sicken, and so die.
That strain again! it had a dying fall:
O, it came o'er my ear like the sweet sound,
That breathes upon a bank of violets,
Stealing and giving odour! Enough; no more:
'Tis not so sweet now as it was before.

In the second scene Viola, having escaped drowning and washed up onto the shores of a country unknown to her, enters in conversation with a captain and some sailors. As she spoke the words *What country (friends) is this?* I had a sudden feeling of recognition. The second scene is short and introduces the idea that Viola will dress as a man and attempt to enter the service of the Duke of Orsino as a page, while also establishing that she believes her brother Sebastian is dead. The moment Viola left the stage I realized I'd been watching none other than Miranda Reeves in the part.

As we moved into the third scene, which introduces Olivia's

uncle, Sir Toby Belch, Maria (Olivia's waiting maid) and Sir Toby's friend Andrew Aguecheek, I remembered that Sam had mentioned that Miranda did some acting but I had not taken much notice of it at the time. Perhaps that was why she was difficult to get hold of. Viola is a major part.

Maria (in the play) now chides Sir Toby for drinking too much and explains that Olivia does not like it. Andrew Aguecheek makes a fool of himself by getting Maria's name constantly wrong when he is introduced to her. Aguecheek says that he thinks that he will leave the following day because he does not have a chance with Olivia now Orsino is around but Sir Toby flatters him and persuades him to stay.

Then Miranda Reeves appeared again, this time dressed as a man, as Viola takes on the guise of Cesario to become a page in Orsino's service. I could see why she had been chosen. Her boyish looks were perfect for the part and no doubt she had kept her hair especially short recently for that very reason. I was intrigued to know how close a match they had in Sebastian (her brother, at this stage believed dead) as at one point he is mistaken for Cesario (Viola). For her disguise as a man Miranda Reeves wore a simple moustache. She was an accomplished actor. I wondered, not for the first time, how such a talented person could have become embroiled in the mess over the *First Folio*. A line from *King Lear* came back to me: *Fools have little value now, for wise men act so foolishly, And do not know how to use their intelligence.*

Twelfth Night is a funny play but also has some profound things to say about the nature of love and once again I could not help relating some of it to my own circumstances. Orsino seems to be in love with the idea of love rather than love itself whereas Viola, having decided that she loves Orsino is constant to this thought. Was my love for Esther constant like that of Viola's for Orsino or was I, like Orsino, in love with the idea of love?

Whatever else, I knew that, as the play made clear, love was a complicated business. Sebastian, played by a student as was most of the cast except, I thought, for Viola and Sir Toby Belch, was a reasonable physical match for Cesario, played by Reeves, but stood in her shade in terms of the quality of the acting.

As the play nears its end, Orsino's inconstancy is shown when he is prepared to switch his love from Olivia to Viola (now revealed as a woman). There has always been a good deal of speculation about sexual ambiguity in this play as Orsino, after she reveals herself as a woman, continues to refer to Viola as a boy and as Cesario. As they took their applause it was Reeves who received the warmest hand. I was near the front. I think she noticed me, I nodded, but I couldn't be sure if she really saw me.

I looked for Sam in the crush of the bar. I found her and bought her and her two friends, Billy and Cleo, a drink. We chatted amiably. It seemed that everybody knew and loved our bookshop, which cheered me. I discussed the possibility of some work for Sam over the summer holidays. Then we got back to the play. Sam was taking an English Literature Major and was currently writing a dissertation on the role of women in Shakespeare.

'Miranda Reeves was very good,' I ventured.

'Yes, I thought she was excellent,' Sam said.

'But, all this business of dressing up as a man, I wonder sometimes if it is a cheap device.'

This was Billy's opinion but Sam did not agree.

'I don't know, in practical terms it would have been difficult to wield as much influence as a woman. I think that's why she takes on the disguise of a man.'

Sam put her hand to her mouth.

'My God, I'm lecturing!'

I laughed.

'It's all right Sam, I always knew you would make a good teacher from the way you behaved in the bookshop.'

'And it's a good device for all that sexual ambiguity stuff,' added Cleo.

'And it contributes to the humour,' I reminded them, though I was worried that my observations were lightweight by comparison with theirs.

'Anyway, she must be getting used to it now,' observed Billy.

'Of course, she played Portia in *The Merchant of Venice*.'

This was news to me.

'Did she?'

'Though you have to admit that was a doddle compared with this role - having to be convincing playing a man all the way through and that.'

'It was in the last production back in the spring - you know about the time of Nielsen's death. I'm sorry Elliot, you probably don't like to be reminded.'

'No, it's OK really Sam, don't worry. And remind me about the play. It's not one I know very well.'

'Well, you know about the pound of flesh?'

'Yes. It's a bit controversial, isn't it?'

'There was a lot of anti-Jewishness at the time. You might say it was institutionalised.'

'But you could argue that Shakespeare showed a lot of sympathy for Shylock by the fact that he portrays him as human like everybody else.'

Billy launched into a speech.

'If you prick us do we not bleed? If you tickle us do we not laugh? If you poison us do we not die? And if you wrong us shall we not revenge?'

'I think that's enough, Billy.' At this point, Billy feigned disappointment and then walked off with his empty glass in the direction of the bar. 'And right up to the end he insists on having his pound of flesh until Portia - played by Reeves dressed as a lawyer - tricks him by saying that the contract is that he takes exactly a pound of flesh and no more and no less - which of course was not possible - and he ends up by losing half of his money.'

'A clever trick.'

'But going back to the dressing up thing, it seems a bit silly until…' She looked for Billy and realised that he was not there, 'Oh, he's gone…anyway, you realise that she feels that she has to dress up as a man to gain respect and power in order to convince the court …'

'That she is a *bona-fide* lawyer.'

'I don't suppose that there were too many female lawyers at the time.'

'Well who's for another drink?' said Billy returning with

foaming glasses of beer.'

'I'm really enjoying your company but I need to try and have a quick word with Miranda Reeves.'

'Just this last one, then that completes the round.'

'We must be off too, shortly.'

'I have to admit, it's good stuff.'

I downed the pint more quickly than I would have wished, and bid farewell to Sam and her merry friends. As I was walking through the lobby, I glanced idly at the notice board. A picture caught my eye. Next to the photo for the current production was a smaller photo showing Reeves in *The Merchant of Venice* production. I was intrigued and went and had a closer look. While playing Portia as the lawyer, Reeves had worn a hat. It was a very handy device for making her appear more masculine. In the two scenes of *Twelfth Night* that were shown she was hatless. When I looked back to the larger photos of *Twelfth Night* I had a closer view of her features than I had had of her on the stage. I had a flashback to my dream of many months before when I saw Esther take on the face of the murderer. I slapped myself on the back of my neck. How could I not have realised? How could I have been so blind?

I went up to the reception desk.

'Do you know if Miranda Reeves is still here?'

'I don't know. I could check for you.'

She made a quick call.

'No, they have all gone I'm afraid. Sometimes they go for a drink in the bar afterwards.'

I went over to the bar. There were just a few stragglers and Miranda was not one of them. I hoped she had gone back to her flat. It was the middle of the week and no doubt she was teaching the next day.

I went outside into the courtyard by the theatre and rang Esther. I told her about Miranda Reeves's part in the play and briefly sketched out my theory, though the beer that I had drunk was affecting me and I was not too coherent.

'It's her, I'm sure of it.'

'Elliot, what are you talking about? You've been drinking,

haven't you? Your speech is all slurred.'

'Only a couple or three, but that's not the point. It's Reeves, she played Portia in *The Merchant of Venice*. I'm going to go and see her - if she's there.'

'No, Elliot, wait, I think you should consider this a bit more carefully. It would be better if we talked about this in the morning.'

'I might not have the courage for it then. *Carpe Diem* and all that.'

'You had best go home - I will pick you up at the station if you like.'

The drink was affecting me more than I had realised. I had not had any supper before the play.

'Couldn't possibly trouble you. You have to look after your chickens.'

I knew I sounded silly. To make it worse I hiccupped just at that moment.

'Elliot, I really think you should get the next train.'

'It will be all right Esther,' I said, forcing myself to sober up. She began to break up. 'I'll see you later,' I said and then, knowing she could not hear, 'I love you.'

32

The walk across the campus helped sober me up. The layout was unfamiliar to me in the dark and it took me a little while to rediscover the annexe to the courtyard where Reeves's flat was located. Of course, I knew she might not be there. I could have phoned to check but thought it best to try to catch her unawares.

As I negotiated the twists and turns out of the courtyard I passed a couple of good humoured students on the way back from the bar, slightly the worse for wear. I hesitated for a moment at the foot of the stairs that led from the foyer. A strange feeling of unreality swept over me and for a moment I was tempted to leave any thoughts of a meeting for another day as Esther had suggested. However, my instincts and my drink addled brain drove me on. I climbed the stairs, paused for a moment outside the door, took a deep breath and knocked.

'Just a minute,' I heard. A few moments later she opened the door.

'Hello, can I help you?'

She was quizzical, peering out into the dimly lit corridor. Perhaps she was expecting someone else?

'Elliot Todd,' I announced formally, though I could tell she recognised me. 'I'm sorry to catch you so late without an appointment but I have something urgent I would like to discuss with you.'

She paused for a moment then gave what I considered was a rather forced smile and opened the door.

'Of course, Elliot, do come in.'

She motioned me over to the sofa.

'Would you like a glass of wine?'

'No thanks, I've just had a drink.'

'Well I'm going to have one if you don't mind. I'm on a bit of a high.'

'Of course, you deserve one. I saw you in the play. I thought you were excellent.'

She nodded. I wondered again if she had seen me in the audience.

'Yes, it's a wonderful play. One of my favourites. It's very funny and says a lot about the nature of love.'

She sat in the armchair facing me. Some of the make-up that she was wearing for her role remained about the eyes and her cheeks were a little red. In my inebriated state, I thought it made her look even more striking than usual.

I took another deep breath.

'This is difficult for me to say.' I looked into her intense dark eyes and willed myself not to lose my nerve. 'I believe that you had something to do with the death of Harry Nielsen.'

The glass of wine was on the way to her mouth. It froze abruptly for a brief moment and a few small drops spilled onto the cream carpet. However, she recovered instantly, took a sip of the wine and deftly passed her foot over the stain.

'You are joking of course? I thought you had come to ask me about the *Folio*. I'm sorry I didn't get back to you. I was busy with this play - but I have now written a letter to the university authorities explaining the situation.'

'I really do wish I was joking.'

She rose from her chair and, glass in hand, walked over to the music system in the corner.

'Well, if you are serious, you had better explain your outlandish accusation.'

She flicked a switch and some music started up gently in the background - not Shakespeare songs this time but Courtney Pine.

'I believe you came from the rehearsal of *The Merchant of Venice*, dressed as a man, as Portia - to my bookshop - and confronted Nielsen.'

'Why would I do that? We were work colleagues.'

'You were lovers. You kept your relationship secret.'

She considered for a moment.

'Being lovers is not a crime.'

This did not sound too dissimilar to what Katarina Budonovka had said earlier.

'But murder is.' I said dramatically.

'I think you should leave now. You have obviously had too much to drink.'

I stood up and reached into the back pocket of my trousers.

'This picture was taken of you at our bookshop on the night Nielsen was murdered.'

She looked at it briefly then handed it back.

'Do you deny it is you?'

She walked a few paces away from me with her glass in her hand before swinging round and facing me again.

'Even if I was there it doesn't mean that I killed him. Besides, why would I harm someone I loved? It doesn't make any sense.'

'Because I believe that by that time you were no longer lovers. You were incensed because he'd fallen for a student, Katarina Budonovka.'

Her eyes flickered.

'She is just a cheap little nobody. He'd soon have tired of her. That pathetic boy Tom came to me in tears and said that there was something he thought I should know. I told him…' she paused, 'that Nielsen would get his just desserts.'

I could see now that I had not fully understood what Tom had said to me. It made sense now.

'Why would he go off with someone like that when he could share his life with me, his soul mate, who knows as much or more about Shakespeare than he does?'

Surely she meant "did" in the past tense. But I did not correct her.

'Nielsen might have been clever but he was weak-willed. Couldn't he see that all she was after was a good grade and was prepared to do anything to get it?'

She turned her back to me and addressed the wall as though contemplating a certain point above the mock fireplace. A Shakespeare line came into my head. I said it out loud.

'*I am driven on by flesh, and he must needs go that the devil drives.*'

Maybe Nielsen could just not help himself? I thought of the Helmut Newton nudes I had seen at his house following the memorial service. She turned back to me.

'*All's Well That Ends Well.*' She could not resist sourcing the quote.

'I can't justify Nielsen's behaviour,' I continued, 'from what I can gather this was not the first time Nielsen had an affair with a student. But surely he didn't deserve to be murdered for it?'

She had put down her glass of wine and was pacing up and down the room. She clasped her hands together and thrust them towards me.

'All right, I can see why you would think that but I didn't mean to hurt him.'

She slumped down on the chair with her head bent.

'I was angry and I just wanted to have it out with him. Since he had started this affair there was a kind of malice in his behaviour towards me, as though it was my fault, and he had become very lax about acknowledging my academic input. That stuff about Jaques and his speech, that was all a result of my research and he didn't acknowledge it once. It was like he was deliberately trying to hurt me, first going off with that whore, then rubbing my nose in it by riding rough-shod over my work.'

'*Of all pains, the greatest pain, is to love, and to love in vain.*'

She looked at me critically.

'That's not Shakespeare?'

'No, George Granville. But I'm afraid I know the sentiments very well.'

'For a moment, I thought there was something I had missed.'

'I'm sure there's nothing I can tell you about Shakespeare.'

She smiled. The tension had eased a little. She sat down on the chair opposite me and leaned towards me.

'Look, it was an accident. I pushed him, hard admittedly. I was angry with him but I didn't mean to hurt him. I wanted him to accept that acts have consequences.'

'You pushed him against the spike of the *pickle helmet*.'

'I could not believe what was happening. Almost as soon as he went back he began writhing in agony. There was nothing I could do.'

'You could have called for an ambulance?'

'I could tell he was dead. What good would it have done?'

'It would have been … the right thing to do.'

'I suppose I panicked. I just couldn't bear the thought…'

'And you took off the beard you were wearing, masquerading as a man?'

'Yes, I came straight from rehearsals. I don't know why I left it on when I got there. I was into my character, I suppose. Part of me thought it would be a wheeze to be taken as a man in a real-life situation. Harry had invited me to the talk a few days earlier. He read through some of what he was going to say, told me about using the Jacques piece. We had a bit of a disagreement about it then. I told him that he should acknowledge my research. He said in an offhand way that if it was in Shakespeare it was knowable - or something like that.

'I had a tutorial that day with that Katarina Budonovka. I knew she was having a lesson with Nielsen later that week and I mentioned to the class that there was a particular point that they should raise with Nielsen about sexuality in Shakespeare - it's a topic that comes up regularly. At the end of the class she came up to me and said that she would be seeing Nielsen later that night and that she could bring it up with him then. Then she made some silly remark like sex was his strong point, especially with the younger woman. It was like she was goading me. I was so angry. It was obvious that she knew of my involvement with him. It was only a few weeks before that he had been in an intimate relationship with me. The more I thought about it the more angry I became. I sent a letter to his office stating that if he used my research for the talk that evening I would make a formal complaint to the university authorities and would consider taking legal action. I castigated him for his relationship with Katarina for which I also threatened to inform the university.'

Tears began to form in her eyes.

'I knew I was acting irrationally but I felt so hurt and violated. When he didn't even acknowledge my letter, I was so upset that I determined to go to the talk at the bookshop straight from my rehearsals. When I heard his lecture and he made no mention of my research, I decided that I had to confront him.'

I shuddered at the thought that, just as I was reading my little excerpt from Jaques, I was in some way participating in the prelude to a murder.

'I can understand your emotion. It was a crime of passion. It would probably have been looked on compassionately.'

'But, the press, the university… I couldn't bear the thought of the notoriety, losing my job…'

'But, set against a man's life ending.'

She touched me on the knee.

'I know. I should have stayed and faced the music.'

She rubbed her eyes free of tears.

'I'm sorry. Look, let's have a proper drink.'

She went over to the cabinet and poured a generous tumbler of whisky for each of us. I stood up and took my glass.

'Cheers.'

She clinked my glass.

This was all getting too cosy. I had to re-focus to ask the next pressing question that was on my mind.

'And what about your relationship with Grindley?'

She laughed, a cruel, cynical laugh.

'Grindley was the scum of the earth. He got what he deserved.'

'Even common criminals deserve not to have their life taken away from them.'

'You don't know how it was. He was blackmailing me.'

'Over the *Folio*?' I speculated.

'He had worked out what had happened with Harry. When I came back to the university from the bookshop I realised that I had to retrieve the letter that I had sent to him, otherwise I would be immediately incriminated. I went to his office to find it - I had access to the code for his door lock, he to mine. I found it soon enough on his desk. It had been opened but returned to the envelope. Unfortunately, just as I was about to leave, Grindley turned up, torch in hand. It was late and he had seen the light on, said he was just doing his rounds. I told him there were some urgent papers I needed but I knew I didn't sound very convincing and he could see the letter in my hand. Then I saw him looking at my sleeve. There was blood on the cuff. It must have got there when I checked for a pulse on Harry's neck and realised he was dead. The next day he had put two and two together and came to see me, though rather than turning me into the police he tried to blackmail me. That is when he had the idea of me helping him to steal the *Folio* - it was his idea of payment for keeping quiet - a one off he said. One good sting and he would be out of the country before I knew it and I wouldn't get any of the blame.

'I went along with it so far but in the end, I couldn't go through with it. You see when I say I love Shakespeare, I really mean it. I stole it to protect it. If he had my collusion it would have been easy for him but I knew once the idea was in his head he would find a way of stealing it whether he had my help or not. I put it into a safe deposit box in a bank and gave him a fake one with an old cover from another old piece of early literature. He didn't notice at first until he had made some enquiries and then when you came to me I realised that he knew it was a fake and that he was trying to offload it on to you.'

'So, you didn't have anything to do with those phone calls to me?'

She shook her head.

'I had made a point of making myself a bit scarce and staying away with friends whenever I could. But, eventually, he caught up with me. We had some fearsome arguments. He came to my room late one night. He said I had to come up with some money or give him the real *Folio*. I am a university lecturer and comfortable enough but that doesn't make me a wealthy woman. I offered him what I could afford but it wasn't enough for him. I was desperate and confused. I just couldn't bear the thought of this vile person having such a hold over me...' she began to sob, 'any longer.'

'It's OK,' I said. 'Here.' I handed her a tissue but was conscious I was being manipulated.

'I had to stop him somehow. I grabbed the first thing I could - the heavy metal lamp next to the bed - and struck him on the head with all the force I could manage.'

She drank down the rest of the whisky in one gulp and continued.

'I didn't know what to do. I panicked. Then I decided to make it look like an accident.'

She gave a guttural cry.

'I think I need another drink.'

'Here, let me.'

The bottle was empty.

'I know, I have been drinking far too much recently. It's the pressure of the remorse. There's some more whisky in the cupboard.'

I rummaged for the whisky in the bottom of the cupboard and, while I did so, pulled my mobile phone from my pocket (which was, thankfully, switched on). While I grabbed a couple of glasses I texted Esther, 'Police now Rs flat.' It was the fastest text I had ever managed and I hoped I had got it right, while at the same time wondering about my next move. Would she try to escape? Should I try to contact the police myself?

I poured the whisky for both of us and brought the tumblers over to where she was sitting. It was as though she was relieved to be unburdening her conscience.

'What happened then?' I asked.

'Then I moved him into the hallway at the bottom of the stairs.' She took another long hard slug of the whisky.

'You realize, I'm going to have to tell the police all this.'

'I know how bad this looks - murder for God's sake and I have never had anything more than a parking fine before.' She laughed through her tears. 'Look, you understand books.' She sat down beside me and clasped my hands in hers. 'We could do something together, with our combined expertise. We would make a great partnership.'

I could feel the warmth of her body. There was no doubting her attractiveness. Neither Nielsen nor Grindley came out of this in a good light but I could not condone what she had done. That saying came into my head, *There but for the grace of God*, but I knew there was much more to it than that. There was a large measure of calculation and artifice in her actions.

'I'm sorry,' I said, 'I have a responsibility.'

With a degree of reluctance, I pushed her hands gently away. She was quiet for a moment.

'So, what are you going to do, handcuff me and march me off to the station?'

'I've already contacted Esther. The police should be on their way.'

'Yes, I could see how that little vixen had got her claws into you.'

This was an unexpected switch in emotion and was in complete contrast to her sentiments a moment before. I recalled something that Sam had said earlier: *Some of the things she says, I'm not sure if she is always quite sane.*

'It's not like that between Esther and me ...'

She rose from her chair and began pacing, not appearing interested in what I was saying. I stood up also, wondering in my own mind what to do should she try to flee her flat. She did not make for the door, though, and turned back towards me.

'Well, I suppose we might as well be civilised while we wait.'

'Yes.'

I was afraid for a moment she was going to suggest another glass of whisky. I did not think I could manage another one. However, she pointed above her decorative fireplace where there was a sword displayed on the wall.

'This is a fencing sword believed to be from Shakespeare's time. Despite his brilliantly crafted language Shakespeare was aware that the audience of the day also craved a good fight scene, such as when Hamlet fights Osric in Act Five of *Hamlet* or Romeo when he slays Tybalt.'

I was a little unnerved by another apparent switch in mood, but also relieved at this retreat into academia which I found less threatening. There was no doubting her intellect and academic prowess.

'I suppose it was an important skill for the actor to learn,' I said, feeling as if I was taking on the role of interested student, though I was also keen to keep her in good humour.

'Yes, an actor would learn in a fencing school and if he was not up to scratch the audience would soon recognise it and he would be booed off the stage.'

She went up to the sword, running her hands gently along the blade.

'And, of course, there were accidents too. Samuel Pepys in his diary told how an actor killed his opponent in a stage duel. In Amsterdam in 1672, the actor playing Macbeth used a real dagger and killed the actor playing Duncan during a performance of the play. Violence in those days was a much more accepted part of society...'

She looked around at me and into my eyes for a moment and gave a little laugh. I should have taken warning. In one easy movement, she swiftly removed the sword from its fastening on the wall and brought the flat side of the blade down against the nape of my neck. I fell clumsily to the floor. The next thing I knew she was astride me with the sword pointing down at me. I looked around frantically for anything that I could use to defend myself. The coffee table was next to me with the large *Folio* facsimile peeking over the edge. Somehow, I managed to grab it and hold it in front of my face - just in time as she struck. Though I felt the force of the blow through my neck, the book had saved me for the moment. Unbalanced, she stumbled - no doubt the whisky was playing its part. The pain in my neck was excruciating and I felt unable to move. I could only watch helplessly as she recovered her stance and stood over me again with the sword raised above her head. I winced in anticipation of a further strike while at the same time I was conscious of another regular thumping sound in my head. There were footsteps on the stairs.

'No!' shrieked a voice, so loud it hurt my ears.

Reeves hesitated, the blow did not come, a dark blue uniform crossed in front of my face obscuring my view. Then Esther's concerned face appeared very close to mine, the wound on her face prominent. I smiled and watched strangely transfixed as I saw a large tear form in her eye before splashing onto my face. Immediately afterwards Esther faded from view and I lost consciousness.

33

'You have received a nasty bruising and a strain, or possibly a sprain, to the neck as you fell. I need to keep you in overnight.'

This was the verdict of the doctor when I was admitted to the Accident and Emergency Unit of the local hospital on the evening of Miranda Reeves's confession. I had regained consciousness soon after the arrival of Esther and the police but I had a severe headache which convinced them that I should receive medical attention. Esther had stayed with me until I had fallen asleep. However, she was back early the next morning.

Something had been bothering me.

'How come you arrived at the same time as the police?' I asked Esther.

'It was just a coincidence. I was in town eating in a restaurant with Felicity when I received your text. I was only five minutes away. It was quite funny really, I was running like the clappers from one side of the courtyard to the staircase up to Reeves's flat and nearly ran into the Policeman, Hedges, running from the other side of the courtyard.'

'I didn't find it quite so amusing.'

'If you are looking for sympathy you're not going to get it from me. If you had listened we could have dealt with this in an orderly manner through the police the next day.'

'I thought you would be pleased. You are always trying to get me to get more involved in things.'

'But this was different.'

'Besides she might not have confessed so readily the following day. And, it was worth it, just to see your concern for me.'

'I think something went in my eye when I was running across the courtyard.'

'Regardless, I was very pleased to see you. You couldn't pour me some water, could you?'

She poured a glass of water into the cheerless plastic beaker while I attempted to sit up in a more comfortable position in the bed.

'I don't know if anything will seem normal at the bookshop again,' I said a little gloomily.

'Nonsense,' she said, 'I have just had a reply from that ex-Foreign Secretary chap to say that he would love to come and do a talk.'

'Good, perhaps things are looking up after all.'

'And, there is something else that pleases me.'

'What's that?'

'You owe me £20.'

My mother phoned.

'Elliot, I heard you were in trouble.'

'Yes, someone attacked me with a sixteenth century sword.'

'You are joking.'

'Well, I try to think of it as a joke. What were you ringing to tell me?'

'A mother doesn't need a reason to ring her son, does she?'

'No, of course not.'

She was making me feel guilty again.

'The truth is, I have something important to tell you.'

I sat down, believing I knew what was to come.

'Elliot, are you still there?'

'Yes, mother, go on.'

'Well, you know I said I went to my doctor.'

'He said you were as fit as a flea. Nothing's changed, has it?'

'No, I'm fine, just as I said.'

'The reason I went,' she continued, 'was because I was taking stock. And though the doctor said I am very fit, well, you know, I am nearly 70.'

'But I'm sure you've got years in you yet.'

'Nevertheless, I wanted to make sure everything is in order and I wanted to assure you that I am leaving you and Dominic equal shares. It doesn't matter that he is the older son and has a wife and children. As far as I am concerned you are equal in my eyes. Anyway, it may be that you will get married one day soon and who knows, I know you're leaving it a bit late, but you might even have children.'

I bit my lip, trying to ignore this further incidence of emotional blackmail.

'The truth is, I don't really think either of us should expect to get your money. I hope you live a good long time yet and spend it all as you deserve to.'

'And there is something else. Now don't be cross with me but I have decided that I'm not going to marry Nicholas.'

'Oh, I thought you were getting on like a house on fire.'

'We were getting on, that's true, but a house on fire, I should think that is the last phrase that you would use to describe Nicholas Pearson. Your dad was a bit quiet but he was also wise and determined. Nicholas, well, I do like him and I have to admit he's very attentive. The trouble is he's too attentive. I like someone I can argue with occasionally. You know, me and your dad, we were not the perfect couple.'

I laughed to myself.

'You know we did have the odd argument.'

That was something of an understatement.

'The truth is, and I realise that this might sound unkind, but I find him a little boring.'

'Thank God.'

'What?'

'Thank God you realised in time.'

'Yes, well I'm glad you're not too upset. I wanted to tell him before things became too serious.'

'Oh, well, mother, *All's Well That Ends Well*.'

Acknowledgements

Thanks to Jo, who read the book more times than is reasonable, corrected the book and found more mistakes than I thought possible; Jill McHale and my sister Vivienne, who read the book in its final stages and gave some valuable insights and corrections; and Lucy, my daughter, who has designed a revised version of the cover. Thanks also to Ben Crystal, who gave an enthusiastic talk at our real-life bookshop some years ago based on his book *Shakespeare on Toast,* and from whom I learnt much about the design of *The First Folio* and who acted out the example that I used in the speech by Jaques. I wish to acknowledge a line from Julia Copus's poem, *In Defence of Adultery.* My good friend Madeleine was the basis of some of the elements of the character of Aggie. Finally I would like to give thanks to all our loyal customers at Brendon Books (the bookshop we have run since 1989), who encourage Jo and myself to *keep on keeping on.*

Elliot Todd Mystery: 2

Roman Holiday, the second in the *Elliot Todd Mystery* series will be available in 2024.

Copies may be ordered direct from Onyx Publishing at the following address:

c/of Brendon Books, Bath Place, Taunton TA1ER
01823 337742 brendonbooks@gmail.com

We would prefer if you ordered either direct from us or your local independent bookseller or online from bookshop.org who work on behalf of independent booksellers. However, it will also be available from other High Street and online retailers.

9 780953 287659